Fleur Blüm is a Melbourne-based writer, performer and musician.

Her blog can be found at https://fleurblum.com/blog

Also by Fleur Blüm:

Sophie's Path: A choose your own romance adventure

Discovering the Franklins

My Mother's Secret

Singular Focus

Sins of the Father: a Barrett Women novel

First edition 2022

Copyright © 2022 Fleur Blüm
ISBN 978-0-6483654-4-0

Editor: Annie Seaton
Cover Design: Charmaine Ross

Published by Fleur Blüm, Melbourne, Australia

The Mother's Fault

A Barrett Women novel

By Fleur Blüm

For all the women and girls out there who have had difficult experiences and come out the other side.

Chapter 1

2015

Chloe Barrett looked at the incoming call from her mother on the screen of her mobile phone and sighed. She declined the call and turned back to her friend, Mel. They were out on the town, Mel's boyfriend was the drummer in a band, *The Inflatable Cocks,* and they were playing at Red Plum Bar. It wasn't Chloe's usual scene, slightly too grungy in her opinion, but she wanted to support her friend, who wanted to support her boyfriend. Plus, Mel had promised to be her wing-woman for the night.

The bar was down one of Melbourne's many alleys, still hanging onto its pre-gentrification vibe. On the door frame as they entered, along with a sign stating: 'No shoes, no shirt, no service' the management had taped an additional rule: 'NO DICKHEADS'.

The rule was somewhat redundant given Chloe couldn't tell the difference between patrons and staff; they all looked pretty rough.

She tugged the hem of her short, flared, neon orange skirt.

'No one wears colours at Plum,' Mel said earlier in the evening as they were dressing.

'Pretending I'm more of a rock chick than I am isn't going to get me anywhere,' Chloe had replied.

'Alright, you can keep the skirt but you'll have to wear a band t-shirt on top.' Mel scrunched up her face and held out a tight black tee with a band logo on the front. Mel dated exclusively from a never-ending pool of grungy musicians who were destined to be 'the next big thing' in the Melbourne band scene, so had quite a collection of T-shirts. Lead guitarists and front men held the most social capital, then bass players, placing drummers lowest in the hierarchy. Keyboard players didn't rate a mention, if the band had keys, they weren't hard-core enough for Mel.

Despite any reservations about getting in with Chloe's outfit, the bouncer barely glanced at their ID before waving them through. The venue was cave-like;_ dark, narrow and long, painted black with huge paste-ups of famous rock musicians plastered on the walls. The bar took up several metres directly in front of the door with more photos of musicians hanging in dinged-up frames above it. Back lights shone through opaque white and tan plastic masquerading as marble, below the countertop.

The stage at the far end of the room covered in scuffed black paint_ was backed by a deep red crushed velvet curtain. It stood empty for the moment, but music loud enough to make conversation difficult pumped through the sound system. A few people milled about, not many, but it was still early.

'The band room is this way,' Mel said, pulling Chloe behind her in the other direction, away from the stage, past the bathrooms which smelled relatively fresh, to a nondescript door. Mel knocked a couple of times before barging into the room.

The room was larger than Chloe expected but still cramped with the four members of *The Inflatable Cocks*, their gear, their respective girlfriends and guests.

'You made it, babe!' Mel's boyfriend, who went by Robbo, said from her left. He was a towering, bulky man, which made sense for a hard rock drummer. His long dirty-blond hair and biker-beard were not to Chloe's taste.

'You remember my friend, Chloe,' Mel said to no one in particular, before standing on tip toes to kiss Robbo with rather more enthusiasm than was necessary. Chloe looked away. She'd met the guys in the band a couple of times before but was still not comfortable enough to hang out without Mel as a buffer.

Though quieter in the band room than in the main bar, the music was still loud enough to make silence seem like _her best response. When Mel and Robbo separated, Mel dragged Chloe over to a decrepit-looking black vinyl couch, pulling her down to sit beside her, with her boyfriend on the other side.

'Are there other bands on tonight?' she asked.

'Yeah, we're headlining, so we're on last, but we gotta be here early coz the other bands use our drums and amps,' the lead singer, whose name might have been Steve, said. Chloe nodded. The group went back to discussing their set and other band-related stuff, Chloe sat quietly; she had no experience with the band scene.

Chloe's hands felt unnaturally empty without a drink in them, and the buzz from the couple of wines she had before coming out were starting to wear off. 'I'm going to the bar, does anyone want anything?'

'Get me a JD and coke, babe,' Mel said.

'Sure.' The band members were drinking beers from the fridge, no doubt part of the rider, and didn't need anything else, why buy drinks when you can get these free?

Chloe was bombarded with music which was much louder than she remembered. The bar was more crowded but nowhere near the sweaty crush she expected when the band played. She ordered two JD and cokes; they weren't her drink of choice, but it was easier than screaming two different orders across the bar.

As she waited for the barman to return with the drinks, Chloe noticed the man standing next to her. Slim and wiry_ and over six feet tall_, he stood half a head taller than Chloe, even in her high heels.

'Hi,' he said leaning towards her so she could hear him over the music. When he turned to her it felt like he could see straight into her mind, and all her secrets.

'Hi.' She was surprised how good he smelled; orange, leather, and musk perhaps. He wore tight black jeans and a black T-shirt which hugged his slight frame under a battered leather jacket.

'I'm Eddie.' He held out his hand toward her.

Her cheeks warmed in a blush as she took his hand. A slightly crooked, aquiline nose sat in a strong face, which made him look intriguing, rather than detracting from his appearance. The eyes which seemed to see deep into her were pale, perhaps hazel or very light brown, hard to tell in the dim light of the bar.

Chloe giggled; he was so hot, and his hand still held hers.

'What's your name sweetheart?' he prompted.

'I'm Chloe.' As she looked down, finally able to break his gaze, her drinks appeared on the bar. 'It's lovely to meet you.'

'What?' he said, yelling over the music.

'I said it's lovely to meet you,' she said, leaning in closer and catching his scent again. It was rare for her to go to pieces over a man, but something about him threw off her equilibrium.

'Both for you?' Eddie's eyes fell on the two drinks she held, one eyebrow cocked.

'No, my friend is in the band room.'

'Why don't you take her drink to her, then meet me in the alley? We can talk out there. I need a smoke.'

'Okay.' Chloe could feel the stupid grin plastered on her face, but couldn't seem to pull herself together to act cool. She rushed back to the band room.

'I'm going outside for a smoke,' she said, handing Mel her drink.

'You don't smoke,' Mel replied, a knowing grin spreading across her face. 'Have fun. The boys are on at eleven.'

Chloe nodded.

Out in the alley a group of about fifteen people clustered around a couple of tin boxes on the ground which served as ashtrays. She had tried smoking a few times in her teens, but given her mother had been a heavy smoker it had never seemed attractive. More like a waste of money and terrible for your health. Smoking inside venues had been banned for eight years now, since before she was legally allowed into bars and nightclubs. She much preferred bars without the smoke haze.

Eddie leaned one shoulder against the graffiti-covered wall of the narrow laneway. His collared leather jacket reminded Chloe of James Dean, the cigarette dangling from his lips adding to the impression.

'Chloe, you found us.' He grinned and beckoned her to stand by him. She hadn't brought a jacket with her, usually she spent enough time inside dancing, surrounded by other people. She crossed her arms across her chest, hugging herself for warmth, her cold drink dangling from her fingertips.

'You want one?' Eddie offered her a smoke.

'No, I'm okay.'

He shrugged and turned back to the conversation, which seemed to be focused on the latest football results. Chloe didn't care for sport much, but she knew enough to follow the talk.

'You cold, hun?' Eddie turned to her as he stubbed out his cigarette.

'A bit.' She wanted to appear tough, but after ten minutes in the chilly laneway she was thinking of going back inside.

'Here,' Eddie opened his jacket and wrapped it around her, pressing his body against hers. She was sure it wasn't just the alcohol or the jacket that warmed her cheeks. As she pressed up against his trim, lean torso, the attraction deepened. 'You smell nice,' he murmured, his warm breath brushing her cheeks.

'Thanks.' She had no idea what an appropriate response was. Clearly, he was interested, using his jacket as an excuse to get close. He was hotter than the guys she was usually attracted to, and seemed kind and thoughtful. Maybe she'd struck it lucky early in the night.

Eddie finished his beer and stubbed out another cigarette. 'The music will be starting soon, you coming in with me?'

'I should check on my friend.'

'You know the guys in the band?'

'The drummer's girlfriend.'

'Wow, you'll have to introduce me. I hang around the scene a lot, but I don't know many of the guys personally.' Eddie squeezed her shoulders inside his jacket. 'Come on, it's freezing out here. Find me on the dance floor when you're done.'

Chloe smiled and nodded. She started to pull away, out of the coat, but Eddie held her close to him until they were back in the venue. With a wink, he slipped his jacket off and went toward the stage where the first band of the night was setting up.

'How did you go?' Mel asked, grinning. She and the others were hanging out near the bar now to watch the other bands. Perhaps the riders had run out too.

'Alright. Hung out with the smokers for a bit.' Chloe couldn't help grinning.

'You must have scored, you look smug. What are you doing in here then? Get back to the boy and close the deal.' Mel winked.

This was exactly what Chloe hoped would happen, but she still felt guilty leaving her friend. She stepped back into the main room and worked her way to the front where the first band had started to play. Eddie had a beer in hand and she wished she'd bought another drink. It would have to wait now; it was rude to go to the bar while the bands were playing.

The music was hard, fast, loud, and heavily distorted, Mel had described it as a punk and metal night. The vocalist screamed incoherently into the microphone, but the band members were in time and probably in tune. Chloe caught herself bobbing her head along with the rhythm of the guitar, and was impressed, not for the first time, at the proficiency of the double kick pedals the drummer was using. Though not her cup of tea, she usually listened to pop or classical music, she appreciated the passion and talent of the band.

Eddie bounced next to her enthusiastically. Too sparse yet to be called a mosh-pit, it certainly had the energy of one already. A couple of times he put a hand on her lower back, sending thrills of excitement up her spine.

The set lasted about forty-five minutes; the audience whooped and clapped their appreciation for the musicians who were all drenched in sweat from the vigour of their performance.

Eddie leaned over to her. 'Let me get you a drink, then I need another smoke.'

'Okay.'

'What are you having?' he asked.

'Whatever you're having is fine.' Chloe was thirsty and would have asked for a soft drink or water if she hadn't been worried he would judge her as uncool and unable to hold her alcohol. Although she usually preferred a subtle white wine, she would be happy with whatever he bought.

She hung back, not wanting to get caught in the crush at the bar. Mel gave her a nod from across the room, where she and Robbo were chatting with the band that had just finished as they packed up.

'Here you go, you had JD last time yeah?' Eddie handed her a small tumbler filled with dark brown liquid, her face heated as their fingers brushed as she took the glass.

'Well done for remembering.' It was more expensive than the beer he held in his other hand.

'I have a few skills; knowing someone's drink is one of them.' Now he had one hand free, he pulled her behind him out to the laneway. As impolite as it was considered to buy drinks during the bands it was worse to go out for a smoke, and the alley was bustling with people getting their nicotine fix.

Eddie found a patch of wall to lean against a little way from the crowd. There was something about the way he stared at her that made her believe she was the only person who mattered; her belly fluttered and her mind seem to work slowly.

'So Chloe, what did you think of the music?' he asked, eyes roving over her.

'I dunno.' She giggled. 'I'm sure they're very good, but I'm not very hard-core when it comes to music.'

'I loved it. I like all kinds of music though.' He sipped his beer. 'What's your go to album these days?'

'I listen to Lady Gaga when I work out. Mostly whatever is on the radio though.'

'I see.' He nodded and seemed about to say something else but decided against it.

'I know it probably… sounds like a cop out… I guess I'm not very musical.' Her words wouldn't flow in his presence.

'I've never been able to play an instrument, my parents never pushed me that way, but I've always thought the music industry was a fantastic business to get into.'

'You work in the industry then?'

A slow smile spread across his face. 'I have my fingers in a few different things. I was a band booker for a while for a place in Brunswick, but that didn't pan out. I mostly work for myself.'

He must be very driven to be self-employed.

'I'm sure you'd do very well at whatever you put your mind to.'

'Are you flirting with me, Miss Chloe?'

'No, I mean … a little.' Despite the cold, her cheeks were burning.

'Glad to hear it.' He leaned his head close to her ear, his breath warm on her neck. 'I think you're hot.' He stood up again and took a long, meaningful drag on his cigarette. 'I'm sure you hear that all the time though.'

Chloe turned away, her heart racing. 'No, not very often.' She turned her eyes back to him to see his hand pressed against his chest in mock surprise.

'I can't believe it. A girl as cute as you who doesn't know it. How did I get so lucky?'

Chloe never had a man as handsome and charming as Eddie interested in her, she wasn't sure what to do with his attention. Mel would tell her to go with the flow, but her mind spun ineffectually. Should she try to kiss him? Or wait until he kissed her, but risk him thinking she wasn't interested. Eddie stubbed out his smoke and flicked it into the tin nearby.

'Sounds like the next band is on.' He cocked his head toward the door and sauntered back inside. She followed, good job making interesting conversation.

It wasn't like her to be flustered by the attention of a handsome man. She prided herself on the ability to connect with people from all walks of life. Perhaps the slow burn in her groin was to blame for her apparent lack of verbal skills.

The next band was a six-piece, with a trumpet and trombone added to the usual guitars and drums. They played a punk ska set with complicated slap-basslines and infectious beats. Chloe finished her drink part-way through their third song and found Eddie standing behind her, his hands on either side of her waist encouraging her hips to sway. Her stomach tensed and she felt out of breath; it wasn't the dancing that took her breath away.

As the set progressed, Eddie's hands moved their way forward, around her waist, lying against her stomach. His lean form was now pressed up against her back, his groin against her buttocks. She might have imagined it, but she thought there was a hint of hardness there.

'This is our last song, you guys have been great,' the singer announced, his jet-black hair stood stiff in a two-inch-high quiff covered in so much hair spray it hadn't moved through the entire performance. The guitarist struck the opening chord just as Eddie moved around to face her.

He stared into her eyes, the music faded away and there was nothing but his gaze holding hers. He kissed her, his lips soft and tender at first, then little by little, more insistent.

She felt like a teenager, making out in front of the stage. Despite being kissed many times before, it was as though this was the first time. Everything was new; sensations threatened to overwhelm her. Her groin was hot, pulsing, and she knew there would be slickness there, her nipples were pert and sensitive where she brushed against him. The warm place under his hand where he held her lower back felt as though it belonged to someone else.

At some point she realised Eddie had pulled away and was applauding the band taking their bow. She stood for a moment, frozen and dazed from the kiss, before managing to clap her hands.

'You're a great kisser, you know,' he said.

'Thanks,' she replied, still a little breathless. 'So are you.'

'I was going to suggest we ditch the last band and go back to your place, but I know you came with them, so that would be very bad form on my part to tempt you away from your friends.'

'You're right.'

'Another drink?'

She nodded, watching him as he walked to the bar for her again.

'You didn't say he was that hot, babe, damn.' Mel had appeared at her elbow without Chloe seeing her approach. She must really be smitten to be so oblivious.

'He's not bad.'

'I saw you two locking lips in that last song.'

Chloe smiled, unsure what to say.

'You absolute slut.' Mel batted her upper arm playfully. 'I don't think any of the band would notice if you snuck off early. Just saying.'

'Don't say that, I don't need any more temptation today.' Chloe shook her head. 'I have a rule about hooking up on the first night.'

'There are always exceptions, and for someone who looks like that, who only has eyes for you by the way … I would.'

Eddie waved to her from the bar and pointed to the door, obviously headed out for a smoke. 'As long as you won't hate me if I disappear. I'll text you to let you know, so you don't worry.'

'Thanks, babe. You know I need to be sure you haven't been murdered.' Mel followed her gaze to the door. 'You better follow, I know your mind is there anyway.'

Chloe smiled, gave her friend's hand a squeeze and bounded after Eddie into the laneway.

'Am I approved then?' he said, holding her drink out for her.

'I don't know what you mean.'

'I know what girls are like, your little debrief there was definitely getting the seal of approval from your wing-woman.'

'Who has been giving you all our secrets?' Chloe took a sip from her drink, this one had a lot more JD in it than the last, she wondered if he was trying to get her drunk, although he didn't need to. 'Mel said the band probably wouldn't miss me if I happened to leave before or during their set.'

'Oh really?' Eddie's eyebrow pulled up. 'You don't seem the type to go home with a stranger.'

'I'm not.'

'But?'

'It seems like a good bet I won't regret it in the morning if that kiss was anything to go by.' Before the kiss, she had been all hormones and nerves, but now she tapped into some hidden confidence. Perhaps she was just the right amount of drunk, or her hormones had kicked in, Chloe didn't want to question it.

'You wouldn't regret it. That's an Eddie Travers guarantee.' He watched her from under half-closed lids. 'I'm going to finish my drink, and then I'm going to get into a cab. I'd love you to join me.'

Chapter 2

For a moment, Chloe considered not following Eddie into the taxi. She'd had rotten luck with men she'd hooked up with on the first date in the past, plus she knew nothing about him. Despite their physical connection he hadn't told her anything of substance about himself. She bounced on her toes for a beat, then followed him.

'You had me worried there for a while.' Eddie winked at her, holding the door of the cab so she could slide into the back seat.

'I don't usually do this.'

'Of course not. You're not a slut, I knew that as soon as I saw you.' Eddie's thigh pressed against hers, he laid his hand on her knee and she twitched.

'Is that okay?' he asked.

'Yes, sorry.' Chloe took his hand and replaced it on her knee. She wasn't sure why she was so jumpy; he had been nothing but a gentleman to her, and she was certainly interested. His hand was heavy, resting on the black pantyhose she wore. Mel said her skirt was too short, as well as being too orange, to wear without pantyhose at a place like Red Plum without attracting the wrong sort of attention. She was right, Eddie was the right kind of attention.

'Where are we headed then?' Eddie asked, breaking into her thoughts.

'Pardon?'

'I'd love to come to your place, I live with a guy who's a bit messy sometimes, I wouldn't want to make a bad impression letting you see that before I've had the chance to clean up. I wasn't expecting company tonight.'

Chloe giggled and told the driver where to go. She had a one-bedroom flat in Richmond, just near the train station. It wasn't fancy, but it was clean and had everything she needed. A space that was just hers, no one would walk in in the middle of the night or steal her stuff, or something worse.

Eddie's hand remained where it was for the short cab ride, traffic was thin. He leaned forward to pay the driver.

'Let me,' she said. 'You bought me all those drinks.'

'Don't be silly, I'm not keeping score.' He waved her money away.

'Follow me. I'm at the top of the stairs just at the back.' Her apartment complex had several freestanding buildings, each with six apartments. Hers was on the second floor in the building at the back. The taxi had dropped them off on the main street, she led Eddie down the side passageway, under the unflattering fluorescent lights to her building and up the stairs. He was curiously silent all the way, when she turned to check on him, he brought his finger to his lips in a shushing motion.

'Don't want to wake the neighbours,' he whispered. She nodded.

As soon as they were inside her front door Eddie grabbed her by the waist, spun her around and kissed her. Chloe tensed in surprise but quickly melted into the embrace. Where he had been tender and exploratory on the dance floor, now he seemed filled with a hunger for her. He pressed his hands up under her T-shirt, flat against the skin on her back. The chilly air in the room a delightful contrast to the heat in his hands.

There was no mistaking the erection that grew, pressing against her this time. She put her hand between their bodies to rub him through his tight black jeans.

'Not yet.' He pulled her hand away. 'We don't need to rush.'

Chloe shivered in anticipation. There weren't many men, in her experience, who wanted to go slowly. He dropped his jacket onto the floor, then peeled off his black shirt. His torso was tight, lean, and hairless except for a couple of patches around the nipples, and a trail leading from his belly button to his waistband.

His skin was as hot as his hands, and when he pulled her shirt off over her head and drew her in for a kiss their torsos were on fire. Her breath caught as her desire for him soared.

'Bedroom?' he asked, inclining his head to the half-open door to his left.

She nodded, not sure if she could still form words. Her room was tidy as always, she didn't have much stuff and she liked to keep it boxed away where it would be found easily if needed. Her mother seemed to have no organisational skills and had constantly misplaced things as she grew up. Not having many possessions certainly helped.

Chloe was still wearing her pantyhose and skirt, and after pushing her onto her back on the bed, Eddie reached up to pull them off. His mouth followed the line of her thigh, following the retreating pantyhose. Once they were off, he traced back up her legs to her groin, flipping up her skirt and pressing his mouth against her panties. His hot breath felt like electricity.

'I think we'll leave these here,' he murmured, not lifting his mouth away. She started to speak, but he shushed her, and pushed her knees further apart.

He explored her skin for what felt like and age. Her arousal building and building until she had soaked through her panties completely. He refused to move them aside, teasing her with his mouth and hands through the fabric.

'Do you want me to fuck you?' he asked, he crawled up the bed to lie beside her. His erection clearly outlined against his jeans. Chloe put her hand out and started to rub him.

'If you'd like to,' she said.

'I want to know what you want,' he purred in her ear, his groin grinding against her hand. She wanted him so badly.

'I want you to fuck me,' she said, before she moved her hand to slide it down his belly and under the waistband of his pants. When she touched the sensitive skin on his cock he twitched and let out a small moan.

All at once he unzipped himself, rolled her onto her side, pulled her panties down and slipped into her from behind. She sighed in pleasure; it was as though he had been made to fit her.

Slowly at first, and then with more vigour, he fucked her. Finally gasping and spasming to orgasm a few minutes later. Chloe had been close to orgasm herself, after being so thoroughly teased before he entered her it was the closest she'd ever come to it on a first time with a man. Often, she wouldn't come with men at all, only on her own, unless her boyfriends were very patient with oral sex or had good stamina.

It wasn't until Eddie had slipped out of her, she realised they hadn't used a condom. It was too late now, but she'd need to get a morning after pill just in case. Her last serious boyfriend had dumped her several months ago and since then she'd seen no reason to keep taking her birth control pills. A consideration for later though, she should focus on the warm body behind her, his breath slow and steady as though he'd fallen asleep.

She must have dozed off, because she woke up to find her right arm asleep and her neck stuck in an awkward position. Eddie was still sound asleep behind her. She kicked off her panties, they had been down around her knees, and extracted herself from Eddie's arms to visit the bathroom.

Funny that he had spent so long at the start of their encounter and then finished in a flurry without removing his jeans or her skirt. Not that it mattered, he was an excellent kisser and a very good lover. Perhaps if they saw each other again he would be the first man to make her come. She smiled to herself, it would be good to see him again.

*   *   *

'Morning, sleepyhead.' A deep voice crooned next to her. For a moment Chloe had forgotten she had company and jumped to hear a man's voice. Then she remembered the handsome man she'd taken home with her. She rolled over to find he had snuggled up behind her in the bed. On returning from the bathroom, she had gently rearranged him so she could get under the covers. It was usually hard for her to sleep with someone in the bed, especially after getting used to being on her own again, but not last night.

Chloe rolled over, taking in the angular planes of his face, strong nose, a little stubble, and brown hair worn long. Her eyes flicked down for a moment, and she realised he was nude. And she was nude. He kissed her and she remembered how good it had felt to be with him.

They had sex again before getting up, Eddie didn't take as much time on the warm-up this time but lasted a little longer. She didn't usually admit it, but missionary was her favourite position, being able to look into her partner's face, to feel his weight on her.

'Do you want coffee?' she asked, her fingers trailing lazily up and down his forearm.

'I never say no to coffee, especially after amazing morning sex.' He smiled and the cheeky twinkle in his eye made her laugh.

'I'll be right back.'

Chloe slipped on her blue fluffy dressing gown and made coffee. The apartment was cold, her feet a little chill on the lino in the kitchen, but the lingering warmth of what she had done with Eddie kept her mind off her cold toes.

She had nothing much in the house for breakfast, usually having toast or porridge. Perhaps she could scrape together passable scrambled eggs if Eddie was hungry.

'Do you want milk?' she asked from the kitchen, there was no response, so she left it black. When she went back into the bedroom with Eddie was fast asleep, one leg hanging out of the blankets.

She perched her bottom on the bed next to him and wafted the coffee under his nose. Eddie opened his eyes and smiled.

'That smells good.'

'I asked if you wanted milk or sugar, but you had fallen asleep.'

'Oh, yeah. Do you mind putting some milk in?'

She sighed, placing her coffee on the bedside table and heading back to the kitchen. 'I don't have much for breakfast. Do you want to get brunch?'

Eddie was sitting up in bed holding her coffee. 'This is great by the way.' It shouldn't have annoyed her, the cup was clean and it was no different to the coffee she held in her hands, but something about the way he'd taken hers while she was out of the room set her hackles rising. She put it to the back of her mind.

'You didn't give me an answer about going for brunch.' She scooted back into the bed beside him.

'I've got some stuff I need to do today, otherwise I would totally stick around here. I didn't plan on staying the night with anyone when I went out last night.' He ran a hand through his tousled hair; it fell back across his forehead almost immediately.

'Work stuff?' Chloe asked, curious to find out more about this handsome stranger still naked in her bed.

'You could say that. I work for myself, so I spend a bit of time trying to set up deal, you know, schmoosing and getting people on board, it means I sometimes have weird hours and irregular pay, but I hate working for the man.'

'I understand. There have been times I've thought about whether having a boss was just a way to make myself miserable.'

'What do you do then?' He turned towards her, lying on his side, head on his hand.

'I'm a teacher's aide. I work with special needs students who are still okay to be in regular school as long as they have a bit of help.'

'Sounds like a nightmare.'

'I like it. I really bond with my students. Sometimes I get to stay with one student for a few years and see them grow. It's very rewarding.'

Eddie nodded. He didn't seem impressed. It had always been her dream to be a teacher but with everything that happened in Year 12 she didn't get into the program. Instead, she did a Certificate III and IV at

TAFE as a steppingstone to get into a Bachelor of Education but she had enjoyed the work so much she'd decided to stay where she was for now. There was always the possibility to go to uni later.

After a while, Chloe realised Eddie was staring at her. 'What?'

'I was just watching your mind ticking over. You seemed very deep in thought.'

Chloe looked down and away. 'Sorry.'

He kissed her cheek, bringing a waft of fresh coffee with him. 'I better shoot off, love.'

'Okay, then.' She sighed. It had been a lovely way to wake up, too bad it couldn't last a little longer. 'Do you want to shower or anything?'

'No, I'm right.' Eddie was out of the bed and slipping on his boxer-briefs and skinny jeans with a surprising speed for someone who had fallen asleep in the time it took to brew coffee. She watched him as he redressed, remembering the feeling of his skin against hers, his body pressing up against hers.

'I don't have your number,' she said as he slipped the black T-shirt over his head. He hesitated for a moment, as though weighing up whether to give it to her. Chloe felt she might be sick, it was the longest moment of her life, she was sure.

'Sure,' he said finally, waiting until she had her phone in her hand to type in the number. 'Shoot me a message sometime and we'll get together again. Maybe even have a proper date.' He winked and turned to walk out the bedroom door.

Chloe sprang out of the bed, she had thought he might draw out the goodbye, or at least come over to her for a kiss, but he was all business now. She jogged after him to the front door.

'I'm definitely holding you to that date. Dinner some time. I hope your … work today goes well.' She held his hand. He turned to kiss her goodbye, his free hand cupping her jaw, reigniting all the feelings in her groin which had been dormant.

Without a second glance Eddie strode off down the stairs and out of the apartment. Chloe shivered, realising how cold it was outside and shut the door.

Sundays were her day for lounging. Often, she would go out with Mel, or one of her other girlfriends on Saturday night and she didn't like to make plans for Sunday in case things got messy. Her tummy grumbled; without company she couldn't justify the expense of brunch out. Her salary, although good for the industry, was largely taken up by her rent. Living alone had its drawbacks but she wouldn't change it for anything. She sipped the last of her coffee before putting both cups in the sink to be washed later. A warm sticky feeling between her thighs reminded her she needed to get a morning after pill, and to find the prescription for birth control she had around somewhere. As cute as Eddie might be, she was in no position to have a baby right now.

*　　　*　　　*

Chloe showered and walked down to the chemist in the shops not far from her apartment. She lived not far from Victoria Street, a bustling part of Richmond in Melbourne's inner east, lined with a curious mix: Vietnamese restaurants, Asian grocers and interesting-smelling butchers' shops, and an increasing number of gentrified hipster bars. Chloe had been living in Richmond for a couple of years, and there was a time she'd had trouble getting a good caffe latte on Victoria Street, these days it was being slowly taken over by well-off couples in their late twenties and early thirties, with no kids and plenty of disposable income.

That wasn't to say the massive housing commission estates had disappeared, nor had their tenants. Mostly low-income people, recent migrants, and their families, there was still a real heroin problem in the area. Every other week she would find used syringes around the bins at the back of her building. At least the crime in the area didn't seem to be rising.

The older man behind the counter at the chemist looked over his glasses at her with disapproval when she asked for a morning after pill. She also handed him her script for contraceptives, which had taken a good ten minutes of searching to find it. He raised an eyebrow as he read it over.

'I've started seeing someone, you see,' she said, the urge to explain herself was overwhelming.

'Ten minutes,' he said, then grumbled something unintelligible. She nodded, then turned to head up the street to get a Vietnamese iced coffee and a *banh mi*, an extravagance but only half the cost of brunch.

*   *   *

A couple of hours later, Chloe was lazing on the couch watching a British crime procedural on DVD when her phone rang. It was her mother, again, she'd ignored the call last night.

'Hi Mum.'

'Why didn't you answer last night?' Janine's words were slightly slurred, perhaps she'd been into the Valium.

'It was late and I was out with Mel.'

'Of course, silly me. You know how I get with time sometimes.'

Chloe did know. Janine didn't work, at least not with any kind of regularity, and constantly mixed prescription medication with wine, it was a wonder she knew what year it was sometimes. 'Do you need something?'

'Why would I need something?'

'You called me, remember?'

There was a pause. 'Oh yes. Gary went out of town with his fishing buddies, and I need you to come for dinner. I don't like to be alone too long. You know I get sad when I'm left on my own.'

Chloe never really bought into her mother's implied threats of self-harm, but all her training and experience meant she couldn't ignore them completely. 'Okay, I'll come over later.' She glanced at the time, a little before four o'clock. 'Have you got anything to eat? Or will I bring something?'

'I don't think there's much in the fridge. You're a dear, looking after your old mum.'

'You're not old, Mum.'

Janine was in her mid-forties, although a hard life and mistreatment of her body meant she looked older.

'I'll see you at about six then? Could you grab me some ciggies too?'

'Of course.' Chloe ended the call. As long as she could remember it had been the same, her mother behaved more like the child in their relationship. Bouncing from one boyfriend to another, they would move in and move out with dizzying speed sometimes. Her relationship with wine and pills went up and down, at the moment she seemed to be going downhill. Chloe would need to be careful not to get sucked into Janine's vortex of self-pity—there was a fine line between helping her mother and enabling her. She'd never been able to afford therapy but had read up on dysfunctional parents in her spare time. It had helped get perspective on when Janine was being manipulative and when she was struggling.

*   *   *

The house was a mid-fifties style, yellow brick veneer bungalow. The fittings hadn't been replaced since Janine moved in just before Chloe was born; dark brown carpet, pine panelling on some of the walls, small dark brown tiles in the kitchen that never looked clean, and a brick archway between the kitchen and lounge which housed a battered brown velvet lounge suite. Often, she would choose to sit in the dining chairs when she visited, hating the feeling of being swallowed by the lumpy couch. Her mother had started draping the cushions in other fabric, as the velvet had worn away so much in some places there was gaffer tape holding it together.

The drive from Richmond was about twenty minutes in good traffic, on Sundays it was usually clear. Her mother didn't drive, more often than not she couldn't afford the upkeep on a car and she had let her licence lapse at some point when Chloe was starting high-school. Though she didn't seem to have many friends, she always managed to convince someone to give her a ride if she needed to get anywhere, not that she went out much.

'My baby! It's been so long since you were here.' Her mother tottered out of the house to meet her in the twilit street.

'I was here last week. I usually come every other Sunday.' Chloe spoke softly, her mother was sensitive and would fall into a deep depression if she was too hard on her. 'Where's Gary?'

'He's fishing, I told you. I've been on my own all weekend.'

It was unusual for one of Janine's partners to have any time away from her, she made sure they were joined at the hip most of the time. Perhaps he was on a romantic getaway with his mistress Chloe thought darkly.

Janine hugged herself, her body a strange combination of scrawny and flabby thanks to her diet, habits and lack of exercise. She looked a little more drawn than usual, until Chloe remembered she was out of cigarettes.

'I got these for you.' She held out the pack, trying not to look at the rotten teeth on the government health warning and ugly grey-green colour of the plain package. They'd changed the law a couple of years ago but Chloe suspected it had done very little to deter smokers, especially ones with as long a habit as her mother. Janine snatched at the cigarettes, ripped off the film of plastic wrapping and produced a lighter from some hidden pocket. One long exhale and the tension in her shoulders seemed to release.

'Come in, come in. No good standing around in the cold.' She smiled, her teeth were yellowed but at least they didn't look purple with wine yet. Perhaps it wasn't such a bad day after all.

The pantry and fridge were almost bare, except for a few condiments and a bag of flour that could have been there since Chloe left home. She'd been to the supermarket on the way and grabbed hamburger patties, bread rolls, tomato, lettuce and cheese.

'I'm making hamburgers. Does that sound alright?' Chloe said, popping her green reusable bag on the dining table.

'That's fine, baby, I'm not that hungry anyway.'

Chloe had never been a big eater, given her size a normal serving was too much, but her mother was worse. Sometimes she went through phases of barely eating anything at all except jelly snakes, cigarettes and wine, and other times she would stop taking so much Valium and get on a health kick. It was after these that Chloe would sometimes find vegetables in the bottom of the fridge in various stages of decay.

Despite the lack of a role model in the cooking department, Janine's go-to meal was sausages and chips, made from potatoes if she was feeling especially fancy, Chloe had grown up to have a discerning palate. She loved watching cooking shows, often making up big batches of food to store in the freezer. Her small apartment meant she needed to be very careful what she bought and cooked, or it wouldn't fit in the kitchen or fridge. School lunches were especially useful for her to prepare in advance and the teachers and other staff frequently commented on how colourful and healthy they looked. She was going through a salad in mason jars phase at the moment, though she may need to switch to soups as the weather got cooler.

Janine, having called her daughter to keep her company, stayed in the lounge room and watched TV while Chloe prepared dinner. At least she didn't have to do the dishes first this time.

'How's Gary's job going?' she called from the kitchen doorway. Her mother was watching a home renovation competition with the volume up far too loud to invite conversation.

'Hmm?'

'Turn the TV down, Mum.'

Janine made no move to lower the volume or turn away from the screen, Chloe sighed and returned to flip the patties. *So much for company.*

They ate the burgers together in front of the TV, both sitting on the threadbare brown velvet sectional couch. It too, had been there longer than Chloe had been alive.

'Do you ever think about getting a new couch? This one is so—well, it's manky. I don't even want to think about how many bums have sat on it.'

'It's still perfectly good. No use throwing something out when it's still good.' This was her mother's answer to everything; the couch, her bed, the piles of junk in the spare room. Ever since Chloe had moved out years before, the room that used to be hers had started to fill up with random stuff.

'Did I tell you Gary threw out some of my boxes without telling me?'

Chloe raised an eyebrow. 'No. What was in there?'

'I don't know, I couldn't look after he'd thrown it away.'

'Was it really so important if you can't even remember what was in them?'

'You're as bad as he is. He says I'm a hoarder.'

'Oh?' Chloe bit her tongue before any further comment could slip out.

'Yes. He says I can't possibly need all those things, and that they're escaping the spare room now and he won't have it. He wants to turn the spare room into a home gym you see, so he wants to get rid of all my precious collections.'

All the childhood clothes I grew out of, and toys I stopped playing with, Chloe thought. 'I'm sure there are

38

some things worth keeping, like the macaroni art I made you in prep, or some of your paintings, but most of it is just rubbish. Not even worth going to the op shop.'

'I might need it sometime, and you know I can't afford to buy things whenever I need them.'

Chloe nodded; a lot of her mother's hoarding tendencies came from being incredibly poor when Chloe was a child. Her mother had bought the house with her inheritance, so rent had never been a problem, but it also meant Janine had very little incentive to go out and get a good job. She tried a few things; letter dropping advertising materials, although that was too much walking, she'd worked for the electoral commission a few times, but that was always seasonal work, and if she managed to get a steady, normal job, someone would say something to her, or look at her funny, and she would spiral into depression, unable to get out of bed for a week or more, and they would have to let her go. If she'd managed to stay anywhere longer than six months it would have been harder to fire her, but she'd never managed to hold herself together that long.

Chloe pitied her mother, she'd been working at the same school for three years, developed friendships with the other staff, and watched her pupils develop and move into high school much better off than they would have been without her help. It gave her a sense of achievement and satisfaction her mother had probably never felt.

'When is Gary back from his trip?'

'He said he'd go straight to work from the country tomorrow and he should be home around dinnertime.'

'You'll have to go to the shops.'

'Mmm.'

Chloe doubted that her mother would make it. She seemed to be heading into one of her dark times. 'Did something happen? You seem less chatty than usual.'

'I don't know what you mean.' Janine shifted in her seat, picking at a piece of fluff on the hem of her hoodie.

'You're avoiding my questions. Something's happened. Has Gary left you?'

'Why would you ask that? Gary and I are as strong as ever.' Her cheeks flushed and she looked at the ground.

'Is he really on a fishing trip? Or has he moved out? Is that why you need company and cigarettes and have no food in the cupboard?'

'No.' Her voice was so small Chloe only just heard it.

'Really?'

'No.'

Chloe reached for the remote and put the show on mute. She knew better than to turn the TV off completely, that would have set her mother off, either crying or yelling that she was missing something important. 'Are you okay, Mum?

'He said he was going on a fishing trip. That much is true. I just...' she sighed. 'I don't think he is. I think he's off with some floozy. And I don't know if he's coming back.'

'Have you asked him about it? Has he been fishing before?'

'Yes.'

'Yes what?'

'He's been fishing before.'

'What's different about it this time?' Chloe didn't want to assume her mother was just being a drama queen for the attention, but she had done it before.

'The way he looked at me when he said he was going.'

'I see.' Chloe paused, allowing the silence to draw out. 'Do you think you might be reading a little bit too much into it?'

'No!' her mother said, clenching her fists. 'I'm not crazy.'

'I didn't say you were.' Chloe had said the wrong thing, that much was clear. The window for talking her mother down from the metaphorical ledge had passed and she would be in too much of a state to bring her down now. 'I'm sorry, I didn't mean it. I know you're not crazy.'

Janine got up from the couch, snatched the plates from the coffee table and stomped into the kitchen.

'You can go now. If you're not on my side then you're against me, and I don't need any more enemies.'

Chloe sighed. 'Do you want me to wash up for you?'

'I can do the dishes myself, thank you, Chloe.'

'Alright, I'll see you in a fortnight then. I love you.' She picked up her handbag and the empty green fabric shopping bag and went out to her car. She hadn't expected things to go so badly so quickly, usually she was a better judge of her mother's mood.

Chloe walked to her car, started the engine and headed home.

Chapter 3

As tempting at it was to check in on her mother, Chloe did her best to put it from her mind. The number Eddie had given her was stored in her phone. She typed out and deleted a message to him several times that night as she lay in bed before deciding it was too soon.

The next day at work it was easy not to contact him, as her phone stayed in her bag while she was in class.

'What did you get up to this weekend, Chlo'?' Mary asked. They sat across the table from one another at the large table in the staff room.

'Not too much, went to see some bands on Saturday night. What about you?' Chloe knew Mary really wanted to talk about her own weekend. Being the school librarian would have made her a quiet and retiring if stereotypes were to be believed but Mary was a gossip the likes of whom Chloe had rarely seen. In her mid-fifties, Mary had never had children and her marriage had ended about six months after Chloe started working at the school. For some reason Mary decided to make her an ally and would tell her all about her life, and the life of anyone ill-advised enough to tell her their business.

'Do you remember I told you I was going to a lingerie party on the weekend? My friend has recently become a rep for some really gorgeous stuff and of course I wanted to be supportive. I didn't realise how fabulous the garments were until I got there.' Mary took a sip from her coffee; instant with two spoons of coffee and two of sugar with at least two fingers of milk in the top. 'I ended up spending far too much money. I did think about becoming a rep myself, my friend Ange says the parties aren't too much work and she makes good commission. Plus, if I sign up she gets a bonus, and who wouldn't want that?'

Chloe nodded, it sounded like a pyramid scheme, but she would never say so. No doubt Mary would work it out, or else spend all her money on lingerie she didn't need and get bored of the idea. 'What did you buy?' she asked, hoping to give Mary enough room to talk without needing to contribute to the conversation too much. While she was talking, Chloe's mind started to wander, filled with steamy memories of the man she'd met on Saturday night.

Maybe he was a bit of a bad boy, he certainly dressed that way, but she had dressed for the venue too, so she shouldn't get too hung up on that. Working for himself showed initiative but it could also be code for chronically unemployed or flaky. The only way to really know would be to spend more time with him.

Oddly she hadn't heard from Mel since Saturday night. Usually if Chloe hooked up with anyone, or even got a phone number, Mel would text her constantly offering advice, whether Chloe wanted it or not. But now she'd got Mary started describing her purchases she couldn't take out her phone and message either Mel or Eddie. It was one thing to only listen with part of her attention, it would be another thing entirely to start typing on her phone.

'Are you listening?' Mary was frowning. Clearly something that required a response had been said and Chloe hadn't provided it.

'I'm so sorry, I was miles away.'

'I can see that. I was asking if you were ever in the market for some nice undergarments?'

Chloe's first thought was to refuse, why should she spend her precious discretionary money on something so frivolous, but on the other hand. 'Well, I did meet a nice young man on the weekend. Perhaps it's something to think about.' Her cheeks heated.

'You weren't even going to tell me?' Mary put her hand to her chest in mock outrage.

'I didn't want to jinx it by mentioning it too early, but I guess it's out of the bag now.'

The bell rang and Chloe was saved from being grilled about this new man. Her own friends and family didn't ask as many questions as this primary school librarian did.

*   *   *

During the quiet periods in her afternoon Chloe composed the perfect text to Eddie, and to Mel in her mind. When she got into her car ready to head home, she typed and sent it.

> *Hi, it's Chloe, from the other night. I had a really nice time. I wondered if you'd like to go out for dinner some time? There are a few good spots near me.*

Once the message was sailing though the ether, she realised she hadn't tried calling him while he was there, it was possible he'd given her a fake number. She hoped not, but her mind tended towards more suspicious than not.

How were the Inflatable Cocks? And the rest of your Saturday night? I hope the boys didn't notice my absence.

Several days without any word from Mel could mean she was pissed Chloe had ditched the band for a boy, but it could also mean she was busy with Robbo or a hangover. It wouldn't be the first time Mel had needed to take Monday off work after a really big Saturday night.

Monday nights were for Chloe's boxing class. She drove straight to the gym from school, did the class, got sweaty and made it home by seven. After the workout she was ravenous, and put a container of home-made cottage pie into the microwave.

Three seconds before the microwave dinged, her phone started ringing in her handbag.

'Hello?'

'Hey, babe!' Mel said. 'I can't believe you didn't even call me to tell me about the guy you ditched me for. I hate you.' Her voice sounded cheerful.

'Sunday got away from me and you know I can't talk at work.'

'I'm only teasing. Tell me all about it immediately.'

Chloe took her pie out of the microwave and sat at her tiny kitchen table. She took small bites so she could talk and eat without appearing too rude. 'Sorry, I'm starving after the gym, you'll have to hear about Eddie while I eat.'

'Eddie is his name? Seems so normal for someone with a face like that. Oof. Yes please. I mean I would have been after him if I wasn't with Robbo. His nose is slightly too big, but I think that's allowed. Did you go home with him?'

'He came to mine.'

'Interesting, could mean his place is a shithole, or he doesn't know how to wash sheets.'

'Don't be gross.' It hadn't occurred to Chloe to wonder why he wanted to come to her place. She was happy to be in her safe place with him, some other guys she wouldn't have been so keen to allow them in her inner sanctum. Thinking back on it, it wasn't entirely smart to let a stranger know where she lived. He could have robbed her while she was asleep, not that she had anything worth selling.

'And he stayed the night?' Mel asked.

'Yes, I offered him breakfast, but he had to dash off to do some work thing. That's what he said anyway.'

'Thank goodness! The worst thing about a one-night stand is if they won't leave in the morning.'

'Who said it was a one-night stand?'

'It wasn't?'

'I don't want it to be, I hate the idea of hooking up with people. Not that there's anything wrong with it, but I like people to get to know me for more than just my body.'

'You're a prude, you know that?' Mel said.

'Maybe.'

'I know all about your mother and her string of boyfriends and having a few nights of good fun doesn't make you like her. Plus, she's a serial monogamist which isn't you at all. You're a smart, funny, independent woman who is not dependent on prescription drugs and wine. You'll never be like her.'

Chloe sighed, her breath a little ragged from keeping her emotions in check. Mel always knew exactly the thing she was worried about. Sometimes it was comforting to have a friend who knew her so well, but other times it felt like a slap in the face. She wasn't sure whether this time it had been a little of both.

'How was the rest of your night?'

'The band was awesome, obviously. We hung out at Plum till they threw us out at about three, then Steve's mate invited us to his place in Prahran. He had some coke, so we took a few lines of that, then Robbo got really toey so we fucked in the bathroom. We stayed up till about ten the next morning before calling a cab and crawling home. I barely made it to work today.' She laughed.

Chloe wondered if one day Mel's antics would land her in hot water. 'How could you trust Steve's mate's coke would be safe?'

'You're such a grandma.' Mel laughed. 'He had some first, I always wait till someone else has some first. I mean I guess it wouldn't help if the coke was cut with something dumb like heroin but the chances of that are pretty slim. YOLO babe.'

She wasn't wrong but Chloe still thought it was wiser to be a bit cautious. Then again Mel had grown up in a nice, upper middle-class family in Burwood. They were the safest people she knew. Mel seemed to have a need to create drama and rebel against her boring, predictable, nice childhood. Chloe had had an extremely disruptive childhood and her mother was constantly on the verge of addiction or depressive breakdown. Sometimes they didn't have enough money for food and Chloe would go to school with nothing for her lunch. Safe and reliable was what she craved.

'Since you're not into one-night stands, when are you seeing him again?' Mel asked.

'I don't know yet.'

'You did get his digits, right?'

'Of course, just as he was leaving, I wasn't sure he wanted to give them to me, but he did.'

'And what did he say when you texted him?'

Chloe hesitated. 'So far, nothing. I'm trying very hard to ignore the little voice in my head that says it might be a fake number.'

Mel was quiet. 'I'm sure it's not a fake number. Maybe he's busy, or at work. When did you text?'

'Earlier today.'

'It's only been a couple of hours. No need to worry yet. Not everyone is glued to their phones.'

Chloe wanted to be reassured, but she wasn't. She'd eaten half of her portion of cottage pie, but her appetite had left her. She prodded the mashed potato topping with her fork. 'I'm sure you're right.'

They chatted for a while longer, Mel told her about the rest of the night, including a more graphic recount of her bathroom adventure. Despite not thinking of herself as a prude, Chloe wasn't so keen on knowing the intimate details of her friend's sex life.

'Anyway, I better go, Robbo's coming around.'

'Thanks for the call. I'll let you know if anything exciting happens with Eddie.' The knot in Chloe's belly that had eased a little while Mel had been talking was back. She hung up the phone and saw a text had come through while she was on the line.

> *Dinner sounds good. How about*
> *Saturday? I'll pick you up. Let's go local,*
> *I'm sure you know a couple of good places.*

She almost laughed in relief. The number was real, Eddie was interested to meet up again, maybe this would turn into something good after all.

*   *   *

The work week seemed to crawl by; she went to the spin class on Thursday night, and even woke up in time for yoga on Saturday. She had been so anxious the night before their dinner date she'd mostly lain in her bed alternately staring at the ceiling or screwing her eyes closed instead of sleeping. If someone had asked her what the worry was about, she wouldn't have been able to say; just a low-lying sense of foreboding that something was going to go wrong.

Eddie was supposed to come by at seven to pick her up and they would walk down the road to one of the many excellent pho shops in Victoria Street; cheap and cheerful and the quality was guaranteed.

At twenty past seven buzzer for her front gate went. She picked up the handset to speak. 'Hello?'

'Hi babe, come down and let's get some dinner.' Eddie's voice was cheerful.

'I'll be right there.' Chloe slipped on her going out flats, she'd worn huge heels to the bar the weekend before, but she usually favoured flats, despite making her feel short. She wore a knee-length black skirt, black stockings, a black T-shirt and a pink and white polka-dot cardigan all under an elegant grey coat that went to mid-thigh. Chloe much preferred to buy quality clothing and make it last, her wardrobe had to double as school appropriate and date appropriate.

'You look nice.' Eddie smiled as he saw her approaching down the dark side passage. 'If a little bit proper.' He winked.

'Didn't I tell you I'm a teacher? I have to look like this or else they take away my licence,' Chloe joked, hiding the hurt. She was sure he didn't mean to make her feel small, but he had managed to pick on the one thing she was most concerned about.

'You're funny.' He grabbed her by the waist and planted a kiss on her lips. At first Chloe was stiff, she hadn't expected such a show of affection at the gate, especially after the brisk way he had left on Sunday. Once over the initial shock, she melted into his arms. He was a surprisingly tender kisser. 'What's for dinner?'

Chloe tried to her breath. 'I thought *pho*.'

'What?'

'It's noodle soup,' she said. He made no mention of his lateness, not a good start in her book, although she shouldn't be too hard on him, it was their first proper date.

'Lead the way.' He smiled, and the warmth in Chloe's gut spread to fill her. It was hard to be annoyed at him with a face like that.

The restaurant she had in mind was five minutes' walk away. Chloe spent most of the walk babbling on, whenever she seemed to run out of steam Eddie asked her something to open up the story again. It felt very easy to talk to him, although she worried she was dominating the conversation. The dining space was up a slim flight of stairs, despite looking a little worse for wear and decidedly dated, this was one of her favourite places. The food was always of exceptional quality, it was quick and inexpensive, and the wait staff seemed to speak very little English. Eddie raised an eyebrow as they were seated at a wood-look laminate table, a little on the small side, complete with the condiment basket classic to Vietnamese restaurants and dark brown vinyl chairs.

'How was the work thing you had to go to on Sunday?' Chloe asked.

'Huh?' Eddie looked blank for a moment. 'On Sunday? Yeah, it didn't come to anything but sometimes they don't.'

Chloe frowned, it sounded like a lie, or at least not the whole truth, but it wasn't the time to press him.

'How's your work? Did you say something about being a teacher for retards?'

Chloe winced. 'I'm a teacher's aide, and we don't use that term. Some kids have average intelligence but have difficulty taking in new information, some of them have dyslexia or other issues. They're all able to perform in a standard school with the right help from people like me.'

'You wouldn't catch me in that job for anything. You must like kids.' He smiled at her again.

'I do, it's really lovely to watch them blossom and with the right support and skills they can go to high school and need very little assistance.'

'I've never been any good with kids. My brother and sister both have a couple, but I don't see them all that often. They live up near my parents in Shep—that's Shepparton. The kids are nice enough but I don't know what to say to 'em, y'know? I'm the oldest too, so of course it makes me feel old and useless not having settled down and had any of my own.'

'I'm sorry you haven't connected with them. It can be daunting trying to talk to kids when you're not used to it, but if they're anything like my students, you just have to figure out the thing they're passionate about and ask them a few questions and they'll usually tell you all about it.'

'You're probably right.' Eddie looked at the menu. 'What's good then? I don't usually get Asian.'

'I always get *pho*. It's broth with rice noodles and meat, usually chicken or beef, and some vegies and bean shoots. Everything is pretty good but steer clear of the ones that say 'combination', that usually means it has offal and stuff in it, that I can't imagine you're into.'

'Offal like guts?' he said, his eyes going wide.

'Yeah, but just don't order combination and you'll be safe. Do you like hot food?'

'Nah, probably best to stick to mild. My housemate, Max, puts chilli sauce on everything but I reckon it's probably ruined his tastebuds.'

'I put chilli on a lot of stuff too.' Chloe smiled. He seemed a bit rough around the edges but maybe he was kind underneath that bravado. 'Do you want to share? Some people get funny about sharing food.'

'I don't usually share, then again I only ever eat with Max and I have absolutely no inclination to share spit with him.' He laughed. 'Why don't you order a few things, nothing too spicy, and we'll share. I trust you.'

'Alright, no pressure then.' She tried to laugh it off but the idea of having to order for both of them made Chloe's anxiety soar. When the waiter came back, pad in hand, she ordered pork spring rolls, and spring onion pancake, then she got one serve of chicken *pho,* and one vermicelli salad. Hopefully she had guessed the level of adventurousness Eddie had for food without being too bland.

Eddie wolfed down the spring rolls and pancake. She showed him how to wrap the spring roll in lettuce with a sprig of mint and to dip it into the sauce, though he preferred them without.

Their mains came out almost immediately after the starters, and they struggled to fit it all on the table. The soup came with a plate of bean shoots, mint, fresh chilli, and a wedge of lemon.

'The traditional way to have the soup is to put the bean shoots in, then squeeze in lemon, and add hoi sin sauce and some of the chilli sauce. Do you want me to put all that in or do you want to try it plain?' She hoped he would say he wanted to try the traditional way. 'I mean, if you try it and don't like it, I'll happily have all of the soup.'

'It'll give it a crack. Put all that stuff in and we'll see if I like it. Otherwise, I'll stick to the salad.

At least he was game to try it, perhaps growing up in the country had made him sheltered. She hadn't discovered foreign food until after she'd moved out of home at eighteen, her mother was pretty conservative in her tastes and they never had any money to buy takeaway.

*   *   *

Eddie didn't like the soup, though he persevered for a while. After making faces for five minutes Chloe put him out of his misery.

'Can I have the rest of the soup?'

'Is it that obvious?' he replied.

'No, but I do like *pho*.' She smiled, and he pushed the bowl toward her.

When they'd finished eating, he settled the bill.

'Do you want me to put in?' she asked, pulling out her wallet.

'No, my treat.' He waved her hand away.

At the bottom of the narrow stairs out of the restaurant Chloe tried to work up the courage to ask him back to her place, the silence stretched out between them. She didn't want to seem too forward, but at the same time, they'd already been intimate, maybe he would expect it.

'Hey, I'm sorry about not inviting you back to my place the other night.' Eddie was not looking at her. He seemed to be watching a tall thin man painstakingly paint the metal frame of a street vegetable stall. The slow movements and level of concentration seemed unnatural, and Chloe wondered if he might be a heroin-user. The owner of the shop, a small, severe-looking Vietnamese man, watched on. Just as the painter's eyes started to droop the owner would prod him in the shoulder.

'I didn't think anything of it,' she lied.

'I hadn't expected company you see.' He turned back to her; his eyes locked to hers. 'I've managed to tidy up and it's suitable for guests now. You know, if you're interested to see my place.' The left side of his mouth hitched in a half smile.

'Of course. I'd love to see your house.' Chloe's belly filled with butterflies thinking of how anxious he seemed. She could imagine being worried by guests, and usually she would have been just the same, but last weekend she'd been drunk and horny.

Eddie took her hand. 'It's not far, maybe ten minutes that way. You okay to walk?' He pointed across the street to the Abbotsford side. In this area the suburbs changed in the middle of the road, on this side they were still in Richmond, on the other side they were in Abbotsford.

'I love to walk.' She grinned.

Eddie seemed to relax as they walked, his shoulders dropped, and his stride was long and fluid. He lit a cigarette and puffed on it idly. She wondered if he'd spent the entire dinner worrying about the other night, thinking she had judged him. Her chest constricted at the thought he was so sensitive. The area was pleasant, although the evening was quite cold and dark. Chloe didn't like to walk alone at night, despite the gentrification of Richmond, and the neighbouring suburbs of Abbotsford and Collingwood, there were still a few concerning characters roaming the streets. Many were harmless, but some were looking for an unguarded purse to snatch or worse.

She would never forget the time walking along the pavement in Gertrude Street a woman struck her in the chest with her elbow. Obviously, Chloe had entered her space without realising. Thankfully, the woman continued on her way, but it could easily have turned into an altercation.

Eddie was chattering away, Chloe was only half listening, her eyes scanning the street.

'It's pretty safe around here. I know it can get hairy sometimes, but we'll be okay.' He flicked his butt into the gutter.

'I'm sorry.'

He squeezed her hand. 'Once you get back from Victoria Street it's much nicer. That's not to say we live in the lap of luxury or anything.'

'You've seen my place, it's nothing to write home about, but it's mine.' She smiled.

Eddie's house was a narrow, terraced place. Chloe thought of them as trains; with a corridor where all of the rooms came off to one side. Some in the area were very swanky having been completely renovated and restored, others were unloved and on the verge of collapse, this one fell somewhere in between. The paintwork over the bricks, which had once been white, was peeling in places and the windows were filthy with cobwebs, but the structure looked sound.

'Welcome,' Eddie said, opening the front door and holding his arm out to invite her through. He followed her into the narrow hallway, polished floorboards with a faded hall-runner carpet over them. The walls were dull off-white and the decorative corbels looked original and they had survived well. Two bedrooms fed off the hallway to her right, and at the end of the hallway was a dimly lit lounge room. The whole house smelled faintly of bolognaise sauce, perhaps someone had been cooking.

'Have a seat, I'll get us a drink. You want wine?' Eddie asked, indicating to the large, comfortable but slightly worse for wear dark red couches.

'I'd love a wine, thank you.' Chloe sat down, sinking further into the couch than she'd expected. She struggled to push herself back out and perched on the edge of the seat.

Looking around the room, it was clearly a bachelor household; the T.V. took up most of the wall in front of the couch, an Xbox console set beside it, and controllers on the coffee table. Under the television was a large open shelving unit; one side had a glass fronted cabinet holding various types of booze, none more than a quarter full. The right side of the cabinet was closed black wood-look MDF doors. She was curious what might be inside but before she could think too much about it, Eddie returned with the wine.

He placed two glasses on the coffee table and sat down heavily next to her. 'Max is out at work; he won't be back till later.'

'What sort of work does Max do?' she asked, waiting until Eddie reached for his wine before she went for hers. It wasn't polite to start drinking before her host.

'Bartender at a posh place in Brunswick Street. They do overpriced tapas and have, like, twenty-five types of gin. I don't know how he keeps them all straight in his mind, but I guess he's a bit of an idiot savant like that.'

'How do you mean?'

'His people skills are terrible—how he got into bartending is beyond me, but I think he likes knowing the role he's supposed to play. I reckon he might be an autistic or something.'

Chloe took a breath before responding, he was clearly tolerant enough to live with someone who didn't quite fit in with the usual way of interacting. 'It's very possible he's on the autism spectrum. Many neuro-diverse people have trouble with certain aspects but not others. Seems like he's making a good life for himself, living with you and holding down a job. That's what I hope for all my students.'

Eddie grabbed his wine again, red in a stemless glass. 'I've never known him to keep a girlfriend for longer than a couple of dates, but I guess I don't usually fare much better.' He looked away.

Chloe put her hand on his knee. 'I'm sure you're not that bad.'

'You're biased, but thanks.' They sat in silence for a moment, comfortably at first, but as the pause grew longer Chloe started to worry, she'd done something wrong. Perhaps he expected her to say something more, but she hardly knew him. She picked up her wine and had a sip.

'This is really nice,' she said, then immediately regretted it. He might think she was a snob for expecting him to have bad taste.

'Max brought it home from work. An expensive bottle some hipster tosspots ordered then refused to drink. Usually, they try to sell it on by the glass when that happens but for whatever reason he brought it home last night. Left a note for me to say I should have some if I wanted.'

'What a sweetheart. It tastes very expensive.'

'Bloody oath. Much better than I could afford, I'm sure. I mean I'm usually a beer guy, but you seemed more like a wine person.'

Chloe shrugged. 'I don't drink much beer, and when I'm out I have mixed drinks. I'm a bit of a heathen,

although I know enough not to mix too many things—I
learned that lesson when I was in high-school.'

He chuckled, the sound deep and low, rumbling up
through his chest. 'I wish I had learned that. If someone's
buying, I'll drink whatever is on offer.'

Chloe's hand was still on Eddie's knee, her other
hand held her wine. He shifted forward in his seat, as
though preparing for something then sat back and drank
the last of his wine in one gulp. Eddie took her glass and
placed it back on the coffee table before cupping her
cheeks in both hands and kissing her tenderly. She
inhaled his scent, musky aftershave, and tasted his lips,
berry notes of the wine. Every part of her body was
suddenly alive with burning sensation, she wanted to pull
him towards her, to kiss him deeply and have him devour
her, but she held herself in check. They were the only
people in the house, and there was no rush.

Eddie pulled away. 'Shall I show you my room?'
His voice was breathy as though he was barely
containing his need to ravish her as she was for him.

'Yes please.'

Chapter 4

Chloe woke up the next morning to the soft sounds of an unfamiliar house. Eddie was sleeping beside her, his breath calm and steady. Minimalist to the point of being spartan, Eddie's bedroom held a mattress on the floor, clothes, the few he had, were piled into an almost empty built-in wardrobe, a lamp, an ashtray, and a plastic cup of water next to his mattress. On the plus side, his sheets smelled clean, and the washing basket in the wardrobe was only half full.

Lying on her side, watching his face as he slept, Chloe was reminded again how little she knew about this man. Did he have so little because he was uninterested in material wealth? Did working for himself mean he was putting all his money into the business? She couldn't wait to slowly explore him and find out for herself what made Eddie tick.

Their lovemaking the night before had been slow and tender, at times almost torturous with its slowness, but when she squirmed and begged for more Eddie just grinned and told her to be a good girl. She had never known touch like his, to make her feel simultaneously on fire and covered in chills.

Eddie slept soundly on and her bladder was becoming insistent, so she disentangled herself from the bedclothes and padded down the hallway to the bathroom. The long thin house had the bathroom tacked on the end. No doubt they had had an outdoor toilet originally that was brought inside at some point. These terrace houses, especially in Abbotsford, were former workers' cottages and never meant to be more than bare essentials.

She hadn't brought anything to wear in bed, planning for an overnight stay seemed to invite bad luck, so she was wearing one of Eddie's T-shirts, a faded black that had gone a sort of greenish grey that she'd picked up from the clean pile in the wardrobe, and her underpants. She was at least half a foot shorter than Eddie, so she was safe from flashing anyone unless she reached up or bent down. Even so she hoped she would get back to his bedroom without running into Max; having their first meeting half-dressed seemed trashy.

When she came from the bathroom into the kitchen a slender blonde man stood near the kettle. He looked very sleepy, but attractive in a youthful way, though his nose was too broad and prominent for him to be considered handsome.

'Hi,' she said, hovering mid-step in the doorway.

The young man lifted his head and his eyes seemed to slowly focus on her. 'Hi.'

'You must be Max. I'm Chloe.'

'Yeah, Eddie said you might be over. I put a shirt on especially.' His cheeks flushed red as he dipped his eyes to her bare legs.

'Thank you.' Chloe pulled the hem of the T-shirt down. 'I didn't expect to stay the night. I hoped you wouldn't be up yet.' It was nearly ten, but she hadn't heard Max come home.

'I don't sleep much. Eddie won't be up for ages. You want a coffee or something?'

She hesitated. 'Actually, that would be nice. I might go put on something warmer though.' The chill morning air, along with her mortification at surprising Max in his own house, had raised goose bumps all over her legs. Max nodded and pulled another cup from the drying rack next to the sink.

Chloe tiptoed back into Eddie's bedroom, he hadn't moved and didn't seem particularly inclined to get up. Hurriedly redressing it seemed illicit to spend time with Eddie's housemate while he slept, but what else could she do? Sleeping on, was out now she'd been up, and lying next to him, awake, seemed worse than having a coffee with Max.

Max was sitting in the lounge, he'd taken a seat on the second couch, which didn't face the TV allowing her to take a seat on the couch in prime position. Her coffee waited on the coffee table, small curls of steam coming up from it.

'I put milk in, but no sugar. Sorry, I forgot to ask,' he said, his cheeks a little pink.

'That's perfect.' Sometimes she added a teaspoon of sugar to her coffee, especially if it was instant, but she wouldn't tell Max that after he was making such an effort to be hospitable.

'I often watch *Rage* of a morning. Y'know, it's sort of entertaining but also doesn't require much brain power. That'll be on for another hour or so.'

'Sounds good to me.' Chloe slipped her stockinged feet up under herself and reached for her coffee. She took a sip and was surprised how good it was. 'Wow, this is great.'

'Thanks. Eddie doesn't care about good coffee, he's more utilitarian, but I thought you might appreciate a fresh brewed cup over the instant rubbish he has.'

'You're very kind, thank you.'

Max smiled. 'I have this new coffee thing—an AeroPress—it's like a plunger but a deeper flavour and less messy.'

'Two of my favourite things: better flavour and less mess.'

He had pulled his sleeves down over his fingers and wrapped them around his cup. The image made him look even more childlike.

'How did you meet Eddie?' she asked quietly. Something about his demeanour made her think he would startle easily and she needed to be calm, serene, like with a new student.

'At school.'

'You've known him a while then?' She was intrigued, this could be a useful connection to foster if Eddie was reluctant to share stories about himself.

'Yeah, he's been my best friend since year ten. He's had other best friends since then, we drifted apart for a while, but he needed somewhere to stay a while back and I had a room, so here he is.'

She sat quietly for a moment, the TV. played video clips interspersed with a band sitting on a red couch talking about them. She didn't recognise any of the men in the band, all young with hair hanging in their faces, but they must have been important to score the job of programming *Rage*. Max didn't volunteer any further information on his housemate and she occupied herself with the videos and scrolling through Facebook on her phone.

A little after eleven her battery started to die. 'You don't have a charger, do you?' she asked.

'Show me?'

She held out her phone to Max and he briefly squinted at it before nodding and levering himself out of the couch. It seemed they were both squishier than they appeared. A moment later he returned with a small black phone charger. Chloe heard no signs Eddie was stirring, she wondered if she would get hungry before he raised himself.

'Eddie doesn't keep much food. If you get hungry there's bread for toast or something and half a curry, I got on my way home from work.'

'You don't have to feed me.' She smiled. It was sweet of him to worry about her.

'I know. But you seem nice, and Eddie doesn't usually see girls more than once so I'm trying to make a good impression. Sometimes I'm not so good at … socialising.'

'You're doing all the right things so far. First coffee then breakfast, perhaps I should be dating you instead.' She laughed and Max's neck, cheeks and forehead turned bright red. It must have been exactly the wrong thing to say, he looked at the floor.

Chloe stood up. 'Maybe I will have some toast, if that's alright.'

Max nodded but didn't meet her eye. She wasn't exactly hungry but thought it would be easier for him to calm himself if she wasn't in the room. Dealing with young people with special needs was one thing, but adults, with all of the additional layers of flirting and interaction that went with it, were clearly outside of her comfort zone.

She found butter and vegemite and made two slices of white bread toast to have it on. It reminded her of the food she used to have with her mother, one of her boyfriends when Chloe had been about fourteen, had been obsessed with white bread and had it with every meal. Ever since she'd moved out she had brought wholemeal or multigrain. Leaning against the kitchen counter chewing she wondered how her mother was doing; whether Gary had been cheating or if there had actually been a fishing trip. It would be pointless to call her now, she wouldn't be coherent until after midday, even if it weren't incredibly rude to call her mother from the house of a man she'd just slept with, while avoiding his housemate who she'd embarrassed through her thoughtlessness.

The kitchen was clean although perhaps it was more bare than actually tidy. Most of the dishes seemed to be on the rack next to the sink, clean. Perhaps Eddie had done all the dishes in preparation to invite her over. Max said he didn't usually see girls more than once, should she be heading for the door? Or did it indicate he was ready to try for something more serious than a one-night stand. If he was a player, he had certainly been very smooth when they met at the Plum. Believing Eddie was a keeper, and different to every other man she'd picked up in a pub or bar didn't make it so. She should have picked up he was only interested in one thing, and why he didn't give her his number until she'd asked.

What had happened in his life to make him so afraid of being in a relationship? Chloe had plenty of reasons not to trust men, including her mother's complete lack of judgement when it came to partners. Her exes had all been flops, she had a talent for choosing men who couldn't hold their shit together. Eddie was charming and sociable; he was easy to be around despite making her nervous. His country upbringing made him a bit rough around the edges, but she had always found country people more trustworthy than city folk, in what little experience she had.

'I couldn't resist any more. It smells good.' Max came into the kitchen, his cheeks had gone back to a normal colour and he met her eye, however briefly. Perhaps she was forgiven for her ill-chosen words.

'It's pretty good.'

'And *Rage* is finished.'

She smiled. She could see why Eddie kept him around, and hopefully Max was protected by Eddie's street-smarts and social expertise. Chloe glanced at the time, just after half past eleven. She'd been up for over an hour and there was still no movement from Eddie. The longer she stayed in his house without his presence, conscious at least, the more she felt she was trespassing somehow.

'When does he usually wake up?' she asked.

'Sometimes noon, sometimes later. Depends when he went to bed although I am pretty sure you were both asleep when I got in.'

'When was that?'

'A bit after three.'

She nodded, her toast was finished, and she suddenly wasn't sure what to do with her hands. She crossed her arms across her chest, then worried it was too aggressive and dropped her arms to her sides instead.

'Should I wake him? I kinda have stuff I need to do, and as much as I'm enjoying hanging out with you, it feels a bit …' she trailed off.

'It's weird. I know I'm a bit odd.'

'I didn't mean it like that. I just meant—it's not your job to look after me, I'm Eddie's guest.'

Max nodded. 'Want one more coffee in case he's nearly awake? You can go wake him after. It'll be noon by then, surely he can't be too cranky.' The way Max looked at the floor as he said it made Chloe think he would be cranky no matter what time he was woken. Strange that he'd seemed happy enough last Sunday.

'Thank you. You're a sweetheart.' She smiled but Max didn't meet her eyes. If he was on the autism spectrum, he'd learned how to engage with people well, she might have even said he was just shy.

There was nothing in particular on TV; Max flicked through the channels several times, perhaps in the hope something good would appear.

'You play Xbox?' he asked.

'I've never tried. I'm not much into games.'

'We could play a team thing, or Mario?'

'I'm happy to give it a go, but honestly, you don't have to entertain me.'

Max switched the feed to the game console and selected a game. He handed her the black wireless controller and explained what the buttons did.

'I'm going to be rubbish at this,' she said.

'That's okay, we're on the same team for this game. Just try to stay with me and not shoot me.'

Despite being convinced she wouldn't have any fun playing with Max, she found it easy to become engrossed in the action. She did accidentally shoot him twice, but he was very forgiving. Her second coffee was finished and the game about to level up to the next setting when she looked at the time. It was almost half past twelve, she really needed to hurry Eddie along.

She glanced at Max who was looking at her expectantly. He read her expression, and his face dropped. A fist clenched her chest. 'I'd better get going. I'll wake Eddie to say goodbye on my way out.'

Next time she would bring something with her, or perhaps she would suggest they stay at her place so she could get on with chores while he slept late. If there was going to be a next time, she scolded herself, it was too early in the piece to be making plans.

She crept into the front bedroom to see Eddie had spread out across the mattress, his face pressing into the pillow.

'Eddie,' she said, kneeling beside the bed and shaking his shoulder gently.

'Fuck off.'

'It's Chloe.' She waited in case he would say something else but he seemed to have fallen asleep again.

'Eddie. I have to go.' She spoke louder this time and shook him again.

'Off you go then,' he mumbled, without opening his eyes.

'Eddie.' She used her teacher voice. He snapped open his eyes and looked at her.

'What's your problem? Oh … Chloe, sorry, I was asleep.' He reached up, grabbed her arm and pulled her towards him. 'You're not going to leave me here all alone, are you?' His morning breath stank of cigarettes and onions, and after deciding she needed to get on with things, his invitation to come back to bed was not enticing.

'I just came in to say goodbye. I've got stuff I need to do today.'

'What do you mean? What time is it?'

She frowned. 'After midday. I've been up for hours, hanging out with Max waiting for you to emerge, but I can't wait around anymore.'

'It's not that late, I usually sleep in on weekends.'

She said nothing.

71

'I'm sorry. I didn't realise you were waiting for me. Next time wake me before you have to go, eh?'

'Okay.'

'I need a kiss though.' He pointed to his lips. She leaned over to give him a peck and pulled away quickly. She couldn't afford to be seduced if she was going to get out the door anytime soon. It wouldn't set a good precedent if she caved into him every time he kissed her.

'Bye.' She picked up her handbag and was out the front door before he could stumble out of bed after her. She hesitated on the porch in case he was going to follow her and beg her to stay, but the house was silent.

It took twenty minutes to walk back to her apartment. She showered and made herself lunch, leftovers from dinner on Friday. She wasn't seeing her mother tonight and despite her urgency to leave there Eddie's was nothing she had to do. She sat on the couch and regretted leaving in a huff, she'd have to apologise to Eddie later.

*　　　*　　　*

On Monday night, after work, Mel came around for dinner, wine and to help figure out what she should do about Eddie.

'I just don't know why I was so annoyed when he didn't get up. It's not doing any harm, and Max was lovely,' Chloe said, part way through her second glass of wine. She had explained the situation to Mel over the meal.

'It's a conundrum.' Mel stuck out her tongue.

Fleur Blüm

'You're not helping. I honestly don't know what to do.'

'You wanted him to make you feel special. For him to miss you when you got up. It's only natural that you wanted him to pay attention to you, perhaps morning sex wouldn't have gone astray either. The housemate is fine, but it's not the person you wanted to be spending time with.'

Chloe's cheeks felt hot. 'I'm not that shallow, am I?'

'Babe, shallow has nothing to do with it. This is supposed to be the honeymoon phase, where you're obsessed with each other, can't stop thinking about each other, or keep your hands to yourselves, but he let you down, slept through the morning sex window and then missed out on afternoon delight by being a grump.' She drained her glass and refilled it. She'd brought the wine, a rather expensive white to go with the chicken pasta Chloe had cooked. Mel was an executive assistant and somehow managed to have a very high paying job in the city with no qualifications and little experience.

Chloe chewed on her nail absentmindedly. 'What do I say to him? I didn't hear from him yesterday or today.'

'You've got two options, but they both kinda set the tone for your relationship, assuming he wants one.'

Chloe scrunched up her face.

'It's no good looking like that, you're the one who said he didn't usually see people more than once.'

'Max said that. Eddie hasn't mentioned it.'

'Whatever. In any case, sounds like he hasn't got much experience in the being a boyfriend department.

On the one hand you could apologise for leaving in a huff and see what he says, one the other hand, you could send something without mentioning it and see if he apologises. The downside for the first one is you start apologising for him being a moron now and you'll be doing it forever. If you don't mention it though, you run the risk of never getting him to say sorry and you'll just fester.'

Neither option sounded particularly useful, Chloe wondered if there was a third option. She couldn't ask her mother, and Mary at work would be much too nosy. Chloe's circle of friends was quite small, she had always found it hard to make friends and a few of the ones she'd made over the years or through past relationships had fizzled out.

Her phone buzzed on the coffee table. She looked at it, a message from Eddie.

'Is that him? Oh my God, you have to show me.'

Chloe grabbed for it before Mel had a chance to snatch it away. Regardless of what she did next, having Mel reply would be worse than anything else—there was no way to predict what she would say.

> *Hi Chloe. Sorry I was such a grump yesterday morning. I'm not used to having people around. I'm sure I've totally blown it with you, but I think you're really special. So does Max by the way, and he usually hates anyone I bring home. I'd like to try again, maybe I can cook you steaks or something?*

'Well, I didn't need to do either of the things you suggested.' She turned the phone to show Mel the text but was careful not to let her take it.

'Robbo would never say anything as sappy as that.' Mel wrinkled her nose.

'I guess that's why I'm not dating him.' Chloe stuck out her tongue. Having Eddie apologise and realise his mistake validated her. Mel's dating advice was marginally better than her mother's but should be taken with a grain of salt too.

'Give me the remote.' Mel held out her hand for it. 'You're gonna agonise over that reply for ages and I'm missing my show.' At least she was smiling, as abrupt as she could be Mel was always straightforward. She told you her opinion, usually without prompting, but Chloe never had to second guess her motivation either.

Crafting the perfect response to the text message did take her almost an hour.

> *I'm sorry too. I felt like a potato hanging around in your house without you. Maybe if you come here, I won't feel like I'm intruding. Steak sounds amazing. When suits you?*

Short and to the point. Once they were more used to each other she was sure to feel more at home at his place. Maybe she had picked a good one this time.

Chapter 5

The weekend seemed so far away and now Eddie had apologised, Chloe was in danger of falling for him. She tried to keep her mind on the task at hand, but her thoughts kept drifting to his cool blue eyes, his dark hair, the way his skin felt hot beside hers every time she touched him. Inappropriate thoughts to be having at school.

Each time she caught herself in a fantasy she would shake her head and promise not to let it happen again. At the lunch table in the staff room on Thursday, Mary was telling her about how she'd roped a friend into the lingerie party business when she frowned.

'You haven't been listening to a word I've said.'

'Yes, I have. It sounds like a great opportunity for…' Chloe trailed off; the name of Mary's friend had completely fallen out of her brain.

'Leslie. I assume you have a good reason to be constantly staring out the window like a teenager.'

Chloe's cheeks heated.

'I'm onto something aren't I? Tell me everything.'

'There's nothing to tell, really.'

'Nonsense, you've been seeing someone and you never said a word. You know my love life is miserably boring these days. I need young people to help me live vicariously.' She was trying to be friendly, but the way her face lit up made Chloe uncomfortable.

'I met him a couple of weekends ago in a bar—'

'Good, classic meeting, go on.'

'He seemed nice; we've had a couple of dates—'

'And was there any action on these dates?' Mary interrupted again, wriggling her eyebrows.

Chloe swallowed. 'Some. That's not the point though. He seems very charming, he's very interested in me, he likes to hear what I think about things.'

'I'm so glad you said that. You know I'm all for the, uh, physical aspect, but if you have nothing to say to each other it won't last. Good for you.' Mary patted her hand; Chloe had to concentrate very hard not to pull her hand away.

Now, having extracted an admission from her, Mary went back to talking about the lingerie parties. It sounded like a pyramid scheme and she worried that the older woman was being taken advantage of, but it would be useless to try to tell her so. Mary was good company for lunch times, but she wasn't interested in hearing what Chloe thought about the big issues. Not like Eddie, he could get her to talk about anything. It was so nice to find a man who was such a good listener.

*   *   *

On Saturday night, Eddie came to her apartment at six. He wanted to make sure he had plenty of time to get everything set up. He brought steaks the size of her entire hand, pounded them out with a mallet he'd brought from home, and would serve them with mashed potatoes and green beans.

It took him a long time to get anything done, especially if he was mid-conversation. Perhaps there was something to the idea men could only do one thing at a time. They ate a little before eight, Chloe couldn't finish all of hers, but he was happy to take the leftover steak onto his plate and finish it. She didn't allow smoking in the apartment, so he stood on the tiny balcony, not big enough for the both of them, every so often to get a nicotine hit.

Chloe surveyed the state of her kitchen. Eddie had managed to get stuff all over every surface in the small kitchen and used most of her pots. She started to tidy up, making the pile of dishes neat, and wiping down the benches, stovetop, and dining table. His place was so clean she wondered if he ever cooked for himself, or if Max cleaned after him.

Eddie let himself back into the small apartment after another cigarette and sat at the table, watching her. It seemed fair she should clean after he had been generous enough to make her dinner, although she would have liked him to make a smaller mess, and to say thank-you. Then she remembered Robbo couldn't even cook, when Mel wanted to spend time with him, they had to eat what she prepared or get take away. He would live off corn chips, chocolate and potatoes if it were up to him.

'How's work going?' she said, filling the silence.

'It's pretty slow at the moment, I admit.'

'What do you do again?'

'This and that. I booked bands for a while, but the venue manager got annoyed at me and I decided it was time to go, and I have a friend, Johnno, who slings me landscaping work every now and again, so I don't get completely destitute. I have a couple of days with him next week actually.'

Chloe nodded. On the one hand, it sounded a lot like he didn't really have a job, on the other hand he might know enough people who needed odd jobs done he would keep out of trouble. Unless this landscaping job paid very well, she wasn't sure how he made enough to pay the rent on the place with Max. She scolded herself; you've no right to go prying into his finances.

Eddie stood and looked her up and down, he had a hungry look in his eye. 'Don't let me distract you.' He walked over to her, his eyes burning into her, and stood behind her. She felt him, hot against her back, and when he pushed his pelvis against her bum, she felt hardness there. Chloe kept wiping over the counter, she wanted to wash some of the dishes, but she was tempted to turn around and kiss Eddie. Perhaps it would be fun to tease him a little, to feign disinterest and see how much he wanted to seduce her.

A moment later his lips were against her neck, kissing and nibbling, causing goose bumps to rise along her arms and her nipples to tighten. It was delicious, but what else would he do if she continued to ignore him.

The hands that had been on her hips moved around her body, one arm tight across her waist, the other pushed between her groin and the bench. His lower hand kept travelling down, to the hem of her woollen skirt, and up under it. She shuddered in pleasure as he ran his knuckles over her.

'You're a very bad girl, aren't you?' he purred. She turned her head, and he kissed her hard.

*   *   *

In the morning, Eddie would want to sleep in. They had kept each other up for a couple of hours after dinner in the bedroom before falling into a satisfied, exhausted sleep. She was not used to having another person in the bed, listening to his breathing and occasionally sticking one leg out of the covers—he really did run hot.

She didn't wake him when she slipped out of bed, showered, and started on her Sunday morning rituals. She cleaned the kitchen was first, then she made herself a coffee and some breakfast before settling on the couch with a novel. This one was a crime procedural set in Scotland. She could never read crime novels at night, she became too anxious, but sitting in the weak winter sunlight coming in through the glass balcony doors was cosy enough to make the excitement of the novel tolerable.

Chloe was taking scalloped potatoes to her mother's that evening; Gary would be cooking a fish he'd caught on the notorious fishing trip a fortnight ago. She hoped he'd frozen it otherwise it would be no good to eat.

Janine had called during the week, while she was in class, and left a rambling message that Gary was amazing, and she'd been wrong to ever doubt him. It seemed odd it would have taken over a week to come to this conclusion, but perhaps it had taken that long for her mother to work up the nerve to ask.

As Chloe was sprinkling the top of the potatoes with cheese, she heard the bedroom door open. 'Morning, sleepy.'

'What are you making?' Eddie said, rubbing his eyes. He looked very cute all ruffled and sleepy. It was well after midday, but she knew he would sleep in on weekends and didn't have to worry about annoying his housemate this time.

'It's for Mum, I'm going over there for dinner. Her boyfriend is making fish.'

'Looks good. I can cook a couple of things but it's pretty limited. I hope you realise that steak was my "impressive meal" to woo you after being such a grouch last week.'

'I'm sure you can cook; it was very nice steak.'

'Yeah, steak I can do.' He smiled, running his eyes over her body.

'Do you want coffee? Something to eat?'

'That'd be great, but no rush, finish your... whatever that is.' He waved his hand at the baking dish. Chloe bent to pull open the oven and slide the potatoes in.

'I usually put them on for slightly less time than they need so when we reheat them later, they're not totally gross and overcooked,' she said.

Max had a fancy coffee contraption, but with her limited income, Chloe made do with the standard French press. She only bothered to make what she called real coffee on weekends. There was a coffee machine in the staff room at work that made a decent cup, and she liked to get in at least fifteen minutes early so she had a buffer in case anything went awry. She drove, not that it was very a long way, but after having to catch public transport home with the school students a few times, it was much too awkward for everyone concerned. Plus, she had a car space on the grounds.

She handed Eddie his coffee and sat with him on the couch, he had flicked on the TV while she was making his drink and had found a football game about to start.

'Is that your team?' she asked.

'Nah, I go for Brisbane. My dad used to go for Fitzroy, so when they merged with the Brisbane team he decided to stick with 'em. I don't follow it fanatically but I enjoy the games when they're on.'

Chloe nodded. She hadn't made herself a cup and now regretted not having anything to occupy her hands. It was too early in the relationship to know whether Eddie would welcome her cuddling up to him, she had little interest in the football, but sitting on the couch with a handsome man was not a bad way to spend the afternoon, especially with her potatoes already in the oven.

'Come here then.' Eddie put his arm out, beckoning her closer.

'I wasn't sure.'

'I could tell. It's still early days, I don't know if I mentioned I have very little experience in this dating thing, and even less in having a relationship. I will probably make a fool of myself a few times, but you can ask, if you want to know things.'

She snuggled up to his side, curling her feet under her. She watched the action on the screen for a while, Saint Kilda and Essendon were playing, one in red, white and black, the other in red and black. At least the umpires were wearing fluoro green making them easier to distinguish. When she was a child, the umpires had worn white, earning them the nickname "maggots". One of Janine's many boyfriends had tried to teach her about AFL, but she had avoided spending any time with him. Her mother wanted them to bond and would disappear doing errands or gossiping with neighbours to let them have time together. Chloe hated it, it wasn't that Terry ever hurt her, not like some of the others, but he was a brittle, unpleasant man who had very little interest in a teenaged girl who didn't like sports.

'Given you just said I should ask about stuff ...' she trailed off.

'Yeah?' he turned to look at her.

'Are you seeing anyone else? I mean, I'm not, and I guess it would be nice if you were also not seeing anyone else.'

'Jeez, we've only been dating for like three weeks and you want to have the exclusive talk now. You move fast woman.' His eyebrows had crept up his forehead.

'You're right. I'm sorry, it's too soon.'

'As it happens, I'm not seeing anyone else. I think about you all the time, and I really don't want to spend time with anyone else, so it's not like it's a chore, but—'

'But?' she prompted.

'I didn't want to jinx it by being too keen.'

Chloe laid her hand on his chest. 'I don't pretend to know everything there is to know about relationships, but I say we follow our hearts. Mine says you're a good one, so I want to keep you around if I can. If your heart says the same, then let's go with it.' She smiled; it was faster than some of her other relationships but what did that matter?

'You're right.' He kissed the top of her head and turned back to the TV. She wanted to tell someone about the news but her phone was on the dining table, out of her reach. No good spoiling the moment by getting up to grab it. She should try not to be so reliant on the thing anyway, she caught herself absently checking it frequently.

'Dinner with your mum, then?' Eddie said during an ad break after a goal to Essendon.

'I have dinner with her every other Sunday usually.'

'Sounds like you're pretty close.'

'I guess so.'

Eddie was silent for a long moment. 'Ever bring boys to meet your mum?'

'Uh, I don't think we're at that stage. Despite what I said about not seeing other people.'

He barked out a laugh. 'I wasn't angling for an invite.'

'Of course not. Sorry,' she said, her cheeks warming as the blood rushed to them.

'I mean, I'd love to meet your mum some time. I've never really done meeting the parents. And yes, I know it's pathetic, I'm twenty-six years old and have never had a relationship long enough to meet her parents, y'know, excluding girls in high school who lived at home.' He laughed, but it seemed strained.

'I've taken one or two serious boyfriends to meet Mum. It's—' she sighed. 'Mum can be, I don't know the best word, intense, difficult. I worry it will scare people off.'

'I'm sure she can't be any worse than my mum. She'll be on you like a rash as soon as you're in the door, asking what your plans are, and whether you're going to sort me out.' He frowned and looked back to the football.

'Mmm,' she said. It seemed inadequate after such a vehement response.

They sat in silence until half time, Chloe was reluctant to get up while Eddie still seemed to be in a funk about his mother. She got up to check the oven, the potatoes were nearly ready but needed a little longer. She boiled the kettle to give her a reason to stay in the kitchen.

'Do you have any brothers and sisters?' she asked.

'Hmm? Yeah, one of each, both younger. My sister got pregnant at eighteen, so she married the father and they're up to three kids now. One each year if you can believe it. I wonder if I need to have the birds and bees talk with them.' He laughed, at least he seemed to be in a bit of a better mood. 'Me sister works part time doing reception or something, but her husband is a hot shot salesman. I'm surprised he's made anything of himself, he always wanted to go to uni and be a fancy man but the kids needed feeding, so he had to put that on hold. Plus they live up in the country near my mum and dad so they get free babysitting.'

'Sounds like they have their hands full.'

'You can say that again.'

'You want another coffee?' she asked, the kettle had boiled and clicked itself off.

'Yeah, ta. My brother, he's the middle child, he became a mechanic after spending his childhood in the shed with my dad.'

'What did you do as a kid?' Chloe plunged the third pot of coffee she'd made that day and made a mental note to get more grounds on the next trip to the supermarket.

'Me? I dunno, got up to no good if you ask Mum and Dad. I guess I had my own stuff. I wasn't really academic but I always had people around me, especially kids with older siblings who could do things for us. Didn't spend much time at home.'

Chloe took a seat next to Eddie. His childhood sounded lonely. She hadn't had much opportunity to get out of her house as a child, her mother seemed delicate, and they never had any money to do activities. If they had, she would have learned piano, or flute; they seemed like good instruments. Violin had always sounded screechy when the other kids played, although the boys who learned guitar, especially in highschool, were popular.

'Did you ever get into music?'

'Nah. I told you I was a booker for a while? That was about as close as I got. I had a few friends in high school who were in bands, they wanted to be the next Kurt Cobain, but I couldn't play anything. I guess I could sing but I'm not much chop at that either. It was a good reason not to hang out at home though, pretended I was the band manager, or the roadie.'

The oven timer went off. 'Shit, my potatoes. They're gonna be overcooked now, I meant to check on them before.'

'I hope you're not blaming me,' he said with a wink.

'It is very nice to hang out with you on the couch, I admit.'

She took the tray out and rested it on the stovetop to cool. When she turned, Eddie was standing in the middle of the room, the hungry look back in his eyes.

'I have to get back to my place, leave you so you can get ready for your mum's later, but I do have time for a little bit of fun before I go.'

'You're insatiable,' she said, grinning.

'You're delicious. I can't help it.' He stepped forward and wrapped her in a deep, hungry kiss. Her body had started to get used to his smell and responded almost immediately. It wasn't often she would have this much fun with a guy, so she was going to milk it for all it was worth.

Eddie's attentions were not as thorough as they had been last night, but she wasn't complaining. It was nice to be desired, to have someone look at her the way people on TV shows did. If he stuck around long enough, she would love to introduce him to her mother, but would have to do a bit of prep work to make sure he knew she was fragile and Gary could be touchy. No good putting him into a situation where he would be on the back foot, especially given his inexperience with parents.

She lay in the tumble of sheets left in the wake of Eddie's visit. He had rushed off and she didn't have to be at her mum's for another couple of hours. The bed smelled like him, and like sex. It was just as well she'd sorted out the birth control after the first time he'd stayed, he wasn't into condoms and since they'd not used them the first time it seemed pointless to ask him to start now.

*   *   *

It was dark when she got to her mum's place in Brunswick at quarter to six. The potatoes would need fifteen minutes in the oven, but Gary was in charge of dinner tonight and he wasn't one to be rushed.

'My darling girl.' Her mother shuffled out to meet her, cigarette between her lips. She'd dressed up, as much as she ever did, in leopard print leggings and a beige knitted sweater which looked like it had seen better days; covered in little balls of pilling. Janine was a proud op shop scavenger, but this wasn't her finest work.

'Hi Mum.'

'You look well. How is school?'

'Same as always,' she smiled. Her mother seemed to be in a good mood.

'Gary is so excited to make this fish. He's been talking about it all week.'

Chloe raised her eyebrow. Gary was not what she would have called talkative at the best of times, he might have mentioned it once in passing. The only things he was interested to talk about were fishing, football, cricket in the summer, and occasionally complaining about work.

She followed her mum inside. Janine had obviously been on a cleaning spree, the place was tidier than usual and smelled like floor cleaner. Sometimes when she was having a bad week it bordered on squalor, especially since Gary didn't deign to do any housework.

'Not my house, I don't have to clean it,' he'd said once when Chloe had asked why. He had a house in Reservoir, a suburb northeast of Janine's, that he still considered his home, although the amount of time he spent there would have been one night a week, if that. Perhaps he could tell himself he wasn't really committed if he had somewhere to bolt to. It also conveniently meant he didn't have to contribute to the bills or expenses if he didn't want to.

Chloe took her oven dish into the kitchen, where Gary was fussing over descaling the fish.

'Hi Gary,' she said. 'Are you ready for potatoes?'

He grunted a greeting. 'This'll need a good half hour in the oven.'

'Righto. The potatoes need about fifteen minutes to warm, so I'll wait till you're in. What is it?'

'Golden perch. Got it with the boys up on the Murray. Never thought I'd get one, but there you are.'

'It looks like it would have put up a fair fight.' The fish Gary was cleaning was at least the length of his forearm plus half again. She wasn't sure it would fit in the oven but would never say so aloud.

'It did alright.' Gary went on to tell her about the trip and the men he went with and how he'd caught this perch. Chloe made herself a cup of tea and stood in the doorway to the kitchen. She had little interest in any of what Gary told her, but when he was in a happy, talkative mood she wanted to keep him it that way so she feigned interest and tried to follow what he said. Her mother had a talent for dating men with mean streaks, and though his only came out rarely, it would ruin dinner and probably send her mother into a depression, something Chloe would do almost anything to avoid.

Janine buzzed around the living room, setting the table, and going in and out of rooms down the hallway. Chloe could hear her opening and closing doors, and cupboards, even over Gary's droning story. She frowned, what was she up to?

'Do you need a hand, Mum?' she called through the house.

'No. I'm okay.'

'You should go see what she's doing. I think she's cleaning out the spare room. God knows why.' Gary said over his shoulder. He'd managed to fit most of the fish into an enormous baking tray Chloe had never seen before, presumably one of his.

Her mother was kneeling in front of a cardboard box in the spare room.

'Are you alright?' Chloe asked quietly.

'Of course I am.' Her mother's skin had a sheen of sweat.

'An odd time to be spring cleaning. Usually you want to hear all about my week.'

'I was trying to find the box of stuff Gary moved a few weeks ago, you remember I was complaining about it? Well, I realised I've had some of this stuff since before you were born, and really it seemed like a perfect time to start getting rid of things.'

'What's the hurry?'

'No hurry.'

Chloe sipped a cup of tea and watched her mother look through the contents of the box, examining each item before replacing them all and closing it up. She seemed to have a lot of energy and not a lot of focus. 'Have you got new tablets or something?'

'How did you know?' Her mother frowned up at her.

'Just a guess.' Chloe had known her mother misused prescriptions, she always had a supply of Valium and various painkillers, this was something new. Maybe diet pills? Or had she managed to convince her doctor to give her Ritalin. Whatever it was the come down would be on its way, she dreaded to think what it would look like.

'You said you were worried about Gary's fishing trip on the phone?' Chloe tried to steer the conversation away from medication but had chosen a topic just as fraught with tension.

'Keep your voice down,' she whispered, before beckoning Chloe closer. 'When he was away for the weekend, I was sure he was seeing some flooszy, but he came back on Monday morning even though he said he would go straight to work, and he stank of fish. God knows what he'd been doing up there but it wasn't showering.' She spoke hurriedly. 'He got ready for work here, you know all his things are here now, and then headed off twenty minutes later. Told me to put the fish in the freezer.'

'Fascinating.'

'You can put the potatoes in now,' Gary's booming voice carried up the corridor to them. Chloe excused herself and went to tend to it. Her mother had been through a few phases of drug misuse, the worst was when she was in late primary school, her boyfriend at the time was a very important salesman, apparently, and they would go out, often staying out all night, and come home wired. Chloe was left on her own, apparently capable of looking after herself, something she wasn't keen on despite being a 'big girl'.

The first few times her mother had stayed out all night, Chloe had lain in her bed wide awake, waiting for the car to come home. It was as though she'd never really heard the night before then, startling at every sound, creak, scratch, bird cry, passing car and tap of branches against her window; waiting for something to get her. After that first night, Chloe was not as frightened of the empty house, although she would wake up whenever they came home, apart from being loud and drunk or more likely high, it was a relief to know her mother had made it home safely.

All her grandparents had died by the time she was five, and without any other family she knew about, Chloe could have ended up in foster care. As poor a mother as Janine might have been, it was predictable. Everything she'd heard about foster care kids was horrific. Chloe would have done just about anything to avoid that.

*   *   *

Janine had a couple of glasses of wine with dinner, Gary had three beers, and Chloe had one wine as she had to drive home. By the end of the evening, her mother was nodding off on the couch.

The fish had been delicious, with a subtle flavour of lemon and salt, and moist from being baked in foil. Her potatoes were not as overcooked as she'd feared, but there was nothing else, salad or other vegetables, to go with the meal. Gary had forgotten to mention it and Janine had nothing in the fridge. There was almost an argument until Chloe had said, 'the fish smells so good it will be cold by the time we eat if we aren't quick.'

Gary's desire for food outweighed his need to be right about the vegies.

'I'd better head off. Don't want to fall asleep before I get home.' Chloe gathered up her handbag. 'Will you eat the rest of the potatoes? Should I put them in a Tupperware for you?' The dish had only been half eaten, and though she didn't need to take the leftovers home, she would need the baking dish for her meal prep over the next fortnight. Lasagne was one of her staples when she was cooking up meals for her freezer, and she was almost out.

'Yeah, leave it. I'll take some to work.' Gary worked in a factory that made window frames. Chloe hadn't ever asked what he did there, but his hands were calloused and worn as though he used them all day.

Back at her apartment, she could still smell Eddie. She smiled as she inhaled his scent. It was hard to deny she was falling in love. Her previous attempts at dating had been slow burners, one was a friend who had turned into more, they met at TAFE, and the other had taken her out to dinner four weeks in a row before attempting a kiss. They had both turned out to be no good for her. Mel was always the one to jump into things quickly. She and Robbo had sex the first night they met, in the bathrooms at the bar where he was playing later. Mel considered it a conquest, no doubt he did too, and they'd barely spent a night apart since then.

Having watched her mother's anxious attempts to keep men interested in her, Janine was almost never single and moved straight from one dreadful man to another, Chloe had tried to be comfortable with being a single woman. She had a career she loved, one or two close friends, and her relationship with her mother was better than it had been for years, partly owing to only seeing her once a fortnight. And yet the moment she met a handsome man who showed an interest in her, she fell head over heels for him.

On the other hand, Eddie was charming, attentive, hot and really into her, so why wait? She dropped the baking dish into the sink and filled it with water to soak off the remaining cheese and pulled out her phone.

It was nice to wake up next to you this morning. Good night, babe x

Eddie might think it was clingy to be texting him when she'd only seen him a few hours before, but she hoped he would see it as romantic.

Chapter 6

The next weekend Eddie invited Chloe out to a bar in Collingwood, it was well known for having great bands and had a bit of a reputation for being rough, so he said.

As she was dressing to go out, the buzzer for her front gate went off.

'Hello?' she said into the handset.

'It's me, buzz me up.'

She pressed the button and hung up the phone. A minute or so later she heard a knock on the door.

'Hey, gorgeous,' Eddie said, grinning widely. He grabbed her waist and pulled her into a kiss. Though she was surprised at first, it quickly turned into building arousal. When he pulled away, she was almost as surprised as when he pulled her in.

'You seem perky.' She closed the apartment door and tried to regain her equilibrium.

'I got some speed off a mate of mine. I know it's not really your scene but I got enough for you too.'

'Thanks.'

Eddie perched on the arm of the couch, his left leg bouncing.

'I'm not quite ready yet,' she said, waving a hand over her face and hair, which were only partly done.

'No stress, babe, it's not the sort of place where you need to be on time.' He barked a laugh. Chloe went back into the bathroom to finish putting her left eye makeup, the rest of her face was done. Then she needed to do something with her hair, probably an up do if it was going to be a sweaty, crowded sort of place. As she carefully swept the winged eyeliner over her lid, she considered Eddie's offer. She didn't usually take illicit drugs, although she had certainly tried weed a couple of times in her TAFE days.

'What do you think?' she said, stepping into the lounge and giving a twirl. She had decided to wear her hair in a ponytail, keeping it off her face but still allowing some movement and showing off the length of straight brown hair.

'Wow.' Eddie stood up and walked towards her, his eyes glittering with a hungry look. 'I'm tempted to take you right here and blow off the bands.'

Chloe giggled and looked away; his gaze was intense. When she looked back, he was standing in front of her, as though about to pounce. He dropped his head a little to kiss her, pressing their bodies together. She felt a hardening in his groin as they kissed, her own arousal building, her breath becoming more urgent.

'But that would be so rude,' he said, breaking the kiss. 'Can I tempt you then?' He dangled a tiny plastic baggy filled with white powder from his fingers.

It wasn't the drugs he was dangling that she wanted at that moment, but it seemed unlikely he wanted to follow through with sex right then.

'Do you need some money for it?' Her budget was too tight to pay for party drugs.

'No, babe. I want my special girl to have a nice time.' He ran a line of kisses down her neck. She shivered with delight.

'Alright, I haven't ever tried it.'

'We'll just give you a little bit to start with, and there's more if you want.' He pulled away and cleared a space on her coffee table. Eddie made three lines of powder, two of which he snorted, and one for her. As she looked down at the table she suddenly wondered if this was a good idea.

'You'll be fine, babe. It's not even that strong.' Eddie squeezed her knee.

'Okay.'

*   *   *

The pub was an old-style building, consisting of a number of smaller rooms, each feeding into the larger band room. When they arrived the first band had already started playing. She felt a little light-headed, and she wanted to dance.

'I'll get some drinks.' Eddie shouted over the loud punk music coming from the stage. The room was a little under half full, busy for so early in the evening, she thought.

Eddie returned with drinks. 'Come out for a smoke.'

The courtyard out the back was more crowded than the band room, perhaps they were there for the later bands. Eddie seemed to know a few of the people there and struck up conversations easily. He had slung his arm over her shoulder, and she was glad to be included in the conversation, despite having little to contribute.

They moved between the bar, band room and courtyard for the next couple of hours. By the end of the headline band's set the dance floor was jammed with sweaty heaving bodies pressed against each other and bouncing to the music. The frenetic double kick driven music wasn't her usual style but the atmosphere drew her in. She whooped and clapped at the end of the set, as Eddie grabbed her hand and pulled her back to the courtyard.

Once outside, he lit a cigarette and seemed to calm down a little.

'Paulie, you know, that I was chatting to earlier, he and some of the band members from the headliner are going into a club in the city after this. We should go with them, what do you say?'

Chloe tried to catch her breath. 'I don't know if I should.'

'If I give you another line you'll perk up.'

She hesitated. 'I think I've had enough for today.'

Eddie opened his mouth, then compressed his lips into a line, as though he was about to say something but changed his mind.

'I'd really like to go.' He exhaled a plume of smoke.

'I don't mind if you go without me.' As soon as she said it, she regretted it. If he went off to a club she would go home alone, and with the kisses and the music and the drinks, she wanted him to take her home and have his way with her.

'Mmm.' He dragged on his smoke a few times in contemplation. His silence felt even more profound against the background of music and chatter and laughing in the courtyard. 'I'd rather you come, but I know it's not really your scene.'

She nodded.

'However,' he said, a cheeky glint appearing in his eye, 'what would you say to coming into the bathrooms with me before you go?'

Chloe felt her cheeks heat, her mouth seemed unable to form words. She'd never done anything like that before, it was something Mel did, something other, bolder women did, not plain old Chloe Barrett. He flicked his cigarette away into the ash tray on the ground and pulled her into one of his deep, probing kisses.

He pulled away. 'Say yes, Miss Chloe.'

'Yes.'

*   *   *

Over the next few weeks Eddie stayed with Chloe more often. Sometimes he would invite her to his place, but he said hers was nicer, and they didn't have to worry about Max hearing or interrupting them. Max was sweet and always welcomed her at their place; he seemed to have taken a shine to her.

Chloe wished Eddie would contribute to the food he ate at her place, he insisted he wasn't a good cook and would frequently show up empty-handed. She would have thought, growing up in the country, he'd have learned better manners. He had said from the start, he'd never had any lasting relationships. Whenever she brought it up or mentioned she was struggling financially, he would go quiet and after the time he left in a huff, she stopped mentioning it. She preferred having him around than to be alone, even if it meant being tighter with her money.

Last night, Tuesday, he had turned up at her place at half past eight, he'd been drinking but wasn't drunk yet.

'Hey, I missed you.' Eddie leaned on the frame of her front door when she opened it.

'I'm just doing stuff for school. You can come in, but I need to work, okay?' It was the first time he'd arrived unannounced on a weeknight and she wasn't sure how to respond. She was pleased to see him, but her work needed to be done for school tomorrow and it would have been better if he'd called first.

'I promise to behave. Be quiet as a mouse, I'll just watch some telly and you can do work.' He leaned in to kiss her, he tasted like beer, but he was happy and said he wouldn't get in her way.

'Okay then.' She stepped back and let him in. He sprawled on the couch, dropping his backpack on the floor next to him with a clank of bottles. Chloe frowned, but said nothing. If he wanted to get quietly drunk on her couch, that was fine as long as she could get her work done.

Her marking, lesson plans and notes were set-up on the kitchen table along with her laptop. She usually listened to classical music or soft pop when she worked, she turned her music off to answer the door and Eddie put the TV on, playing reruns of *Friends*.

Chloe thought about whether she should offer him a drink but after hearing the sound of his bag hitting the ground, he was unlikely to want a cup of tea. She sipped hers; peppermint to help digestion and concentration without keeping her up all night.

Eddie laughed loudly as something on the screen. 'Jeez, I love this show,' he said. Chloe glanced at him, her eyebrow raised of its own accord.

'Sorry, I'll keep it down. I'm a man of my word.' He reduced the volume, chuckling to himself occasionally. Chloe took a moment to consciously roll her shoulders back and down, trying to will away the tension of having her plans disrupted. He hadn't done anything wrong—it was natural for him to want to see her on a whim. If she had been more forceful, told him to go home that she was busy, perhaps she would have felt better but she knew well that he would put on his sad puppy-dog face and she would have let him stay anyway. He was very good at getting his way when it suited him. She looked over to his profile, he was beautiful, she shouldn't let little disturbances in her routine upset her. It smacked of stubbornness and rigidity, two things she hated in other people. In ten minutes, I'll take a break and give him a cuddle, she thought to herself.

Once she found her rhythm again, Chloe was able to block out the sound of the TV and the occasional comments from Eddie. He was halfway through his beer before she realised it had been much longer than ten minutes. She stretched and stood up.

'I don't suppose you want a cuppa,' she said.

'Nah. I'm good babe.'

'I'm having a little break.' She flicked the kettle on to boil, rinsed her cup and put in a fresh teabag. Sometimes she reused herbal teabags, which were usually potent enough to do two cups, but she was being a little bit extravagant.

The show had changed to some reality program set in a jungle. It looked hideous; she couldn't imagine why anyone would want to torture themselves like that.

'Who's winning?' she asked.

'You can't really tell that yet, but that little guy,' he pointed to a celebrity she vaguely recognised, a small-time actor perhaps. 'He's got immunity for the next elimination, so I think he's winning for the moment. I'm sorry I didn't text you to see if you were free. I forget you have homework to do like the kids.' He kissed her forehead.

'It's okay, I'm glad to see you. I feel bad that I can't hang out with you though. I need this stuff finished by the morning.'

'I get it. Max got called in to work and I was just at my place alone and it seemed like if I wanted to drink beers, it would be less weird if I did it in company than on my own.' His grin was lopsided.

'You can admit you like me.'

'Never.'

Chloe stayed until the next ad break and then went back to her work. Another half hour and it should be done.

*　　　*　　　*

Once she finished, Eddie was onto his third beer. He seemed cheerful but sleepy. She wondered how many drinks he'd had before he arrived.

'Are you alright?' she asked.

'Why wouldn't I be?'

'Drinking on a weeknight, I haven't seen you do it before.'

'We don't hang out on weeknights much.'

'Mmm.' If she were drinking on a weeknight, it would be in celebration or commiseration for something. She didn't drink much, especially if she had to work in the morning. She'd seen enough of her mother trying to function permanently hungover to be very careful with her drinking habits.

'Johnno cancelled a job on me,' Eddie said after a long pause.

'Oh?'

'Said I was late too many times. I guess I was a bit more pissed off about it than I wanted to let on. I haven't had as much work this month as usual and I'm gonna be short on my rent.'

'Oh.' Chloe shifted her position. Every time he'd spoken about his work, and about his friend Johnno, it had been so positive. She had no idea he would be struggling for money. It felt stingy that she had been considering asking for a contribution to her food bills when he was struggling to pay rent. On the other hand, she didn't want to end up in a relationship where she had to carry the other person; she barely made enough to keep herself let alone support someone else.

'I'll go if you're gonna be like that,' he said.

'Like what?'

'I can feel you judging me, Chloe. Honestly, I've had it all my life. I thought you'd be different. It's a tough time for me, and I need people around me who will be supportive, not fair-weather friends.'

'I'm sorry … it's unexpected. I thought you were doing really well.'

''Course you did. I was trying to impress you, keep up the line about my own business, I wanted to be stable and worthy of a relationship with someone as great as you. I guess I'm just as much of a piece of shit as I've always been.'

Chloe turned to him, his cheeks were flushed red. 'You are worthy. I'm sorry. You don't have to go. I'll do whatever I can to support you until work picks up a bit.' Everything except give you money, she told herself.

Eddie yawned, his jaw creaking. 'It's past your bedtime, should we retire?'

'Sure.'

When Chloe had finished her night-time routine and crawled into the bed next to Eddie, he was naked and snoring softly. It must have been a real blow to his ego to have his income taken away like that. Perhaps she could keep an ear out for odd jobs and other things that might help him while his business got off the ground.

'Goodnight,' she whispered into his hair.

*   *   *

Her alarm went off at half past six, and Chloe got out of bed and straight into the shower. As she dressed and did her hair and makeup, Eddie was still fast asleep.

'Time to get up, sleepyhead.' She gently shook his shoulder. He stirred a little. 'I'll make coffee, I have some toast too if you want it, but you have to come with me when I go, okay?'

At this early stage in their relationship for him to be staying in her apartment while she was at work put a rolling ball of anxiety in the pit of her stomach. He wasn't homeless and it didn't cost him anything to be at his own place during the day. She was going to be firm on this point.

Eddie was back to snoring when she brought his coffee ten minutes later. She roused him again.

'I'm awake, I'm awake.'

Chloe needed to leave the house by eight at the latest, she needed plenty of time to get to work and settle in without feeling stressed. At five to eight, Eddie was still in her bed.

'Come on. I know it's early for you, and you don't have work, but you need to get up. I can't leave you in the house.'

'Why not? I'll be fine. I'll just kip for a bit longer, and snib the door on my way out. I won't break anything, or steal anything, I won't even raid the cupboard. Cross my heart.' Beside him, the coffee was untouched. Chloe gritted her teeth. What was really so wrong about leaving him while she went to work? He couldn't get up to too much mischief.

106

'Alright, just this once. Text me when you get home.' She kissed his forehead and hurried out the door.

*   *   *

All that day at work Chloe thought about Eddie alone in her house. It felt wrong not to trust him, but it gnawed at her to leave him alone. She checked her phone during breaks and there was no word from him.

'You expecting a call, love?' Mary asked as she was packing up to leave for home.

'My boyfriend was supposed to text me,' she said, as the words left her mouth, she realised they had never agreed that they were together, something for her to mention next time they hung out. 'He was still at my place when I left this morning, he didn't have to work today.'

'And you feel funny about leaving him there?'

She hesitated. 'I know he won't do anything but, it's my house. If he's still there when I get home, I'll be annoyed.'

'Men are pretty clueless I've realised in my years of experience, especially when it comes to household matters. Try not to think about it, I'm sure he doesn't mean anything by it.' Mary patted her shoulder and walked out of the staff room. She was probably right, men could be strangely clueless about things. Given he didn't understand why she felt strange being left with Max it wasn't surprising Eddie didn't understand this either.

Chloe grabbed a couple of things from the supermarket on her way home; more milk and cheese, and something to make a pasta bake. She had meals pre-packaged in the freezer but this would be a treat for having had a stressful day at work worrying about Eddie.

When she walked into the house, she knew immediately he'd left. His smell still lingered in the apartment, but she could see he'd done some tidying; the papers all over her kitchen table were neatly stacked, the dish rack was full of clean dishes and her bed was made.

Thanks for cleaning up, babe. I'll see you soon.

She texted him, relieved to find not only was her stuff safe and sound, but Eddie had made an effort to leave the place nicer than he'd found it. A lifetime of her mother's bad boyfriends had made her cynical but it wasn't fair to him to be suspicious.

*   *   *

For a while after that first time leaving him at her place Eddie was on his best behaviour. After swearing to cut down on his drinking and be more reliable Johnno had taken him back on the work crew. They knew each other from high school, a friend of Eddie's younger brother, Johnno was a master builder and often had a number of jobs on the go. Eddie got the landscaping jobs because he didn't need a certification to be there, unlike carpenters or electricians.

The weather started to change; warmer but windier, and rainier. Spring in Melbourne was a season for pollen and hot days followed by cold days followed by hot days. Now Eddie's income was more stable, he took work with Johnno a couple of days most weeks, he was restless to go out.

Although they had met in a bar, Chloe was generally a home body, only venturing out when she had someone to drag her along with them, usually Mel. She had her hobbies, boxing, spin and yoga classes, and she didn't go out often, not least because she usually couldn't afford to spend a hundred dollars or more on drinks.

One Friday evening in late September, Chloe was at Eddie's place for dinner. Max was out at work and Eddie had shouted them pizza.

'Come out with me tonight,' he said, grabbing another slice from the box on the coffee table.

'I don't think I can, this week at work has been really intense and I want an early night.'

'You never want to do anything. I thought you were fun.'

'I am fun.' Chloe frowned. Was she really a bore? 'I'll come out with you tomorrow, how about that?'

'I've had a shitty week too, that's why I wanna go out and get wasted. Why don't you support me? You know I don't like to drink alone.'

'You could go to Max's bar, then you wouldn't be drinking alone. I won't be good company tonight babe, honestly. Any other time, I'd come out, but I'm knackered.'

Eddie harrumphed and sat back in the squishy seat of the maroon leather couch, munching his pizza in a sulk. Chloe didn't have the energy to argue with him let alone go out to a bar. She should have cancelled, the whole week one of her regular students had been driving her mad with his outbursts. Usually a quiet and compliant kid, this week Lee had been disruptive, loud, and had tried to hit her more than once. Something was going on at home, she was sure, but he wouldn't talk to her about it. His behaviour regressed when he was under stress. Next week she would continue to gently probe him, hopefully he would open up.

She and Eddie had planned to go out on Friday after work all week, but when she got home her head was pounding. A couple of Panadol and a glass of wine had helped take the edge off the pain a little, but she was more inclined to go to sleep than out for drinks.

'Do you still have a headache, babe?' Eddie asked.

'It's not letting up.' She rubbed her neck with her fingers.

'I'll give you a massage. Lemme put this left over in the fridge and we'll sort you out.'

'That'd be great.' Perhaps she was being too hard on Eddie, he'd been looking forward to going out tonight, and it wasn't his fault she had a headache.

When he returned from the kitchen, Eddie took Chloe's hand and led her to his bedroom. 'Take off your shirt, and I'll give you a massage.'

'You don't have to.'

'I want to. You look tense.' He guided her to the mattress on the floor, he hadn't been able to afford a bedframe yet, he spent all his money on beer and takeaway. Chloe took off her work shirt and lay on her stomach. Eddie had produced massage oil from somewhere, she assumed the bathroom, and brought it with him. He pulled her jeans and underwear down to expose the top of her buttocks.

'You relax, let me make you feel special.' He unclipped her bra with one hand and she felt cool liquid dribble onto her back. He worked with his hands all day, so he would be strong but she hoped he had some idea of what he was doing. Even if he just pushed the oil around her back it would no doubt feel nice.

Eddie had some skill in massage, he started with the long thin muscles up her spine, then moved out across her shoulders and upper back. His strokes were firm and confident, she felt the tension she had been carrying start to melt away. He moved further down and started to work on her lower back and glutes.

'Let's get rid of these, I wouldn't want to stain them with the oil,' he said, tugging her jeans off, then her underpants. The cool air of his bedroom touching her skin made her shiver a little, goose bumps popped up along her arms and the backs of her legs.

Eddie straddled her legs and started to rub her buttocks. It seemed more like fondling and less like massage now, as though he'd lost some of his focus. His hands slid up and down the back of her thighs and buttocks, then dipped between her thighs, skimming over her groin.

'I'm not in the mood, babe. The massage is really nice though.' She was sleepy and relaxed, but not the least bit turned on.

'What if I do this?' He pressed his shirtless torso against her back, she could feel his erection on through his pants.

'I said no. If you don't want to massage me anymore, that's fine.'

Eddie was moving his hips against hers, the feel of his hot skin on her back was pleasant, but she wished he would listen. She sighed and tried to enjoy the feeling.

As much as she might have preferred to go home to bed, Chloe's body started to respond to his touch.

'You naughty girl, you're so wet,' Eddie said. She heard him peel off his tight black jeans and toss them aside with a jangle from his belt buckle. The next moment he was on top of her, inside her. It wasn't unpleasant, but she wished he'd listened when she said she wasn't interested.

He didn't need much input from her, thankfully, and was done in a few minutes. He rolled off and ran his hand up and down her spine.

'I didn't expect a massage to end like that,' he said. Chloe didn't believe him, but she smiled anyway.

'You wanna come out with me now you're all loosened up?' he continued.

Chloe sighed; he wasn't listening at all. 'Thank you for the massage, it was lovely,' until you made it about sex, she thought. 'I'm really tired, I think I should go home to my place.'

'Seriously?' He got up and started to dress, angrily shoving his feet through his pant-legs. 'I go to all that effort and you still won't come out.'

'I'm sorry, babe, I'm really exhausted.' Chloe fought back the tears that threatened to break through. After a long and difficult week, she thought her boyfriend was being nice and thinking of her, but it was just a manipulation to get her to change her mind about going out. The sex, which she hadn't wanted, was clearly for his benefit.

'Fine. Go home. I don't need you, I'll get drunk on my own.' He stomped down the hallway and slammed the bathroom door. Chloe found her clothes and dressed. The massage oil would probably stain her white shirt but it couldn't be helped. She didn't want to be here when Eddie came out of the bathroom, she would definitely cry and didn't want to give him the satisfaction.

Chapter 7

Chloe drove home from Eddie's with her hands clenched around the steering wheel and her jaw set. She would not cry. Exhausted, her skin sticky from massage oil and sex, she felt dirty and angry, but most of all stupid. How could she not have seen what Eddie wanted? She should have been clearer that she wasn't up to it.

In her apartment she locked the door behind her, dropped her bag and stripped off her clothes and stood under the shower. She turned the water up as hot as she could tolerate and stood with her head under the stream for a long time. After a while it occurred to her how much water she was wasting and she started to soap herself down and washed her hair. When she stepped out, she rubbed herself vigorously with the towel; her skin still soft and red from the hot water stung a little at her scrubbing.

She had a robe she used sometimes, satiny material with floral print, which she wrapped around herself. The pizza she'd eaten earlier sat in her belly like a congealed lump. She was tempted to make herself vomit to bring it back up, but she didn't want to slide back into less functional coping mechanisms she'd left behind in high school.

The only alcohol in the house was three beers Eddie had left in her fridge. She gave a hollow laugh when she saw them, how perfect to be planning to drown her sorrows with his leftovers. Chloe sat on the floor in front of her couch, her legs straight out in front of her, and watched reality TV until the beer was gone.

She woke up at some point in the middle of the night, head resting on the couch seat, flickering screen still on, and dragged herself to bed.

In the morning her head hurt. Last night's pizza threatened to come back up of its own accord, but she staggered to the kitchen for water instead. She held the cool glass against her forehead and sighed. What a mess she'd made of it.

Her phone stared back at her blankly. Whatever Eddie did last night he hadn't tried to call or text. No doubt he was still sleeping, he would have gone hard last night. Not that she cared. He was a grown man and could do whatever he wanted.

She finished a second glass of water before crawling back to bed. It was only a little after ten, she could indulge in another hour or so of misery before pulling her socks up and getting on with her day.

*   *   *

No contact from Eddie all Saturday, Chloe started to think they were done.

She texted Mel.

> *Have brunch with me today. I've had a*
> *shitty weekend.*

With work and spending too much time with Eddie, she'd neglected her friend. It wouldn't have surprised her if Mel had decided she couldn't be bothered.

The Mother's Fault

What's happening, babe? I can meet you
at 1. How about the place near the
station?

Mel replied twenty minutes later.

Around the corner from Mel's place was their go to
brunch place, although by one in the afternoon it was just
lunch. Before Robbo and Eddie had taken up all their
time, they met regularly to go over the trials and
occasionally joys of their lives. To think she'd let her
friendship suffer for a boyfriend who clearly didn't care
about her clamped like a fist around her heart.

She arrived first, if they hadn't been so close Mel's
constant lateness might have annoyed her, but her friend
walked in only ten minutes after she arrived.

'Hey babe, you look awful,' Mel said, embracing her
tightly.

'Gee thanks.'

'I mean it, are you okay? Have you been crying?'
They sat, Mel took the bench seat, Chloe on a white wire
chair. It had looked more comfortable than the bench,
with its thin cushions, but she wasn't sure she'd made the
right choice trying to find a position where her chair
didn't dig into her bottom.

'I cried a bit last night. I also had three beers and fell
asleep on the floor in the loungeroom.'

'Oh my God, hunny. What's happened?'

'Nothing. I'm an idiot.'

'You're not an idiot.' Mel took her hand and looked
into her eyes, it was more intense that Chloe was

116

comfortable with, especially after a hard night. 'You are not an idiot, okay?'

At that moment the waitress came over to take their order, she looked about fifteen-years-old and was painfully chirpy. Mel ordered strong lattes for both of them.

'Okay,' Chloe managed to say.

'Things not going so well with Eddie then?'

Chloe let out one gasping moan, before getting her emotions in check. 'I think he's dumped me.'

'He didn't tell you?'

'Not in so many words.' Chloe told her what had happened on Friday night. 'And I haven't heard from him since then.'

Mel nodded. Before she could say anything else the café worker came back with their coffee. 'Do you want to order anything?'

'Bircher muesli with extra yogurt please,' Mel said. She got the same every time they ate here.

'Can I have the scrambled eggs?' Chloe said. The waitress nodded and left them to it.

'Firstly. It may not be over. I know you had a rough night but, really hun, you guys haven't ever really fought, and you said he's pretty new to relationships, maybe he doesn't know what to say.'

They were silent for a moment, Chloe looked at the table.

'On the other hand, if you don't want to be with him anymore then maybe it's a blessing in disguise, a good reason to let it go and find someone who doesn't pressure you to go out if you don't want to.'

A tear slipped from Chloe's eye, she brushed it away. 'I don't want it to be over. He can be so loving, and tender, and thoughtful. I know the stuff with his work has made him stressed and it can be really hard to accept when someone pulls out of plans at the last minute. I would have been disappointed it he'd done it to me.'

Mel raised an eyebrow and sipped her coffee. 'Would you have given him the silent treatment?'

'No, but I—I walked out without saying goodbye. Maybe he thinks I've dumped him?'

She opened her mouth, then closed it again. 'I hadn't thought of that.' Chloe drank the rest of her coffee without really tasting it, the caffeine buzzed around inside her and her mind felt a little sharper after a couple of nights bad sleep and more alcohol than she was used to. She waved to the waitress and pointed to her cup, who nodded she would bring her another coffee.

'Maybe I should be the one to break the silence? If he thinks I stormed out and then I didn't contact him for two days, well, almost two days—what if we're both sitting around miserable because we thought the other broke up with us?' Chloe laughed.

'That would be just like you, babe. You hate conflict. At work you can do it with your eyes closed, but in real life you just let people drift away.'

Chloe raised her eyebrows.

'And don't give me that look, you know you let Jenny go after she got annoyed at you about that dress.'

Chloe's cheeks burned. She had let Jenny pull away from her. They had been friends for a couple of years, after meeting at a party with some of her TAFE buddies, but they had both arrived at a mutual friend's wedding wearing the same dress.

'She was so mortified, I tried to make light of it, but...'

If the ceremony hadn't been in the Yarra Valley, at least an hour and a half away, she would have gone home to change.

'Jenny kept making a big thing of it, if she'd let it go then no one would have worried. Way to draw focus from the bride and groom.'

'It looked much better on her anyway.' Chloe looked down at her hands.

'And then what happened? Did you just stop speaking to her? I told you that it would be okay after you'd calmed down.'

'I... I couldn't. I just wanted to forget it, and every time I tried to call Jenny it was too hard and I just never did.'

'That was years ago,' Mel said, her voice raising in pitch as though she had done something unbelievable.

'I miss her sometimes. She could have called me too.'

'True, but you don't want to leave it so long this time. Why don't you text him now, I need the bathroom. I'm sure you'll feel better once you've sent it.'

The Mother's Fault

Mel walked to the back of the café, Chloe suspected it was a ploy to give her some time to compose a text message without her watching. Her friend could be thoughtful sometimes. She wouldn't let Mel go as easily as she had with Jenny, that lesson had stuck.

> *Hey. I hope you had a nice night on Friday. I'm sorry I left so suddenly. I'd like to see you, maybe we can talk about it? I don't want to lose you over this.* xx

Chloe sent the message before she could think about it too long. The longer she deliberated the less likely she would be to break their silence and now she thought about it, she wasn't ready to let Eddie go without a fight.

Their food had arrived by the time Mel returned from the bathroom. She raised her eyebrows as she sat down.

'I sent it. And I'm not checking if he replied till I get home. I want to be here with you, I haven't seen you for too long.'

Mel grinned. 'Good. Now eat your food.'

*   *   *

Chloe checked her phone repeatedly for the rest of Sunday, but no reply came from Eddie. Nothing still all Monday. On Tuesday, when she pulled her phone out at the end of the school day to check, it was there.

> *I was really angry when you left. I went out on Friday and I hit it hard. I've only just got my brain together enough to send*

*this. Let's talk this weekend. I don't
wanna lose you either.*

There were so many people in the staff room,
gossiping and packing up after the end of the school day.
Chloe wanted to giggle and cry in equal measure. She'd
given up Eddie as having dumped her. Of course, it made
sense if he'd had a really big weekend he would want a
few days to get his thoughts in order before responding.
Maybe he was still mad at her, of course he had a right to
be, she'd walked out without a word. Given his history,
or lack thereof, no doubt he assumed she was leaving
him.

She tucked her phone into the inside pocket of her
bag and drove home. Her mind was spinning a million
miles a minute. They would have to get their feelings
out, if they didn't talk through what had happened they
wouldn't be able to build a strong foundation for the rest
of their relationship. Mel was better at conflict resolution
than she was, but only barely. Her solution to any
conflict with a boyfriend was to shag it out—no one can
be in a bad mood right after sex she always said.

It was dinner time but Chloe was too agitated to eat.
She stared at the phone, her first instinct was to call
Eddie, or to go to his place and beg his forgiveness. To
feel his arms around her and remember what it felt like to
be loved, held. In previous relationships when she and
her boyfriends had fought they would make up and never
talk about it again. Usually she would apologise
regardless of whether she'd done anything wrong.

I'd like to see you this weekend. Should I come around on Saturday? We can have a night in.

There was no point going on Friday evening, as much as she couldn't wait to see him, the possibility of a repeat of last week because of exhaustion after work was too big a risk. And because she said they could have a quiet night in Eddie wouldn't expect her to go out drinking, spending money she didn't have on alcohol and writing off her Sunday in a hangover. Not to mention any unwise words that the alcohol might release from her.

As much as lying around Eddie's place like a lady of leisure appealed, it left her cranky and dissatisfied to spend the whole day in bed and ruined her sleep routine for the week at school. *What an old lady I'm turning into.*

Anything from the boy?

Mel texted her about an hour later, it was almost nine but Chloe needed to talk.

'Did he get in touch?' Mel said when she answered the phone.

'Yeah, he wants to meet up on the weekend. I suggested his place on Saturday.'

'Good one. His housemate works nights, right?'

'Yeah, we have the house to ourselves. His place so it will feel like his turf, and if we don't go out, we won't drink as much, or at least I won't.'

'Solid logic there, hun. You've got this.'

Chloe smiled, having her friend's approval helped calm her. Her mother had been such a people pleaser even when she approved of Chloe's actions it seemed disingenuous and her judgement was so poor it probably didn't bode well. None of Janine's boyfriends' opinions counted for anything if they deigned to share them. It was too bad she didn't have more girlfriends; it was so hard to keep friends and now she was heading into her late twenties it felt harder and harder to make new ones. Learning to mend fences would be an important skill if she didn't want to end up lonely.

No doubt when Eddie introduced her to his friends, she would be able to make new contacts with their partners. Despite talking about all the people he knew, Eddie didn't have many close friends. He hung out with Max, or with people he met at parties or bars. He was great at making conversation, but people only stayed around one night before drifting away, much like his previous attempts at romance.

They would have to make new friends together. Maybe they could take up a couples' hobby, bushwalking or wine tasting or something.

Mel and Chloe chatted about nothing for almost an hour before Chloe started yawning. Now the worry about Eddie had gone all the bad sleep she'd had over the last few days had caught up to her. She washed her face, cleaned her teeth and went to bed with a small, hopeful smile on her lips.

*   *   *

Saturday came around more quickly than she would have thought, the work week flew by and she and Eddie chatted via text every day. They had agreed she would make dinner, his steaks were delicious, but it was her turn to make an apology meal.

Chloe knocked on Eddie's front door, she had brought all her ingredients with her, sometimes she walked to Eddie's as the parking wasn't good and it felt silly when he only lived a short walk from her, but with all the supplies she'd taken the car. Given the state of his kitchen, she had included oil, salt, pepper and other kitchen staples she couldn't be sure he would have in his bachelor household.

'Hi,' she said as he pulled open the door. She grinned broadly to cover up the waves of burning nausea in her belly.

'Hey, I'm glad you came. Want me to grab something?' He reached for one of her green bags full of food.

'Thanks, babe.'

The house was clean, and smelled fresh, perhaps he'd done a spring clean in preparation. 'Max is at work tonight,' he said over his shoulder as they walked to the kitchen.

'That's nice. I thought I'd cook and then we could watch a movie?'

'Sounds good. What are you making? I'm starving, I got up late so I've only had breakfast today.'

Chloe looked around and saw one small plate in the sink, it had a smattering of crumbs on, perhaps it had been toast.

'I'm making crumbed lamb cutlets with mashed potato and beans. An old boyfriend used to make them for me, and I've always thought they were a good special occasion meal. Especially good if I don't want to spend all afternoon simmering something or make stir fry.'

'Anything that involves meat gets my vote. You want a beer while you cook?'

'Sure, why not?' she said. 'I owe you three beers by the way. You left them in my fridge but I drank them the other night—I was upset.'

He handed her a chilled bottle from the fridge, she didn't recognise the name, but it was a pale golden liquid in a clear bottle. 'Let's not talk about that now, eh? Don't wanna spoil our appetites.'

She nodded. 'I didn't bring any pans with me, I assume you have a fry pan and a couple of pots?'

'I might be a bit of a light-weight when it comes to cooking but we do have the basics.' He laughed. 'If I was being strict about it, Max has the basics. I use his stuff. He doesn't mind.'

'That's good. He's a lovely guy. It's a shame he doesn't have a girlfriend.'

'I tried to hook him up with someone on Friday night. After you left, I went to his bar. He managed to get her to come home with him, but she didn't give him her number.'

Chloe had found the pans she needed for the meal and put a pot of water onto the stove for the potatoes, they would take the longest to cook. 'Poor Max.'

'I mean he got his leg over, so that's a plus, but yeah. Would be nice to get a girl to stay more than one night. He's such an awkward fish it's hard to get anyone who'll see him again once they sober up.'

Chloe looked up, frowning, from where she was peeling potatoes into the sink. It was such an unkind thing to say she was surprised at Eddie.

'His words, not mine.' He held his hands up in front of him in a gesture of surrender.

'Maybe meeting people at his bar is not the right approach. Does he have hobbies or anything? Perhaps someone with a mutual interest would be a better bet.'

'Maybe. I mean, most of the time he plays video games, or sleeps, or works. I don't think he does have any hobbies.'

'There are girls into video games.'

Eddie laughed. 'Oh, you're serious. Have you ever seen them?'

'What do you mean?'

'They're not hot.'

'Not everyone needs to be hot. If Max has trouble making lasting connections maybe changing who he goes for will be better for him.'

'That's true.' Eddie took a sip of his beer. 'People like me have girlfriends like you, there's a kind of equivalent level of hotness, but Max is different. You're right, I should stop trying to get him girls I'd like.'

'It's sweet you look out for him, but it might work better if he was his own wingman.' With her students, fostering independence and confidence always worked much better than trying to do things for them. 'How long have you two been friends?'

'I've known him since high school, but we didn't really hang out much before I moved in here. I guess four years?'

'You've been living here that long?' She dropped the peeled and chopped potatoes into the pot of now boiling water.

'You sound surprised.'

'I thought you had moved in recently.' Chloe thought of the mattress on the floor, the clothes in piles on the floor, the empty wardrobe. She had assumed it was disorganised because he'd moved recently, but four years was a long time to live like that.

'Nah, been here a while. I'm pretty settled. Max and I have a good rhythm, for the most part.'

'I'm glad. It's good to have stability.'

While Chloe set about tenderising, crumbing, and frying the cutlets, Eddie wandered away. She heard him switching on the TV and the repetitive clanging, droning and chimes of a road racing game. She sighed, it wasn't very interesting to watch someone else cook, but after what they'd been through last weekend, she thought he would have wanted to clear the air between them, to recover some of the ground they'd lost.

'How's it coming? The smell is making me hungry,' he yelled from the loungeroom.

'I'm about ready to serve, you want to eat in here or in the lounge?'

'Lounge.'

She hoped this wasn't an indication of what the rest of their relationship would be like. Her mother had had plenty of boyfriends who were glued to the couch, most of them were watching football or some other sport ignoring her and yelling demands, but video games would be another version of the same poor behaviour. Now she thought about it, Chloe had no idea what Eddie did to fill in his time when not working. And his business, which seemed as nebulous and unrealised as always, seemed to make no money. He lived off the landscaping income he got from Johnno. Perhaps that was why he hadn't bought a bed, such inconsistent earnings would have made it hard to save.

She brought the plates of food into the lounge and laid them on the coffee table. 'You'll have to turn that off while we eat.' She sounded like her mother.

'Of course.' He switched the screen off while she went back into the kitchen for knives and forks. 'Can you bring me another beer, babe?'

'Yep.' She got a glass of water for herself and sat next to him. The coffee table was low to the ground and she had to bend right over her meal to reach the plate. She considered moving to kneel or sit on the ground, but it seemed a strange thing to do in company.

They ate quietly, Eddie more interested in shovelling the food into his mouth than in talking to her. She didn't know what to say to fill the silence and ended up saying nothing.

'That was great. Thanks.' Eddie burped and finished off his second beer.

'I'm glad you liked it.' She reached for the plates.

'Don't worry about that, I'll take care of them later.'

'Thank you. I … was hoping we could talk about what happened last weekend.'

Eddie sighed. 'Do we have to? You said sorry, I said sorry, end of story.'

'I guess so, but I need you to know why I was so upset. It's no good saying you're sorry but not changing your behaviour.'

'Alright, tell me why you were upset.' He crossed his arms in front of his chest and shuffled his butt along the couch so he was facing her.

'I was tired. You offered me a massage, which was lovely, and then it turned into sex, which I wasn't really into, but I enjoyed in the end, and then you wanted to go out.

'I thought because you were giving me a massage you had heard me say I was too tired to go out and you were pampering me, but it felt more like you were trying to manipulate me into going out by doing something nice for me.'

'I see.' Eddie was silent for a while, his knee bobbing up and down as he stared at the coffee table. 'I'm sorry you felt that way. I thought you were feeling more perky after the rub down, I certainly was, so I wanted to see if you'd changed your mind, but I guess it might have sounded like I was pressuring you. From a certain way of looking at things. I'm a bit offended you thought that, if I'm honest.'

'I was tired and sensitive. I didn't mean to make you feel like you manipulated me.'

'I went out and got really drunk, I did some stuff I regretted that night. It would have been so much better if you'd been there, I don't do so much stupid stuff when you're around. I need you Chloe, you make me want to be a better person.' He turned to her then for the first time since they'd started talking seriously, his eyes were glistening and the hurt in them was clear. She wanted to reach out to him, to comfort him, have his forgiveness. It was awful when they fought, the empty place in her heart felt so much emptier when he wasn't around. Not to mention wanting to make sure he had a safe place to come home to so he wouldn't act out while drunk.

'How about this; next time, I'll be more generous when you ask me things, like if I've changed my mind, but maybe you can take my word for it when I say I'm not up to something. I don't need you to stay home because I am, but sometimes I don't have the energy to go out.'

He ran his hand over the jeans on his right leg, obviously using the gesture to give himself time to formulate a response. 'I guess I didn't want to go out on my own. I'm sorry you felt like I was pressuring you. I'll do better next time.' He looked into her eyes, he seemed so lost. There was pain in his face. 'I missed you,' he said.

'I missed you too.'

'Do you…' he trailed off and leaned forward to her, pressing his lips against hers. A chaste kiss, delicate, unlike any kiss he'd ever given her before. At first, she wanted to pull away; she wanted to forgive him, but it was too easy, she wanted him to really acknowledge what he'd done to make her feel so dismissed. He was so close she could smell him, despite her concerns her body responded. She pushed forward, deepening the kiss. As soon as she made her move, she wanted him. He pushed her back to lie on the couch and he was lying on top of her in under a second, his body on hers, his arousal clear, pressed against her legs. She bucked her hips towards his instinctively.

They fucked on the couch, it was hot, sweaty, rough and the best she'd ever had. As they lay together, afterwards, their clothing still mostly on, still joined together, she felt a giggle rising inside her. It felt silly, almost hysterical, but it came bubbling out.

'What's funny?' he asked, a frown shadowing his strong, handsome brow.

'Nothing, I just—that was good.' She laughed.

'Yeah.' He smiled and laid his head on her shoulder. They stayed there for a long time, until her leg started to get pins and needles where it was crushed under his body.

'I need my leg back,' she said.

'Sorry.' He lifted himself up, replacing his jeans slung low around his skinny hips, and straightened his T-shirt. 'You want a beer?'

'Uuhh.'

'Max has some bourbon somewhere; you want that instead?'

'No, beer is fine.' She didn't want to drink Max's liquor, since they'd just violated his couch. 'I just have to go to the bathroom, want me to bring the beers back?'

'Thanks, babe.'

*   *   *

Chloe and Eddie watched a movie, an action film with Stallone and several other past their prime stars. It wasn't Chloe's cup of tea, but she was satisfied to have Eddie beside her. She fell asleep as some point and he woke her when the credits were rolling.

His mattress on the floor seemed more comfortable than the last time she was there, though perhaps a few beers and a better frame of mind helped.

In the morning, Eddie snored on, and Chloe woke a little after ten. It was late for her, but Eddie would sleep for another couple of hours. She had remembered to bring something for breakfast, or first breakfast, they might go out for brunch later, although neither of them could really afford it.

She was making coffee using Max's AeroPress, a giant syringe-like plunger, when she heard his soft footfalls coming out of his room.

'Hey,' she said.

'Oh.' He stopped dead in the doorway to the kitchen. 'You're here.'

'Yeah. I thought Eddie would have told you I was coming round.'

'I—we aren't really speaking to each other.'

'What happened?'

'I shouldn't say. The important thing is you're back.' He hurried through the kitchen to the bathroom. Chloe frowned after him before pushing the plunger down on her coffee. She removed the used grounds and made another coffee for Max. When he re-emerged from the bathroom, he seemed to have calmed himself, his wild blond hair looked like it had been smoothed down with water.

'I've made you a coffee, if you want it,' she said.

'Thanks.' He took it, she'd already added milk the way he liked it. She took pride in knowing how people liked their hot drinks. It always seemed to make such a difference when she didn't have to ask again each time.

'How's work?' she asked.

'Same old.'

With other people silences could be awkward, but with Max she was trying to train herself to be comfortable in the quiet. If he was different, neurodiverse or autistic, it might take him a long time to work out exactly how he wanted to phrase something, or he might be thinking about something different entirely and not be aware of the pressure of silence the way other people were. It would do nothing to help the situation if she prattled on filling the silence or peppering him with questions. The strategies she used for her students worked just as well for adults when she remembered to use them.

'I met a lady on Friday.'

'Oh?' She tried to keep her face still.

'Eddie told you, didn't he?'

'He mentioned it.'

'And that she didn't want to see me again after waking up here?'

'What do you mean?'

'Took one look around the place, the second-hand furniture, the empty fridge and cupboards, the state of the bathroom, and walked out.'

'I'm sorry to hear that.'

'I don't think she was right for me. I mean physically attractive, very symmetrical face and low body fat, but she didn't seem very interesting. We didn't have much of a chance to talk, it's very loud at work and she was quite drunk—' he stopped abruptly.

Chloe waited in case he had more to add, but apparently that was all he wanted to say. 'If you ever want any help in meeting people, I mean, I'm not very good at it myself, but I'd be happy to give you my thoughts.'

'Thanks.' Max rested his hand on the coffee cup as though half-way through a thought. 'You wanna play something with me?'

'You know I'm not much of a gamer. I have a book though, and some muesli. I'll come hang out in the lounge with you.'

Max smiled, it made his face look so different to see joy in his eyes, Chloe was surprised how much sadness was there when he let the smile fade. He must have had a very difficult time going through life, having people constantly misunderstand or mistreat him.

Max played a game which seemed to involve building things with pixelated cubes; he turned the volume down low so as not to interrupt her reading. Time slipped by, and after a couple of hours, Eddie finally emerged from his bedroom.

'You're here,' he said.

'Yes.' Chloe replied.

'I thought you'd fucked off again.'

'You know I don't sleep as late as you. I'm sorry you thought I'd gone.'

'I dunno whether I like you hanging out with Max.' Eddie scratched his hair absently.

'Why not?' Chloe asked.

'He might tell you all my secrets.'

She laughed, but Eddie's face remained serious.

'He doesn't talk much. I'm sure your secrets are safe.'

'Right.' He stumbled out of the lounge and into the bathroom, apparently not bothering to close the door, before relieving himself. When he came back into the lounge he seemed in a better mood.

'You know I was kidding about the secrets? I don't have anything to hide from you.' He smiled and sat next to her on the couch.

'I thought you were. You're not a secretive person.' Chloe squeezed his knee and went back to her book.

'Let's play something else,' Eddie said, picking up the second controller on the coffee table.

The Mother's Fault

The simple domesticity was a welcome relief to
Chloe after a week of turmoil and uncertainty. Max
looked at her a few times, she read some concern in his
eyes, but perhaps he was worried that his routine would
be upset again if they had another fight. She made a
mental note to reassure him she had no intentions of
going anywhere.

Chapter 8

The comfortable rhythm they had had before that dreaded Friday night was hard to find again. Eddie vacillated between overly attentive and avoidant. When he stayed at her place, they would be okay, but when she stayed at his place there was a tension in the air, especially if she spent time with Max. A couple of times she wondered if Eddie was jealous, despite the fact Max wasn't a threat to him.

One Friday night after a particularly good day at work Chloe wanted to go out.

'Should we go hang out at Max's bar?' she asked.

'Why would we do that?' Eddie was sitting next to her on the couch.

'I dunno. I thought it might be fun to go out. You said we were spending too much time at home.'

'Yeah, I did, but why would we go hang out with him? There are so many places, better places, we could go.'

'I don't mind where we go. You know I'm a bit of a home body, I don't know where is good.'

'Have you got a thing for Max?' Eddie turned to her, his eyes narrowed and blazing.

'I don't know what's got into you. I don't have a thing for Max and if you're going to be in a mood then you can go back to your house.'

'Is that how it's gonna be? Throwing me out? Unbelievable.' Eddie jumped up and started pacing the room. Chloe's body tensed; she had never seen him so agitated.

'I'm not throwing you out,' her voice was calm, her words measured, 'but perhaps you need some time to settle down. I can see you're angry, but maybe we can talk about it when you're feeling less stressed.'

'Are you fucking Max?'

'What?' She giggled nervously, her heart beating hard in her chest, and wrapped her arms around herself. 'No. Why would you think that?'

'I get up and you're always hanging out with him. He looks at you and he looks guilty. I'm not an idiot.'

'I never suggested you were. I don't want to wake you by fidgeting in bed while you're sleeping, so I get up. Max is often up too. We chat sometimes, mostly I read and he plays games. I'm not sleeping with him, promise.' She wanted to reach out and soothe him, make sure he was calm and clear headed, her mind went straight to overheard arguments between her mother and whichever boyfriend was there at the time. This wasn't a conversation she would let get out of hand.

'If you were, it wouldn't be the same as what I did...'

'I'm not—wait, what did you do?'

Eddie stopped pacing, his hands clenched and unclenched at his sides. 'Nothing.'

Chloe sat forward on the couch, a cold, hollow feeling started in her stomach and spread through her. 'What did you do?'

Eddie was silent. Chloe's mind whirled, churning over what could have happened. Max had brought someone home the night she and Eddie had fought and both men had been strange around her since. 'Did you do something that night we fought?'

Max had said he was glad she was back, she thought he must have meant it was good to see her, but maybe he was glad it wasn't someone else. Was Eddie jealous because he felt guilty?

'You fucked someone else, didn't you?'

Eddie's face flushed red, he turned away and stared out the balcony windows.

'That night after I left. Did you think we were broken up? Is that why you didn't talk to me for days afterwards?' It was all so clear looking back. He confirmed his betrayal through his silence. If he had thought they were over then she might have been able to forgive him, but he said nothing. He could have been punishing her or sabotaging himself by doing the one thing he knew would destroy their relationship. How Max fit into the situation she wasn't sure, perhaps he was projecting his guilt.

'I'm gonna go,' he said.

'We need to talk about this. I want to know what happened.'

'No, you don't.' He picked his wallet and phone from where they sat on the floor next to the couch. He walked out of her apartment as she watched, stunned. She blinked; her mind felt as though it was spinning out of control but also ominously empty.

The silence after the door closed behind Eddie felt more profound than any she'd felt before. Worse than the silence lying in bed as a kid, waiting for someone to come into her room, worse than the silence after one of her mother's boyfriends had ended a fight planting his fist into her face. Slowly, sounds drifted back in—her heartbeat, her breathing, the hum of the fridge as it clicked on, a pair of high-heeled shoes clip-clopping along the path down-stairs, the booming laugh of one of her neighbours. She couldn't move, her limbs felt heavy and she was trapped on the couch, waiting for her brain to return to operation.

She took a deep breath, then another. Outside the night sky was brown tinted navy, dirty yellow street lights against low hanging loose clouds.

They'd had one fight, he'd pushed her too far and she had pushed back, stormed out and he went straight to a bar to pick up another woman. He might have claimed he was no good at relationships because he'd never been in one, but maybe he had never been in one because no other woman had ever been stupid enough to let him hang around so long.

Chloe didn't know what the woman looked like; she could have been anyone. A picture started to form in her mind of a slim woman with bright, bouncy blonde hair, not like Chloe's boring mousy brown hair that hung straight down her back. She would have worn something skin-tight, probably short, and black to contrast with her hair and complexion. Max had met someone too, perhaps one of her friends, the less attractive of the two because no doubt Eddie would make sure to go after the hot one. Chloe thought she might be sick.

Her hands shook as she reached for her phone. The only person she could call was Mel, and she prayed her friend would answer.

'Hey, babe.' Mel sounded out of breath. 'What's up?'

'I… I think Eddie broke up with me.'

'What? Hold on.' Footsteps echoed and the background noise died down. 'Sorry, I'm at Robbo's getting ready, he and his housemates were having a beer. I went out the front so I can hear you. Say it again?'

'I think Eddie dumped me.'

'What happened?'

'The night we fought, you know weeks ago, he went out and picked up a one-night stand. He just told me, he didn't mean to but it slipped out. I wanted to talk it over but he just walked out. It's over, it has to be. I can't be in a relationship with a man who fucks someone else every time we have a fight.'

'Slow down. Tell me what happened, in detail.'

Chloe paused to gather her thoughts and went over what had happened. It seemed surreal, even saying it aloud for the third time. She felt nothing, other than a growing sense of nausea and crushing dread.

'What are you going to do?' Mel said.

'I'm not sure. I don't want to see him ever again, but I was so used to him being in my life. My mind is full of fog.'

Mel made a soft consoling sound. 'Why don't you run yourself a nice hot bath, and order some takeaway, I know you don't like the expense, but treat yourself today, yeah? I can't come over just now but maybe we can go out tomorrow? There's a party for Jesse, remember the guy from TAFE? It's his birthday. You could be my wing-woman.'

'I don't know.' It was so soon, she couldn't possibly get out and meet new people.

'Promise you'll think about it, okay? Have a glass of wine or two, and a bath, and some junk food and watch a movie. You'll feel like shit for a while, but after that you'll be okay. You got this.'

'Yeah. I've got this' Chloe didn't even believe herself as she said the words.

'You're strong.'

'I know. Thank you.' Her voice wasn't so wobbly the second time. Mel was a social butterfly, a true extrovert, and it wasn't a surprise she couldn't come over and commiserate tonight. At least she'd answered the phone. Chloe's limbs still felt leaden and uncoordinated. She prised herself off the couch and went to run a bath. She poured bath salts into the bottom and turned on the tap.

The fridge was pretty empty, although there was a cask of cheap wine in there. Barely drinkable, she'd bought it for cooking, it would do the job. Her favourite takeaway was Indian, the Vietnamese places on nearby Victoria Street were no good for delivery; the soup didn't travel well. She ordered one of everything she liked, it was more money than she'd spent on herself for weeks, but it was worth it. If she had to eat rice and beans for a week, then so be it; there would be no more cooking for two to eat into her budget.

Her meal would take at least forty-five minutes to arrive, enough time for two glasses of wine in the bath. No doubt it would make her drunk on an empty stomach, so she took the remains of a slab of milk chocolate in with her.

Her apartment buzzer went off a little less than an hour later, her head lolling sleepily against the bathtub, her eyes sore and puffy from crying. Wrapping herself in a towel she buzzed the delivery driver up and waited at the door. It was a mild night, but she was still wet from the bath as the slightly abashed delivery man handed her a large brown paper bag.

'Enjoy your meal,' he said, dipping his head in a nod.

She thanked him, put the food on the kitchen table and went to dry off. Chloe ate in her pyjamas, a little from each dish, as well as garlic naan and saffron rice. She thought she might burst, but at least it was a different feeling to the paralysing sadness, and emptiness, that set in as soon as Eddie left.

There was nothing good on TV and all her movies were romantic comedies or thrillers, neither of which were what she felt in the mood for. She switched it to a reality show where B-list celebrities competed at ballroom dancing, some of them were woeful, the football players in particular seemed to have no rhythm at all.

At about one in the morning, she woke up curled into a ball on the couch. Four wines and a lot of Indian food had put her straight to sleep. Her mouth was covered in a furry carpeting and her throat was dry, she ignored both and crawled into her bed.

* * *

Chloe stayed in bed until eleven, drifting in and out of sleep. Her phone jingled; a message from Mel.

> *Are you up for the party tonight? No expectations, just a little drinking with people who don't know Eddie and who will be thrilled to see you. I'll drive there and back. Pick you up at 8?*

Despite the overwhelming urge to hide in bed all day, Chloe knew getting out and talking to people would be good for her. Naturally introverted and more comfortable with her own company, she had learned a lot of techniques to feel better about talking to strangers as a teacher's aide. Her best trick was to listen to what the other person was telling you and ask a question about whatever it was when they started to slow down. It almost always worked, especially for men who needed to feel important, but women were often able to talk about themselves if given the right opportunity. When she showed interest in others, they often had fond memories of her regardless of whether she gave them any information on herself.

It was a warm night, but likely to get cool later, typical of late October. She wore slim fitting jeans and a sleeveless top, and took a pale blue cotton cardigan with her in case it was cold. Mel picked her up in Robbo's massive four-wheel drive. He worked in construction so it was dusty and a little bit dinged up.

'Looks like I feel,' Chloe joked as she climbed into the front passenger seat.

'It does the job. You doing okay?' Mel took her hand and squeezed it.

'I think I can hold it together, but if I freak out, I might have to get a taxi home.'

'We're going to Footscray, that'll cost you a bomb. If you need to leave come find me and we'll say you had a dodgy prawn or something.' Mel gave her hand one more reassuring squeeze before dropping it to put the car in gear. They roared off down the skinny Richmond side street, Chloe felt so high up it was like being in a boat rather than a car.

The drive to Footscray, a suburb to the west of Melbourne, took a little over half an hour. A lot of young people were moving to the western suburbs to be able to afford a house with a yard to start their families. Jesse had joined them. They pulled up in front of a white weatherboard house with a grey picket fence in front. Both the house and the fence needed repainting, chips and flakes curled all over them. The garden wasn't much to look at, mainly lawn, but it seemed clean. A fixer-upper but it looked solid, not that Chloe had much knowledge of houses.

Jesse had been studying to be an electrician at the same TAFE where she and Mel met. Clearly, he was doing well for himself if he'd bought a place already. Music and ebullient voices wafted through the open front door as she followed Mel inside.

The house was partially renovated, the floorboards were freshly polished and shone like new, but the walls and skirting boards were grubby and covered in dust. A few of the walls had patches on them as though they had been repaired but not yet repainted. The decor was nothing special; a mish-mash of sleek stylish pieces and flat pack student stuff. There were people everywhere; a few of the faces Chloe recognised from her TAFE days but others were completely new. Mel spotted Jesse and made a beeline for him.

'Happy birthday, gorgeous,' she said, flinging her arms around his neck, standing on her tiptoes to reach.

'Mel, you came. That's a turn-up for the books, I thought you were hibernating with that boyfriend of yours, what's his name again? Ricky?'

'Robbo, you duffer.'

Chloe suspected Jesse knew exactly what Mel's boyfriend's name was but had decided to pretend otherwise. There was a bitter look in his eye that said he had not gotten over the fact Mel had never been interested in him.

'And this is…' he looked at Chloe.

'You know my friend Chloe? We hung out together back then, but we're bestest buds now, aren't we, babe?' Mel draped her arm around Chloe's shoulder. Jesse stared at her face intently, eyes narrowed, as though trying to remember her. She remembered him though, he was one of the cool guys. The tradies were much cooler than the teaching aide students, and they knew it. He had trailed Mel around trying to get her to go on a date with him for about six months, and Chloe had been there for a lot of that time, but clearly, she had not registered. She was used to not being noticed by people.

Mel and Jesse were deeply engaged in conversation about various people Chloe didn't know, so she excused herself to find somewhere to put her drinks; she and Mel had gone in for a six pack of pre-mixers, that way they shouldn't get too drunk.

The kitchen was bustling, as was the way of parties in the suburbs. 'Are we putting drinks in the fridge?' Chloe asked.

'There's probably no room, but there are a couple of Eskies out the back with ice in 'em,' said a tall slim blonde woman. Chloe nodded and made her way out to the enormous, new-looking, wooden deck at the back of the house. This must be where all the cool people hung out, small groups clustered on the deck, and a few stragglers had ventured further back onto the grassed area. The lights from the back of the house didn't quite reach them there and they were only silhouettes, the occasional red ember of a cigarette bobbing around in the darkness.

She deposited her six pack of rum and cokes into a large blue and white cool box, grabbed one and flipped the lid down. The can hissed and popped as she opened it and took a sip. She had forgotten how sugary they were, but the second sip was better.

'Are you lost?' A kind voice came from behind her. Chloe turned to see a man only a little taller than herself, chubby, with auburn hair and an enormous auburn beard. He smiled widely at her, teeth gleaming in his round face, and she felt immediately at ease.

'I don't know many people so I'm just soaking up the atmosphere.'

'I'm Ben.' He stuck out his hand, broad and calloused, to shake hers. Despite having a firm grip, he did not crush her fingers.

'Chloe. Lovely to meet you.'

'Now you know one more person. You want to come sit with my friends and me? We're inside, but we have chairs.'

Chloe grinned. He was flirting with her, and she found she wanted to flirt back. Harmless fun—she had no intention of making anything of it so close to the fight with Eddie, but what Ben didn't know wouldn't hurt him.

They walked back inside, music played through speakers outside and was less obnoxious in here, droning non-vocal house music, not her favourite, but at least it wasn't aggressive hip-hop. Ben's friends were sitting in the dining room around the table. Ben indicated to a chair beside him.

'This is Otto and Luke.' He pointed to the two men already sitting at the table. 'Boys, this is Chloe. She doesn't know many people here, so I thought we should take care of her.'

A look passed between the other two men; Chloe wasn't sure what it meant and wondered if she'd made the right call coming to sit with them. Then again, it was a house party and she could leave any time, what did she have to lose?

'Lovely to meet you, Chloe,' Luke said. He was very handsome, and seemed tall, although it was hard to tell as he was seated, muscular, his T-shirt hugged his chest and biceps in a way that made it clear he knew he was hot, brown hair slicked straight back, clean shaven, he had been blessed with a square jaw, strong but proportional nose, and dark eyes she couldn't read. Otto was seated on his other side, his hair was dark and curly, receding a little at the temples though it fell nicely to cover it, his lips were slightly too big to be handsome but she imagined kissing them would be luxurious.

'How do you know Jesse?' Otto asked, his voice smooth and thick like honey being poured.

'My friend, Mel, and he were close at TAFE. I've met him a couple of times, though he doesn't remember me.' She laughed.

'How could he forget a face as lovely as yours?' Ben asked. She turned back to him, her face heating in a blush. From anyone else, such a bald comment might have felt creepy, but Ben's face was clear and open. He seemed to realise he'd overstepped and started to stutter to cover his fumble.

'Ben suffers from foot in mouth syndrome.' Luke moved his chair closer to hers, his knee now pressing against her leg. It was very warm in the house, despite the cool spring night, and she took a long drink from her can.

'Tell us about yourself,' Luke said, his eyes locked on hers, a hungry look in them, perhaps he looked at all women that way.

'I'm a teacher's aide.'

'That's so great,' Ben said. She swivelled her head back to him.

Luke put his hand on her knee, a shiver of arousal ran up her leg from his touch. Men as attractive as Luke didn't usually pay her any attention and her head swam.

She stayed with the three men for quite a while, each of them flirting with her outrageously. For whatever reason, it seemed they were competing for her affection and after a while, suspecting they were teasing her, Chloe stopped worrying about it and accepted their attention.

Ben had gone to get some of his red wine, quite an expensive bottle by the taste; smooth, mellow and warm in her mouth. She'd had a few glasses and was feeling decidedly tipsy.

'Are you trying to get me drunk?' she asked, feigning outrage.

'I would never do such a thing,' Ben replied, putting his hand against his collar in mock surprise, then he winked.

'We're just trying to make sure you're being looked after, a single woman who doesn't know anyone,' Luke said.

'I never said I was single.'

He narrowed his eyes and smiled wickedly. 'You are though, aren't you?'

'Yes,' she giggled. She hadn't meant to tell them, but it was hard to keep her tongue in check with all the attention they were paying her and so much delicious wine.

'It's your turn to get more booze, Ben,' Luke said.

'Fine.' Ben sighed and stood up, his glass was still half full, but Luke's beer had run out.

'Now he's gone,' he leaned over and spoke softly in her ear. 'Are you really going to let that big oaf take you home when you could be with me?'

'I know you don't have any interest; you're just playing some silly game with Ben,' she said.

'I assure you,' he put his hand on her leg again, halfway up her thigh, the heat made her shudder with anticipated pleasure, 'my interest is genuine. I say we give it another half hour then put poor Ben out of his misery and you let me show you what a good time you can have.'

Chloe looked away to where Ben was grabbing drinks from the esky on the back deck. He was sweet and handsome in his way, but Luke was beautiful. If she was going to have a fling with one of them, an idea that was becoming more and more tempting, why wouldn't she go with the hot one? If she and Eddie really were over, perhaps she would be able to hook Luke, and if not, then what harm could there be in a little fun.

'You promise you're not leading me on?' she watched his face as she replied. The smile that stole over his face spoke of victory.

'Cross my heart and hope to die.' His eyes looked straight into her soul and she couldn't look away. She dipped her gaze to his lips, sensuous and full, they were only inches away from hers. In her mind's eye she could taste them against hers. She shook herself and looked away, no need to rub it in Ben's face.

When he returned to the little party with three beers in his hands, he glanced at each of them and his smile faded, as though it were something he'd experienced before. Chloe's heart broke a little for the kind, bear of a man who was constantly bested by his handsome, suave friend. It must have been a kick to his self-esteem, she briefly considered changing her mind, and not going home with any of them, but Luke's hand gave a squeeze on her thigh under the table and she knew she wouldn't say no.

She finished her wine and turned to Ben. He seemed sad, and she couldn't blame him. Luke had moved his chair right up against hers and draped his arm casually around her shoulder. Otto, pretending he hadn't noticed, excused himself, giving a meaningful look at Ben who followed him onto the deck.

'Now we're alone, I want you to come home with me,' Luke said, his intense eyes gazing into hers.

'I don't know … I told myself I wasn't going to be with anyone today.'

'You've been flirting with me all evening, you've broken poor Ben's heart already.' His fingers brushed the delicate, exposed skin on her neck. 'I don't think you really want to say no to me.'

She shivered. Eddie had been with someone else, surely this would make them even, if they were ever going to see each other again, which was not a guarantee at this stage.

'Will it be awkward between you and Ben if I do?'

'You're making excuses, but no. Ben and I sometimes have our eyes on the same lady and, more often than not, she chooses me. When that happens Ben isn't upset, and when she chooses him, I'm not upset. I can't force you to do anything you don't want to do, but I think you'll enjoy it.' Luke moved his head close to Chloe's ear, his breath hot and sweet on her skin.

'I need to tell my friend I'm leaving, she's my ride.'

Luke nodded. 'I'm going out the front, I'll meet you there. Don't take too long, sexy.'

The cold where his hand used to be was like a slap, she wanted to feel him against her, she hardly ever indulged in spontaneous encounters, although Eddie had started that way.

Mel was in the kitchen talking to a woman who looked familiar although Chloe couldn't remember her name. 'I'm heading off.'

Mel raised an eyebrow. 'I saw you talking to those three chaps. Don't tell me one of them has convinced you to accept a ride home.'

Chloe looked away, her cheeks heating. 'I may have agreed to a ride home with a fellow named Luke.'

'Watch him. He's a player,' said the woman in the kitchen.

'Consider me warned.' Chloe had no intention of changing her mind. Despite being highly unlikely to lead to a relationship, she fancied a bit of fun and attention from a handsome stranger.

'I'll check in with you tomorrow, babe,' Mel said. They hugged briefly, Chloe half expected Mel to whisper something dirty or encouraging in her ear, but her friend was silent.

Luke was waiting at the front of the house. He seemed impatient, though she had only taken a minute or two to say her goodbyes.

'Ready?'

'Yes,' *as I'll ever be*, she added to herself.

*　　*　　*

Luke drove them back towards his apartment in South Yarra, in a high-rise building off Chapel Street. The car ride lasted about fifteen minutes and it was a little after midnight when he turned into the gated carpark. The sound of their car doors closing echoed off the empty concrete space.

He came around to her side of his car, a low profile sporty-looking black Mazda. He put his hand on her hips, they were both standing, he was considerably taller, he bent his head to kiss her, his lips were smooth, cool, and just as soft as she'd imagined. Her breath hitched in her throat as he pulled her closer, the kisses became harder, more demanding, as did the shape beneath his tailored black pants.

'What's the naughtiest thing you've ever done?' he whispered in her ear as he started to kiss down her neck towards her collarbone.

'I'm not very naughty,' she said.

'You've never done anything where people might see you?'

'No.' she giggled.

'I think you just need a nudge in the right direction.' He pulled down the shoestring straps of her singlet and bra, and kept pulling until her breasts were exposed.

'What if someone sees?' she said, her voice breathy with arousal and a touch of fear.

'I'm the one who lives here and beside no one will see us.' He pushed her back against the car and took her nipple into his mouth. Her objections were drying up in her mouth, her mind filled only with what his mouth was doing to her body.

'Will you play with me, Miss Chloe?' Luke took her hand and rubbed it over his cock through his pants. Chloe nodded. He unbuttoned her jeans and slid his hand down the front.

'My goodness, what a naughty girl you are,' he said, as his fingers skilfully found the wetness that had soaked through to her knickers. In one swift movement, he turned her around and bent her over the bonnet of the car.

Their backs were to the carpark, a quiver of danger ran across Chloe's skin, but it was quickly overruled by Luke's fingers. He had pulled her jeans down to expose her backside, as he slipped his fingers in and out of her.

'Are you ready for me?' he said, she heard the unzipping of his pants.

'Yes.'

After being with Eddie, the feel of another man inside her was a surprise, but one that sent shivers of pleasure through her. It was sweaty and fast, Luke climaxed quickly and he bent over Chloe to nibble her ear before pulling away.

'Fuck, that was hot,' he said. 'We should probably head inside; we wouldn't want anyone to catch us.' He winked and slapped her bottom, the sound reverberating around the empty carpark.

She followed him and they took a lift to his apartment on the fifteenth floor.

'Have a seat, I'll bring you something to drink. Are you a white wine girl?' he asked, showing her into the apartment. Everything looked minimal and elegant, the furniture and décor were all in shades of black and white. Chloe took a seat on the edge of a vast black leather couch, she felt slightly dirty, her knickers were still slick, after what they'd done in the carpark. She brushed at some dust that had transferred from the car bonnet onto her top.

Luke returned with wine for her and a coconut water for himself. 'I've had quite enough for tonight,' he said. They talked about this and that for a while, mostly his job in financial management. She was two thirds through her wine when his eye fell to her shoulder.

'You've got a smudge on your shoulder there. You're welcome to have a shower, perhaps my car is not as clean as I might have liked.' He winked.

'That's okay... actually, I will have a shower, thank you.' She thought about having to sleep in his bed covered in dirt and old sex.

'Let me get you a towel.' He disappeared and came back holding a tasteful grey towel, a bath sheet really, it was enormous. 'Bathroom is through here.'

As with the lounge, the bathroom was entirely black and white; the tiles in the shower were such a glossy black she could almost see her reflection. She turned on the water and started to pull off her clothes. As she stood under the water, flowing over her hair and face and body from a huge black rain shower head, she heard a tap on the door.

'I thought you might like company,' Luke said, as he strolled in. He was already naked, his body toned like a bodybuilder, his abs rippling as he walked towards her, his cock already at half-mast. She was surprised he wanted to go again so soon, but she certainly wasn't against the idea. They took their time, Luke soaped her up and got her into a lather. He used his hands and his tongue to bring her to orgasm before he took her from behind again.

When they were finished, she was shivering with pleasure. He flipped off the water and wandered into the bedroom, wrapping a bath-sheet around his narrow hips.

Chloe was sure she would have trouble walking; her legs had turned to jelly at some point since she got under the water.

After drying herself off, Chloe followed Luke into the bedroom.

'Hey,' she said, languid and sensual.

'Hey, yourself,' he said, lounging naked under a black sheet. She went to the other side of the bed and pulled back the sheet.

'We can cuddle for about half an hour, then you have to go.'

She stopped mid-way through her movement, the towel had already dropped to the floor. 'I have to go?' she repeated.

'Yeah, you can't stay. I have shit to do tomorrow, and you don't figure into it.'

She couldn't seem to make her mouth work.

'The offer was my cock, not my bed. I never promised you anything other than a good time.'

She dropped the sheet and scrabbled to pick up the towel. 'I don't understand.'

'Clearly.' He sighed. 'I have a sort of … competition going with the boys. That's why Ben is never upset when I win. None of us wants a relationship, it's an exercise in getting girls to sleep with us.' He reclined, propped up on one elbow, the look of the wolf back in his eyes. This was part of the game—the confusion in her face, her embarrassment, her realisation. She was just another conquest. No wonder the woman in the kitchen had tried to warn her off. Why had she not listened? Why hadn't she followed her own rules and gone home with Mel?

It was too late now; hot tears stung her eyes. She would not fall in a blubbering mess in front of this man who cared nothing for her.

Chapter 9

Chloe dressed and left Luke's apartment as quickly as she could. He stayed in his bed, saying nothing as she gathered her clothes and redressed. Outside, she walked to Chapel Street, it was nearly two in the morning, there would be no trams at this time of night, she would have to get a taxi. If she walked it would take the better part of an hour to get home, but she would save twenty dollars. She was an idiot, allowing herself to be persuaded by a handsome stranger when she'd had a ride home. She wasn't wearing walking shoes, but at least they were flats. The streets were quiet, in spite of it being a Saturday night, Luke's apartment was near the river, away from most of the night spots in South Yarra.

Her route home went past a couple of pubs likely to still be trading at this time, but for the most part it was houses and shops. The night was cool enough to need her cardigan, but she was warm once she started walking.

*   *   *

In the morning Mel sent her a message.

> *How did it go with the dapper gentleman? I hope he rocked you all night long, I was stuck making small talk with jerks from TAFE.*

Chloe felt a sick tightening in her belly as she read the message, her best friend's feigned jealousy made her feel even more foolish.

Disaster. Luke kicked me out of his
apartment at 2. Walked home. I have
blisters on my toes.

Instead of a reply, Chloe's phone started to ring.

'What the fuck happened?'

Chloe sighed. 'You know the woman in the kitchen who warned me off?'

'Yeah? Karen?'

'She was right.'

'No.'

'Luke told me he and his buddies have a bet going who can get the most girls to come home with them. He never intended to let me stay over. I managed not to burst into tears in front of him but it was close.'

'I'm so sorry,' Mel said.

'You don't sound like it.'

'Sorry, Robbo is doing a stupid dance. It's very distracting.' Muffled scrabbling sounds came down the line, she must have put her hand over the microphone to tell her boyfriend to buzz off. 'So did you get any action?'

'I don't know if this is the worst part, but yes, twice.'

'Two times and then he threw you out? What a charmer.' Birds twittered in the background; Mel would have gone outside to get some peace.

'It was really good too.' She sighed, having held her tears in since last night, Chloe's eyes stung with them now. 'What is wrong with me?'

'There's nothing wrong with you.'

'Why can't I get a man then?'

'You weren't to know he was a piece of shit, plus you weren't really looking to have a relationship with someone like that guy. He's way out of your league.'

'That's not nice.' Chloe sniffed, she couldn't seem to stop the tears leaking from her eyes.

'I'm not being mean, just realistic. You're cute, but he was a model, and rich apparently, he probably thinks he can do whatever he wants.'

'Clearly. He's betting his buddies he can fuck more girls than they can.'

'Doesn't seem like a very fair game.'

'No, I wouldn't have played if I knew those were the rules.'

'I meant for the other two guys, surely Luke would steal the girls more often than not.'

Chloe clenched her teeth together, appalled her friend seemed to have no sympathy for her bruised ego. 'That's not what I meant. I gotta go.'

'Really? Alright then. I'll talk to you soon.'

'Yeah. See ya.' Chloe hung up the phone and plonked it face down on her bedside table. She wasn't sure why she expected Mel to be understanding, she often misunderstood what Chloe needed from her, but this was a new level of missing the point.

Chloe was exhausted, her feet were sore, and she could still feel Luke's deft hands on her body. If he had been a less effective lover, would it have hurt as badly as it did right now? If she'd known what she was walking into, would she have gone?

For the rest of Sunday Chloe's brain ran through scenarios which did not end up with her out on the street in the middle of the night after being man-handled by a handsome narcissist. It didn't make her feel any better, and the longer she thought about it, the more warning signs she picked up on from the three men. They hadn't told her how they knew the host, they weren't talking to anyone else, as soon as she showed any interest, they were laser focused on her. She should have known better.

*   *   *

'What did you get up to on the weekend?' Mary asked when she came into the staff room on Monday. Immediately Chloe froze, she had told her colleague she'd been seeing a guy, admitting she'd blown that would lead to more questions, not least of which was 'what happened?' But she didn't want to lie to Mary, she was a solid friend, if a little indiscreet.

'Earth to Chloe? Did you get up to anything good?'

She had clearly taken so long to respond Mary wondered if she'd heard. 'I went to a party on Saturday night.'

'Any good?'

'Not really, I didn't know many people, and I left early.' Not strictly a lie, but definitely not the whole story. Hopefully Mary wouldn't want to dig any deeper. 'What about you? Anything fun?'

'Funny you should ask.' Mary started a long and detailed description of her weekend. Chloe should have known it was an opening to tell her about the weekend, and it wouldn't matter what she'd said; a rare instance when Mary's self-involvement was in Chloe's favour.

At school that week, her student, Lee, was quiet. He had a learning disability and some dyslexia but with her help he was able to keep up with his classmates. Being different made him shy but usually in their one-on-one time he was chatty and had a certain level of quiet confidence, but it seemed to have abandoned him.

'Are you okay, buddy?' she asked just before the bell went for lunch on Wednesday.

'Yes. Are you?'

'I'm fine.' Chloe was surprised when Lee frowned. 'What is it?'

'Well, you seem sad. I thought maybe it was me, maybe I was talking too much, or not doing my work properly, so I worked hard and tried to do my best, but you're still sad.'

Her heart broke a little to see her student struggling to make her happy. 'I have been a bit sad this week, but it has nothing to do with you. I'm sorry you thought you'd done something wrong. If it was something we needed to work on, I would tell you, you know that right?'

He nodded, his eyes on the table in front of him.

'I'm not upset with you. If you think I'm sad again in future, you can ask. I might not always want to tell you about it, but I would never want you to worry you'd done something wrong.'

'Okay. What made you sad though?'

'Well…' she hesitated, how could she put this into terms her primary school-aged student would understand. He was pretty clever when it came to human emotions, but he had absolutely no sense of discretion. 'I went to a party on the weekend and I thought I had made a new friend.'

'Was it a birthday party? I'm not good at parties, but everyone says they're fun. And I like friends.'

'It was a birthday party. I was a bit shy because I didn't know many people and I met couple of nice boys but then they said they didn't really want to be friends, it was just a game. I got sad because I thought they liked me.'

'But they didn't?' Lee said, his little face was full of concern.

'No. They were only pretending to like me, having fun at my expense.' When she explained it like that, it was no surprise she hadn't caught on to the plot earlier, they had been covering for each other, smoothing over anything in one of their stories that seemed to undermine the set-up. Chloe still felt like a fool, she'd broken her own rule about fucking on the first date and it had gone about as badly as it could have gone. The mind-blowing sex only made it more confusing.

'Frankie, from Mrs Mason's class, pretended to be my friend one time. He asked me to play hide and seek and I went and hid really well, but they didn't come and find me and I stayed there until the end of school. Mum was really angry.'

'I remember. We were so worried, we couldn't find you and all the other kids said they hadn't seen you. Frankie told them all not to say where you were.' The staff thought Lee had left the campus or possibly had been convinced to go with a stranger. He was trusting and with the right words he would follow just about anyone just about anywhere. Chloe worried about him, if he grew up being so naïve, he would be easily exploited.

'I'm sorry you're sad, Miss.'

'Thank you. You're very thoughtful.' She glanced at the time, 'you better be off for lunch. I'll pack this up.'

Lee grinned, packing up was his least favourite thing. Some of her students were obsessive and enjoyed putting things away neatly, making their environment just so, but Lee was a messy, disorganised kid. They were working on these skills, essential for making it through the world as an adult, but he was coming along slowly. Not that it seemed to have stopped Eddie, she thought of the piles of clothes on his floor, the state of the sheets on his bed, the way he organised his work schedule and ran his business, if you could even call it that. She shook her head, neither Eddie nor Luke were worth the space they took up in her head, she would have to train herself not to think about them.

*   *   *

Occasionally when Chloe checked her phone, she half-expected to find a message from Eddie. Back before their fight, he would send her messages throughout the day, asking what she was up to, sometimes what she was wearing. He liked to keep an eye on her, and sometimes he put in requests for dinner.

Now she only had to think of herself, she went back to her staples for dinner. It was more economical certainly but it was boring and lonely. She missed sitting on the couch with him, watching some nonsense on the TV, she missed watching him play on the Xbox, or trying to keep up when he insisted she play. She missed hanging out with Max on a Sunday morning, even though he didn't say much, she had started to get to know him too. But that was all over now; Eddie had made it clear he wasn't interested in being in contact. He had done the wrong thing, slept with someone else while they were exclusive, and though she had also been with another person, she didn't think it counted against her. He should be the one to apologise, to make it up to her, to beg her to come back, and if he didn't then she wasn't going to start any conversations.

*   *   *

Lee seemed much more settled and chattier now they'd had a conversation about why she was sad. It surprised her sometimes how perceptive he could be, especially for an eight-year-old with learning difficulties. Then again, the learning issue was around reading and writing and not emotional intelligence. Lee was the youngest of five, the other four were much older, only two still at home, and though no one said so, it seemed obvious he had been unplanned. On the one hand, it meant his parents had free babysitting, but on the other hand Lee grew up essentially an only child. He found it

167

hard to make friends with the kids in the class and often would be sitting alone at lunch time, Chloe wondered what he got up to, he didn't read for fun, it was much too difficult for him, but sometimes he looked at the pictures in the science type books from the library.

'What do you want to be when you grow up?' she asked him one day. It had been a couple of weeks since she'd heard from Eddie and she had almost stopped thinking about him.

'I don't know. Maybe I can be a rocket scientist.'

'That sounds good. It's very hard to be a rocket scientist—you'll have to work hard to get in.'

'I always work hard, Miss, you know that.' He grinned so broadly she would have believed him capable of anything. She hoped more than anything he would get his wish. Kind people deserved to have their dreams come true.

'What did you want to be when you grew up, Miss?' The question caught her off guard, lost as she was in her own thoughts. It was happening more and more lately, drifting off in the middle of class, while doing the dishes. Maybe she was coming down with something or maybe after all the stress of the last couple of weeks her brain had just taken a holiday.

'When I was very little, I wanted to be in the police. But then when I was a bit older, I wanted to be a teacher.'

'You are a teacher. That's good you got to be what you wanted.'

'Yeah. It is, isn't it?' Her job was not exactly what she dreamed of when she was at school, but it was lucky she even finished high school.

Janine's boyfriend at the time was a particularly vile man named Kevin although he insisted everyone call him Big Kev, he said Kevin sounded like a paedophile. Just after the end of her year 11, Big Kev was particularly flush during the summer holidays, and her mother had managed to keep a job for almost six months, and they had some money in the bank, so they all went to Rosebud, a beach side town about an hour and a half from Melbourne. It was known for mild beaches, golden sand and cheap holiday caravans near the shore.

Janine booked a place on the phone, told them it was for two adults and one child, but when they arrived it was clear the caravan park had expected a child under ten, not sixteen. All three of them were supposed to sleep in a tiny caravan with only one bedroom. The third bed was made by converting the bench seat in the kitchen. Chloe had no privacy, no where she could go for a moment's peace, and worst of all she had to wait until Big Kev had finished watching TV to make up her bed.

'Come on, love, let's give Chloe some space,' Janine had said on the third night, Kev wanted to watch the late-night run downs of the cricket.

'Don't rush me, woman. You know better than that.'

Chloe and her mother shared a look, in that moment she could have sworn her mum was trying to say she was sorry, though she doubted the words would ever be spoken aloud.

'I'll make it worthwhile, baby.'

'Don't be a slut, Janine, I don't like a woman who's desperate.'

Knowing her mum and her boyfriend would be in the next room, separated by only a thin plastic-covered cardboard concertina room divider was more than Chloe could take. She'd definitely hear Big Kev grunting and she was sure Janine would be whispering sweet nothings to keep him going.

'I'm going out,' Chloe announced, getting up from the bench seat.

'Where do you think you're going at this time of night?' Big Kev was at least two long-necks of beer into the night and had appointed himself as her father.

'I'm going to hang out with some other kids on the beach. If you're just going to watch telly and then fuck my mum, I'd rather be somewhere else.' She hadn't tried being this direct before, there was every chance it would backfire.

'Not if you want to come back into this caravan, or back into your mum's house again. You do as you're told.'

'You're not my father, thank God, and I don't have to do what you tell me.' Chloe had picked up a light jacket, despite the interior of the caravan being sticky and hot, the beach was likely to be windy and chilly at night. She looked at her mother, not expecting to be backed up but hoping none the less.

'Stay here, Chlo'. We're going to bed soon.'

Chloe nodded, that was how it would be. Her mother sided with her boyfriend the way she always had, and she was sick of it. 'Bye then.'

She walked out the door, slamming it behind her, though the flimsy aluminium frame of the fly-screen undermined the drama of it. She walked out of sight, a couple of caravans down and came around the back to listen under the window. Janine might still redeem herself if she stood up for Chloe in her absence.

'I told you she was trouble. Why did we have to bring her?' Big Kev's booming voice was clear through the walls.

'She's my daughter, I can't leave her at home.'

Janine was all she had. Chloe's father, Craig, had left when she was a baby, but not before ripping her grandmother off some two hundred thousand dollars and driving her into alcoholism, poverty and finally death, all before Chloe was a year old. Janine had been declared unfit when the fellow she had been dating at the time punched her grandfather, Janine's father, and landed him in hospital.

Chloe's earliest memories were of her mother's parents; cold, unfeeling and manipulative. They had been determined to keep her but both got pneumonia, one after the other, when Chloe was five and she was shuffled back to her mother's care. Apparently that pesky unfit-to-be-a-mother thing only mattered when there was someone else clamouring to take the baby.

And since then, Janine had taken care of her daughter by making sure there was always a man in the house and taking his side in arguments.

'I'm saddled with some other prick's kid, a rancid teenager at that, and you expect me to tolerate that bullshit? I meant what I said, Janine, she's not coming back in this caravan. And she's not coming home.'

'It's my house.' Janine's voice was so soft Chloe could barely make it out from her hiding spot outside.

'What did you say?' Kev was furious. Janine never talked back to him.

'I said, it's my house. I own it. And I want my daughter to live there with me.'

A sickening thud, a cry, and the tinkling of broken glass followed. 'You do what I tell you. You might own the house, but I own you.' His voice was a gravelly whisper, but Chloe heard it clearly. There were a few slaps after that and then she couldn't stand to hear any more. She spent the night in a caravan in another part of the park after she met up with some kids on the foreshore.

In the morning she came back to check on her mum. There was a note taped to the front of the screen door, which was now locked.

Here's $20. Let Kev cool down. Come back home in a week or so. I'm sorry baby. I love you. Mum.

Chloe laughed, so much for backing her up, her rebellion had cost her mother a beating and now she was out on the street until Janine got Kev subdued enough to let her back in the house. If she hadn't laughed, she would have cried.

That summer was the first and only time she slept rough and did whatever she needed to do to have enough money to feed herself—there were no the retail and hospitality jobs left in the seaside town.

She looked over to Lee sitting in his moulded plastic chair, working his way through a page of basic maths. He was quiet, concentrating hard. Her dream had been to be a teacher, maybe one day she would be able to do the uni work required to qualify, or maybe she would remain an aide for the rest of her career. She wasn't much good at administration and had no desire to go into an office job. It wasn't so bad really, she got to know her students well. The hardest part was when they moved on to high-school and she had to say goodbye.

*   *   *

By the next Friday, Chloe had started to worry about not having had her period. It wasn't always regular, but even so, it should have come on Tuesday. She was on the pill, and nearly finished the sugar pill section. No contraception was one hundred percent reliable and neither Eddie nor Luke had used condoms. It was probably not her best decision, particularly with Luke, who was not picky about who he slept with, apparently.

'You alright, love?' Gina asked. She was the grade teacher for year five, the class Lee sat in. Chloe had been sitting in the staff room poking at her lunch with a fork instead of eating it.

'Yeah.'

'You look pale, you're not coming down with something, are you?' Gina put the back of her hand against her forehead. 'You feel alright. Kids are walking germ factories. It's a wonder we don't all have some illness constantly.'

Chloe smiled, she hadn't been sleeping well and was less and less interested in eating. Maybe she was coming down with something, but maybe she was pregnant. There was only one way to be sure but she didn't want to take a test—once confirmed she would have to make a choice about what to do.

It would be hard to be a single mother, although perhaps less difficult than trying to drag Eddie, kicking and screaming, into adulthood. If it was Luke's and she got back with Eddie, he would find out eventually. Both men were attractive, but built quite differently. She was terrible at keeping secrets, maybe she should just tell him there was a chance it wasn't his.

If she could get Max interested, he would be a good baby-sitter. Despite being a bit odd he was kind and reliable. Definitely someone to keep in contact with, although he would likely side with Eddie if it came down to it; they'd been friends for a long time before she came along.

'Just tired I think,' she answered Gina after a long pause. She would have to get a pee on a stick test and put her mind at ease. Janine had been a single mother, at least in the sense she had never remarried and the boyfriends changed frequently. She imagined telling her mother about the pregnancy and wondered what her reaction would be. Chloe had no grandparents, both she and her mother were only children, so no aunts or uncles or cousins to help her with a baby. Eddie was far too unstable to be a father, he would run away from any obstacle, and if she had to choose between an absent father and an unreliable one, she would choose absent.

What a mess she'd made of everything. The man she had hoped would be a change from her crappy exes turned out to be exactly the same. But he had a right to know.

On her way home she purchased a home pregnancy test. She'd done a couple; once at eighteen and again at twenty-one. Since then, she had been much stricter about taking birth control and making sure she wouldn't have to make this sort of decision. At least she had five years more life experience than her mother had when she was born.

The test took ten minutes to show a result, it felt like the clock was ticking interminably slowly. She paced up and down her tiny apartment though it didn't help much to pass the time.

When it was finally time to check on the test, she picked it up and took a deep breath. She saw one clear dark line, and a second faint but distinct line. Pregnant. Her hands shook and she had to put the test back on the bathroom sink. She had hoped the test would come back negative, that she was imagining it and her cycle would start soon, but now she knew it wasn't all in her mind. She'd been taking the pill but maybe she missed a couple in the turmoil of Eddie's confession. It was too late to worry about how it had happened now.

She looked up whether birth control would hurt the baby and was relieved to find it wasn't harmful. She hadn't decided whether to keep it but if the pill had somehow damaged the foetus her decision would have been made.

Who could she talk to? Her mother was useless when it came to any kind of crisis, Mel would probably laugh or tell her to get an abortion. Eddie had been giving her the silent treatment for over two weeks, but it might be his. She dialled his number and listened to the ringing. It went on so long she was sure he wouldn't pick up.

'What do you want?' Eddie said.

'Hi. Uh—' She didn't know how to tell him.

'What do you want?' he repeated, slowly as though to a stupid child.

'I have some news.'

'You better not have given me some STD, Chloe.'

'Why are you being such an arsehole? I'm not the one who messed up our relationship by fucking someone else.'

'I don't have to listen to this. Tell me what you wanna tell me and let me get on with my life.'

'I'm pregnant.'

'Fuck.' Eddie breathed heavily into the phone. She heard the sounds of a video game in the background, perhaps he and Max were having a game before he went out to work.

'You sure it's mine?' he said. Her hesitation was enough to let him know there was more. 'Is it mine, Chloe?'

'Probably.'

'Jesus.' He was silent again, Chloe felt an immense pressure to fill the void with chatter but it wouldn't help. He needed time to process the information.

'I thought you should know,' she said finally.

'Yeah, well, now I know. Anything else?'

'No.'

'Okay. Bye.' The line went dead.

She had run the conversation over in her mind several times before calling him and that was not the way she expected it to go. She had anticipated anger or possibly shock but this indifference was worse. In the couple of weeks since they'd ended things, he had clearly clamped down his feelings for her.

He knew now, if he wanted anything to do with the decision to keep the baby or not, he knew where she was. She was only a few weeks gone and had a while to decide.

'Don't say anything, okay?' Chloe said down the phone to Mel as soon as she answered. 'Are you there?'

'You told me not to say anything.' Mel's voice was bright with suppressed laughter.

'Why do you always take things so literally.'

'Because it annoys you.'

'You're right, it does,' Chloe said. 'Here's the thing, I need to tell you something and I want you to try to remain objective. Do you think you can do that?'

'I'm your best friend, dummy, what do you think I'm going to say?'

'I don't know.'

'You're really worried, aren't you? Listen, I will always love you. Nothing you can tell me will change that. Unless you've killed a man and need help to bury the body, then I might love you a little bit more.'

'I'm pregnant.' It was the second time Chloe had said it aloud and it didn't feel any less foreign in her mouth.

'Good one. You really had me going for a minute.' Mel huffed a laugh.

'I'm not kidding. I'm four days late and I peed on a stick earlier.'

'Shit.' Silence stretched out. 'You're definitely preggers then?'

'Yeah.'

'Is it Eddie's?'

'Uh…'

'You sly thing, I didn't know you were seeing anyone else.'

'I'm not.' Chloe didn't want to admit to her best friend how sloppy her safe sex routines were.

'You didn't sleep with that fuckboi without a condom, did you?'

'Yeah.'

'Shit.'

'Yeah,' Chloe said again.

'Did you tell Eddie?'

'He didn't care.'

'You gonna tell Luke?' Mel asked.

'I don't know his number.'

'That does present a problem. I could ask Jesse to find out for you. I'm sure he'd know someone who could get his number. Have you tried stalking him on Facebook?'

Chloe didn't spend much time on social media. 'I didn't think of it.'

'Hold on, I'll find Jesse's friends list.'

Chloe heard faint tapping as her friend looked.

'You're on speaker. I found him, Luke Walker. Damn, he's hot though.'

'That's true, but he's also probably a sociopath.'

'Mmm. I've sent you a link to his profile. You should be able to just send him a message.'

'What would I say? Hi I know we only knew each other for one night but I'm pregnant and it might be yours?'

Mel hesitated. 'Are you keeping it?'

'I haven't decided.'

'Because if you don't want to keep it, then you probably don't need to tell Pretty Boy.'

'Do you think I should keep it?'

'Babe. I can't make that sort of decision for you. If it was me, I'd get a termination immediately and not tell anyone. But you're not me; you like kids.'

It was true she had become a teacher's aide not just because it was close to her dream job but because she liked kids. There was something pure about the weird connections they found to things, the stuff they found

179

fascinating that made her feel young. 'I never wanted to be a single mum.'

'I hear you, but your mum was on her own and you turned out okay.'

Chloe sighed. She doubted the way she turned out had much to do with her mother, but it would be hard to be a worse parent than Janine. 'I guess.'

'You can't be very far along, you've got time to think it over. Don't do anything right now, maybe call the clinic and see if there's a waiting list or something.'

'If I'm less than eight weeks along I can have the tablet, no waiting list.' Chloe had looked it up while waiting for the pregnancy test to show.

'Then you're fine. Give it a week or two, let the idea settle, then you can go get the tablet and it will be fine.'

'Thanks.'

'I gotta go, hun, I'll talk to you later, yeah?' Mel said.

'Okay.' As Chloe hung up the phone for the second time that night she felt an emptiness creeping into her no-longer-empty belly. She wanted to have a glass of wine and cry, but if she decided she wanted to have the baby she couldn't have wine. She had no idea what she was supposed to do or not do in the early stages of pregnancy and the thought of looking it up online made her nauseated.

Instead, she decided to go to the convenience store a short walk away and stock up on chocolate. What good was being pregnant if not to lean into the cravings?

The night air was warm, in early November, late spring, Melbourne's weather seemed to vacillate between hot and dry, and cold and rainy; in-between weather didn't exist. The shop was attached to a petrol station on the opposite side of Hoddle Street to her apartment. On that side of the street the suburb changed to East Melbourne, a very exclusive and expensive area, while on her side of the road, Richmond, the demographic was much more varied, owing to the mixture of expensive hipster renovation projects and the Housing Commission dwellings, often side by side.

Though the cars across three lanes of traffic were many, they weren't moving quickly but they were not stopping. Chloe wove her way to the grassy island in the middle of the road before waiting until the traffic crawled to a stop and she finished the trip. Fifty metres up the hill was a set of lights but she felt reckless.

Inside the service station a bored-looking attendant gazed out the plate glass windows at her. She nodded as she put down two large slabs of plain chocolate; despite all the fancy flavours she would always come back to plain Cadburys.

'Just those?'

'Yes, it's an emergency,' Chloe said, handing over her cash.

'It often is.' The attendant smiled wearily, a young woman of Indian appearance she managed to be both overworked and bored.

Back in her apartment, which seemed stuffy and hot after strolling in the fresh air outside, Chloe watched a reality cooking show while devouring half a block of chocolate. She stopped herself before she could eat the rest and hoped it was in time to avoid feeling sick.

Taking out her laptop she logged into Facebook and clicked on the link Mel had sent her to Luke's profile.

Not much to see there, he would have his security settings locked down for precisely this reason no doubt. She clicked on the message icon and a small blank white window popped out to taunt her. What could she say? Would he even see it? If he didn't reply maybe that would make the decision for her.

Hi. I realise you have no interest in anything ongoing, I just thought you should know I'm pregnant. It could be yours, but also possibly not. I haven't decided if I'll keep it. Get in touch, or don't, I really don't care.

She surprised herself a little at how angry she felt. It was one thing to go home with someone for a bit of fun, but to tell her she was part of a game he was playing with his buddies was cruel. Not to mention throwing her out of his apartment in the middle of the night expecting her to have money for a cab home. It must be nice to be rich enough not to worry about that sort of thing. Rolling her shoulders Chloe tried to release some of her tension.

Nothing was happening that weekend, save for dinner with her mother and Gary on Sunday. She would have to get up early for yoga in the morning just to give herself something to do.

*　　　*　　　*

At the yoga class Chloe wasn't sure if she should mention her pregnancy to the instructor. If she wasn't keeping it, there would be no harm in doing what she normally did, but then again, she hadn't decided.

'If you're menstruating, you can do the modified version,' the instructor announced in a sweet, serene voice. Chloe decided that she would do the easy version just in case. After her class she felt a little better and bought a takeaway coffee to walk home with.

If she was going to keep the baby, she would have to do some serious budget calculations. If she couldn't work full-time, she wouldn't be able to afford to keep her apartment and if she couldn't keep the apartment, where would she live instead? A place with two bedrooms made more sense, perhaps somewhere further out where rent was cheaper. Her mother had two spare rooms, one for her and one for the baby, but she'd promised herself she would never live with Janine again. And she would have to deal with Gary, or whatever boyfriend inevitably came along after him. She would not allow her child to be subjected to the same environment she had been.

Big Kev might have been angry, but he had calmed down enough after the episode in Rosebud to accept her back in the house without a fight, though he occasionally muttered under his breath when she was around. He'd made his point and Janine had convinced him it was for the best to let Chloe back in to finish her high school. After not having finished school herself, Janine was surprisingly stubborn about her getting her VCE.

The Mother's Fault

Without a father to help with bills and caring, Chloe couldn't afford the baby. If she ended up on welfare benefits or having to move back into her mother's house, she would be a failure. She hadn't fought to remain independent since moving out in her first year of TAFE just to slip back into the swamp her mother called a life. She'd do almost anything to avoid that.

Chloe had left her mobile at home while she was at yoga class; there was no reason for her to be contacted during that hour and it stopped her checking if Eddie had called, or if Luke had responded to her message. She didn't really want them to; that way she wouldn't have to hear any arguments to keep the baby. On the other hand something in her yearned for a baby. Knowing she had one growing inside her, regardless of how useless it's father might be, it was hard to imagine not having it. As soon as she got home to check her messages, she saw one from Luke.

You were a fun fuck, but this is a bit farfetched. If this is just a manipulation to get me to reply to you, then you're a sad, sad individual Chloe. I honestly thought you were better than this.

However, if it's true, and the kid is mine, which I doubt, I'd be prepared to chip in for whatever costs are associated with making it go away. I have no intention of being a father and would need to see

*something from a doctor to prove you're
pregnant before giving you anything.*

Chloe choked back a laugh that quickly turned into a sob. Given their previous interactions she wasn't sure why she had expected a sentimental or romantic response but this was colder than she had anticipated. Probably not the first time he'd had a pregnancy thrown at him, especially since he seemed to have an aversion to condoms. He didn't deserve a reply, if she kept the baby, he would not be the father.

She busied herself cleaning the house and then sat down with a book on her couch, the sunlight came in through the balcony windows and made her sleepy.

*   *   *

Chloe was woken by pounding on the door. Her neck was stiff from the position she'd fallen asleep in. The front gate buzzer hadn't gone off, perhaps it was one of her neighbours.

The pounding didn't stop.

'I'm coming.' She straightened her top and smoothed her hair down, checking herself quickly in the mirror to make sure she didn't have drool on her face.

'Hi.' Eddie stood on the landing in front of her apartment door.

'Uh, hi.'

'Are you gonna invite me in?'

'I guess—'

Eddie walked into the apartment before she could finish her sentence. 'I've been thinking about what you said.'

'Right.' She wasn't sure where this was going and Eddie's energy was tight like a coiled spring, covered in a sheen of sweat, his fingers fluttering on his thigh.

'I decided—I was thinking, if you want to have a baby, then I'd like to be involved.'

Chloe sat down heavily on one of her kitchen chairs. It was the last thing she'd expected him to say, he seemed to have worked himself up into quite a state. 'Involved?'

'Ideally, I want us to give it another try, a kid should have two parents but I understand if you don't want to after what I did that night.'

He hadn't said anything about what she'd done, she thought.

'If you don't want to give it another go, I wanna try to work something out where I can contribute, you know, financially but also have the kid sometimes. I've always fancied myself being a pretty good dad, better than I am a businessman at any rate.' He hitched one side of his mouth up in a crooked smile, putting himself down to seem humble always made her like him more.

'I'll have to think about it.'

'About me? Or the baby?'

Chloe sighed. 'Both. It's a big commitment.'

'You're right. But sometimes I think the universe gives us signs. We have to take what we're dealt and make the most of it.'

'I said I would think about it, and I will. I promise to give it proper consideration.'

'And what about me in the meantime?'

Fleur Blüm

'I guess we could try to get back on track, see if we can sort it out between us and then, no matter what happens with the baby, we'd have each other.'

'I like the sound of that.' Eddie stood up from where he had been sitting on the couch and walked to her. He took her hand in his, pulling her gently to stand, and then kissed her. She was tense at first, she had been sure he was out of her life, and now here he was, saying he wanted to step up, to make it work, she didn't trust herself not to become overly excited.

He pulled back from the kiss, his eyebrows furrowed. 'Too soon?'

'No.' She shook her head. 'Actually yes, it's a bit sudden. Let's just spend some time together and see how it goes?'

'Okay. You're the boss.'

She smiled, her chest felt a little hot; he'd never called her the boss before, it felt as though something had shifted in him. Perhaps it would be alright after all.

*   *   *

Eddie stayed that night on the couch, he didn't really fit on it, being longer than she was, but he didn't complain when she suggested it. The next morning, he took her out for breakfast, to celebrate he said, before they both headed back to his place.

'Hi Chloe,' Max said when he saw her come in the lounge room. 'I thought I would never see you again.' He looked at the ground, she hadn't known him to be shy around her since the early days with Eddie when the weather was still cold.

187

'It's lovely to see you Max. I hope you didn't miss me too much,' she said, teasing him a little, and hoping Eddie didn't notice. It wouldn't help matters to fuel his jealousy or whatever it was that made him strange about the two of them.

'I told Max.' Eddie slumped into the enormous maroon couch beside Max. Chloe perched on the edge of the other one.

'Okay.' She didn't really want anyone else to know, but she hadn't told him not to say anything either.

'You weren't much help were you, big guy.' Eddie punched Max in the arm a little harder than seemed friendly and he rocked away absorbing the blow. 'Still, he said I had to go try to patch things up. Now we might be having a kid, it was worth another try.'

'Thank you, I wasn't really looking forward to being a single mum, but I still hadn't really finished thinking it through.'

'My mum was on her own with me for a while,' Max said.

'Bullshit, I never knew that.' Eddie looked at his friend, eyes wide in surprise.

'You never asked. When we met, she was with her new husband, I've been calling him Dad since I was fourteen but he's not a blood relation.

'How did your mum end up raising you on her own? That must have been hard.'

'Yeah, double hard with a re—special needs kid like you.' Eddie corrected himself mid-sentence. At least he was trying, even if being respectful in his language seemed to be foreign to him.

'Is it a dinner with your mum week, Chlo'?'

'Yeah.'

'Maybe it's a good time to meet her. I know we don't want to get ahead of ourselves with telling people about the bun in the oven or anything, but it can't hurt to have dinner with them.'

Everything in Chloe's system screamed at her to stop this idea before it rooted in Eddie's mind—Gary was a nightmare, and Janine was either in a stupor or sided with Gary. 'It's too soon.'

'Are you ashamed of me?'

Chloe's face flushed hot with blood. 'I…' she struggled to get the words out.

'Is that why you won't let me meet your mum and dad?'

'Gary isn't my dad,' she said with surprising vehemence. She frowned, surely he remembered the part where her dad had never been around and had shafted them all just after she was born.

'That's right. Janine always has a man around you said, but none of them are your dad.'

'Yeah,' Chloe agreed. Eddie had a light in his eyes, a sort of angry glint, she didn't like.

'So why can't I meet your old lady and her boyfriend?'

She sighed. 'It's not because I'm not ashamed of you. I'm ashamed of them. They're awful, I don't want you running for the hills when you meet them. I couldn't take that kind of shock right now.'

Eddie laughed. 'You're kidding, right? What could they possibly say that would make me think any differently of you?'

Chloe looked down at the carpet, dull grey low-pile with a suspiciously yellow-brown coloured stain near one of the legs of the coffee table, she hoped it was beer. He stopped laughing and put his hand on her knee.

'Nothing your mum says to me will ever change how I feel. I've made a commitment to … well to seeing where this goes and that's between you and me. Not Janine. Not Gary. It's with you and, hopefully, my kid.' Eddie was never this serious usually. He must be really sold on the idea of giving their relationship another go to be this insistent on meeting them, even after all she'd said about their unpleasant qualities.

'Okay, if you really want to meet them today, we'll do it. I have to call Mum and warn her though, she won't have enough food for four otherwise.'

Chapter 10

Chloe went into the back garden behind Eddie's house, such as it was, to call her mother. She hadn't made much mention of him to her, knowing it would only encourage her to ask questions and it was easier not to tell her anything.

'Chloe, baby, I was just thinking about you.' Her mother sounded chirpy and slurred, she'd obviously started on her happy pills early.

'Hi Mum. How are you?'

Janine went on a rambling monologue describing her week. She had a job working reception for an alternative medicine clinic, the woman who ran the clinic seemed inclined to micromanagement and Chloe doubted the job would last much longer. 'What did you call for love? I'm seeing you tonight, aren't I?'

'About tonight—'

'You're not cancelling, are you?'

'No, I wondered if it would be okay to bring a … friend with me.'

Janine spluttered and made a sound in her throat like a cough. 'A friend? Or a boyfriend?'

'I guess a boyfriend.' Chloe regretted agreeing to this dinner already.

'Why haven't I heard about this boy before? What's his name? How long have you known him?' Despite whatever she'd taken, Janine was ready to interrogate her daughter immediately.

'His name is Eddie. We've known each other a while, and I guess I thought it was about time he met you. And Gary of course.' She always had to add Gary to the end of her sentences, otherwise her mother would accuse her of excluding him.

'We'd love to meet him. I'll see you later then. I had better get on.'

'Okay, see you later.' Chloe sighed. Knowing Eddie's ability to keep secrets the pregnancy wouldn't stay hidden for long only added to the already nerve-wracking idea of him meeting her mother.

When she walked back into the lounge Eddie and Max's heads both swivelled towards her expectantly.

'She's very keen to meet you, started asking me questions on the phone and everything.'

'What did you tell her?' Eddie turned back to his video game.

'I managed to get away with only telling her your name. I think you can tell them whatever you feel comfortable telling them, although I would be careful giving them too much. Gary is a horror for using anything anyone says as a way to torture them.'

'I know the sort. If it goes well, we'll have to get you out to meet my family. We can have a competition to see whose is the most fucked up.'

She smiled, remembering how charming Eddie could be, how in love with him she was in the beginning before his business stuff fell through and he became sullen. Maybe it would be okay.

*   *   *

Fleur Blüm

They drove to Janine's brick house in Brunswick in Chloe's car. It was nice he'd told Max about the baby, he needed people he could talk to and although she really didn't understand their relationship, they'd been friends for a long time and obviously it worked for them.

When her mother came out of the house to meet them, she wore an inappropriately figure-hugging jersey dress, with tiny spaghetti straps, pink and black zebra stripes all over it. She wore thongs, and her toenails were painted an eye-watering shade of pink the same as the dress; no doubt she'd done them specially to match. Janine was only in her mid-forties but had lived a hard life and her figure and face wore the signs of it.

'My baby girl,' she said, running towards Chloe with her arms outstretched. Her breasts and belly jiggled under the dress and Chloe saw Eddie turn his head away out of the corner of her eye.

'You dressed up?' she asked, while receiving an overly affectionate hug from her mother. There was nothing like meeting a new person to get Janine to put on a show.

'Of course. I want to look nice for dinner. This must be Eddie.' She turned to look at him, tall, slim, wearing his best, least ripped jeans and a black T-shirt that was still mostly the right shade of black. He'd greased his hair and slicked it back like he was in a gangster movie and he'd shaved, his pale skin gleaming with perspiration in the warm evening air.

'Mrs Barrett, a pleasure to meet you.' Eddie held out his hand to Janine, she ignored it and gave him a hug, pressing her body against him in an entirely inappropriate way.

'Call me Janine, please. You're very handsome, if Chloe isn't able to hold onto you maybe I'll have a try.' Janine winked, and Eddie smiled, apparently taking it in his stride.

'Don't let Gary hear you,' he said.

Janine beckoned them into the house, a brown velvet modular couch took up most of the lounge room, it was bare in some places and had been covered with blankets and throws to make it look less decrepit. It didn't help. Next to the couch was a reclining armchair, also brown velvet but newer than the couch. She remembered when her mother had bought the armchair for Roger, one of her boyfriends, when Chloe was in early high school. She was never allowed to sit in it, only Roger could.

'Where's Gary?' Chloe asked.

'He's out the back, there's a shed where he has some of his toys, he prefers being in the shed if there's no sport on.' Janine smiled at Eddie, touching her long blonde hair flirtatiously.

Another reason Chloe didn't bring people around.

'What sort of toys? I do a bit of landscaping and handiwork if he ever wants a hand with something.'

'I don't know love, it's woodworking stuff, saws and planes and sanders. He makes things but usually I'm not allowed to touch them. He sells some on the internet, but it's just a hobby.'

Eddie nodded as though it meant something to him.

'Do you need a hand with dinner or anything?'

'No, it's all under control. We're having salmon and potato scallops and some greens on the side. The salmon will be another fifteen minutes, I just put it in.'

'Sounds amazing, Mrs Barrett.'

'What did I say about calling me Janine?'

'Sorry,' he said, smiling his best winning smile. 'Janine.'

Chloe knew Eddie was just being friendly, trying to make a good impression, but she wished he wouldn't flirt with her mother. She tried not to think of him as her boyfriend, as though she had some claim to him and they hadn't only been back together since the night before, but it was so easy to go back to the way she felt and thought before.

'Can I get drinks?' Janine said.

'I brought these.' Eddie held up a couple of beers. 'But I wouldn't say no to a glass to pour it into.'

'Right you are, what about you Chlo'?'

'Tea for me, if you're offering.' She hoped her mother wouldn't immediately ask why she didn't want wine or something else, usually when she visited her mother, she needed something to dull her senses, to stop her from acting out but she was pregnant now and drinking was definitely out. She would have to put some thought into pre-natal care if she wanted to make any kind of rational decision. The longer she put it off the more likely she was to have to terminate because she hadn't taken care of herself. It wasn't right to let that happen; if she wanted to make a good decision all the options needed to be on the table.

She needn't have worried; Janine didn't make any comment about her drink choice.

'Your mum sure is friendly.' Eddie raised his eyebrows.

'She's terrible—either she'll be all over any guy I bring home, or will give them the third degree. Usually both, to be honest.'

'You don't need to look so stressed; your mum isn't you. I may not have done meeting the parents before, not in any real sense, but I'm good with people. You know me.' He squeezed her hand as Janine came back from the kitchen with a long beer glass.

'Here you are, dear. Sit down won't you, only not in the chair, that's Gary's spot.'

A mischievous glint shone in Eddie's eye as his gaze went straight for the recliner.

'Don't,' Chloe said. He walked toward the chair, then thankfully kept going to the ancient couch.

They sat next to each other, the cushions were so flattened and lumpy they ended up pushed together. Janine came out after a few minutes with two mugs of tea and sat on the return. Her side of the couch looked a little better.

'When are you going to get around to upgrading this, Mum?' Chloe asked.

'I don't know what you're talking about.'

'The couch is eighty percent duct tape and throw blankets. You've had it since before I was born.'

'I have a lot of memories on this couch.' Her mother stared into the distance, wistful.

Chloe looked down into her mug.

I have a lot of memories on this couch too. She remembered coming out of her bedroom one night for a glass of water, she must have only been seven or eight years old and finding her mother and her boyfriend at the time having sex on the couch. Chloe had been surprised but hadn't really understood.

'You filthy little pervert,' Janine's boyfriend had said. His voice, breathy and rough, had snapped her out of her stupor and she had turned and fled back to her bedroom. Hiding in the dark for ten minutes, listening to the slapping and grunting in the lounge, Chloe waited.

The boyfriend had come into her room, once they were finished, and sat on the edge of her bed in the dark. 'Do you like watching people?' he asked.

'No.' Her voice was a tiny squeak.

'I think you do. I think you know a lot more about it than you let on, Miss Chloe, and I think you and I are going to have to have a conversation about what good little girls do.' He put his hand on her leg, it felt hot even through the covers, and moved it up towards her groin. She wanted to move away but she was paralysed. 'Next time, we'll have a talk. Go to sleep.'

He had slipped out of her room like a cat, he barely made any noise when he walked if he didn't want to, she was never sure when he was around, when she would wake up in the night to find him sitting on her bed.

Chloe pushed the memory from her mind and looked up as the back door opened. At least he was loud enough to let you know when he was coming; over six feet tall, broad-shouldered as though he had been a sportsman in his youth but most of his weight was carried in his belly, firm and round, sticking out in front of him when he walked into a room.

'Chloe.' He nodded in her direction. 'Who's this skinny bastard?'

Eddie stood up and walked to Gary with his hand out to shake. 'I'm Eddie, Chloe invited me to come and meet you two.'

'Did she now? You know about this, Janine?'

'Yes, love. I told you Chloe's boyfriend was coming for tea.'

'Hmm.' Gary's frown remained, but he said no more. He went to the fridge for a beer and returned to the lounge to sit in the recliner.

'What you working on out the back then?' Eddie asked.

'Joinery. I'm making a nice bedside table unit for my sister's kid, he's turning twenty-one soon.'

'Fantastic, it must be so satisfying to make something with your own hands. I work in landscaping and odd jobs for a friend in construction so I can relate to the feeling.'

Gary made a harrumphing noise and took a sip from his beer.

'Is that your usual line of work, Eddie?' her mother asked.

'I do a bit of this and that, but Johnno often needs a hand with projects. He keeps me out of trouble but I'm really an entrepreneur.'

Gary guffawed, but covered it with a cough. 'Isn't everyone these days? Doesn't pay much though unless you've got your head screwed on.'

'You're not wrong, Gary, I've been working on my business plan for a couple of years and if Chloe and I are—' he broke off suddenly, 'well we're looking like getting serious, I'd better put my head down and get the business humming along.'

Silence followed as Gary took a swig of his beer, Eddie followed suit and looked at Chloe from the corner of his eye. She hoped he knew how badly it could go, if he let slip she was pregnant. No one else needed to know until she had decided to keep it, and her mother and her boyfriend were definitely not the first people she wanted to know.

In the kitchen the oven timer buzzed, and Chloe let out the breath she'd been holding; they would have something else to talk about for a while as they ate. Oven-baked fish was one of Janine's impressive meals, usually she wouldn't have bothered with the expense but believed it made her more upper middle class. Chloe didn't remember her mother's parents, her grandfather had died when her mother was fifteen, it had been the start of all her woes if you believed Janine, and her mother had died in a car accident when Chloe was a baby. Her mother didn't like to talk about the accident, or about her grandmother. Janine's mother's parents on the other side had looked after her until their deaths when she was about five, her memories of them were fuzzy, and cold. She had not missed them.

'Getting very fancy with this meal, Janine. I hope that's not solely in aide of this one,' Gary said, gesturing with his thumb to Eddie. Gary and Janine had taken the ends of the table, Chloe and Eddie were sitting on the sides opposite each other.

Her had mother produced a cask of white wine to have with the meal and Chloe refused again. 'I have to drive.'

'Of course.' Her mother narrowed her eyes, but she hoped in her medicated state her mother wouldn't figure out her secret yet.

The conversation around the table laboured along until Gary and Eddie were able to find common ground around sports.

'Honestly, Hawthorn supporters have no right to feel so smug, they might have won the flag three years in a row but no one stays on top forever.' Gary stabbed his salmon which fell apart under his fork.

'They do tend to go on about the three-peat,' said Eddie.

'And who do you support?'

'If I'm honest, Adelaide. My dad's from there so I inherited them. I guess I could have chosen another team, but it didn't seem like the hill I wanted to die on.' Eddie laughed, but there was no humour in it. Chloe would have to ask him later what he meant by it, in all their conversations his references to his father were pointed and bitter.

'Good you stuck with the family team.' Gary nodded in grudging approval. His team was St Kilda, who hadn't won the Grand Final since 1966, a fact he repeated often. Chloe didn't understand why he would continue to support a club that was so clearly either incompetent, unlucky, or both. Then again, it seemed one couldn't change teams once loyalty had been awarded. That was worse than following a team who didn't win.

'Would you like more, love?' Janine asked Eddie.

'If you're offering, I'll always accept a second serving.' He grinned at her, and Chloe was sure Gary would notice the vibe between them. Her mother passed him the serving dish and he took a good-sized chunk of salmon before helping himself to more potatoes.

'I saw Chloe making these potatoes once when I was 'round at her place. Who is the better cook of the two of you?' Eddie asked.

Gary chuckled. 'That's dangerous talk.'

'Not at all. I'm sure Chloe and I have skills in different areas, I might be a better cook, but she's certainly a better teacher,' Janine said.

Having her mother compliment her was a foreign experience. Janine loved her and was proud of her but she had hardly ever said so aloud. Most of the time it seemed the only words her mother spoke to her were criticisms.

'I'll make you the scalloped potatoes some time and you can compare,' Chloe said. She wanted Eddie to prefer her cooking to her mother's but it seemed petty to be competitive. So much of her life had been defined in opposition to her mother. Despite the meal going much better than she expected so far, Chloe was a jangling bundle of nervous energy and couldn't wait to be gone.

*　　*　　*

In the car on the way back to Richmond they were silent for a long time. She put the radio on to fill the air.

'That was weird,' Eddie said as they parked at Chloe's apartment block. She turned to him; he was smiling.

'What do you mean?'

'Your mum flirting with me, and her boyfriend looked like he wanted to punch me—right up until I asked who was a better cook, then he seemed happy to sit back and wait for one of you two to punch me.'

'I did warn you.'

'I had expected more tension.'

She laughed, a strangled sort of release of anxiety. 'You didn't feel the tension? I could hardly breathe, part of me still hasn't exhaled. I'm waiting for the other shoe to drop and you tell me what a nightmare my mother is.'

'She seems a bit mad, but I wouldn't have said she was a nightmare.'

'Really?' Chloe's hands had been gripping the steering wheel of the stationary car so hard her fingertips had turned white.

'You were really worried I'd run off?' He put a hand on her shoulder and it took all her strength not to collapse in a fit of tears. 'Hey, it's okay. Why don't I come upstairs and we can have a nice cuddle on the couch and you can relax? I know you're not allowed any wine, but I reckon you could use just a little bit right now.'

'You're not kidding. I was sure Mum had clocked I wasn't drinking and was going to have a go at me about it.' She opened her door and stepped into the cool evening air.

She and Eddie tramped up the three flights of stairs to her apartment. He was being so caring and gentle, and since her paranoia hadn't settled down, it was hard not to second-guess his motivations. Although she hadn't said anything at dinner, her mother might call her at any time, having realised the situation. Maybe when her Valium wore off.

Chloe made another cup of tea for each of them, there was no more beer, and they sat on the couch to watch whatever crime show was on. She snuggled up to Eddie, thinking how nice it was to have him there.

'Do you think you'd make a good dad?' she asked.

'I dunno. I know what sort of dad I don't want to be.' He looked at her. 'Are you keeping the baby?'

'I haven't decided yet, but if you want it, if you really want to be a dad and to be with me, that will make a difference.'

'It's your body. I'll respect your decision and I'll never leave you up the creek with my baby. That being said, it'd be pretty cool to have a kid to dress up and kick a footy around with.'

'I don't want an occasional baby-sitter; I want a co-parent. Either you're willing to pull equal weight with me or tell me now and I'll figure out whether I want to raise this kid on my own.' Chloe surprised herself with how angry her words were.

He frowned. 'Of course, I want to do my share. I'm not saying I'll enjoy changing nappies, but I'll do it. You have to do the breastfeeding though, deal?'

She laughed. 'Alright then.'

The TV show finished, and Eddie turned to her, where she was resting her head against him. He put his hand under her chin, tilting her face to him and kissed her.

'I don't know if I'm in the mood, it's a bit soon,' Chloe said, pulling away.

'You can't get any more pregnant.' He laughed, before leaning forward to kiss her again. He smelled good, and she had said no the night before. Her body wanted him, even if her heart wasn't sure.

'I guess it can't hurt.'

*   *   *

In the morning Chloe got up and readied herself for work. She kept as quiet as she could, there was no need to wake him. It had been so nice sleeping next to a warm body again, she hadn't realised how much she'd missed his presence.

She tiptoed into the bedroom as she was about to leave and kissed his forehead. 'I'm going to work, you're welcome to stay here.'

He opened his eyes, looked at her drowsily. 'You off then?'

'Yep. Gotta earn my money while I can.'

'Thanks for last night.'

'You weren't so bad yourself,' she said giving him a nudge.

'I meant meeting your mum. I know it was hard for you. They're a bit nuts, but I still want to be with you. Let's talk about what we're going to do, yeah?'

'I told you I needed to think about it.'

'I know. I thought it might be useful to think about it out aloud. I'm sure you have reservations, maybe if we hash it out we'll know whether it's going to work or not.'

'Okay. We'll make time to have a proper sit down. I'll talk to you later.' She kissed his mouth, the tickle of his stubble and the smell of his cologne reminded her of what they'd done the night before. She wondered if it was loneliness or hormones that were making her so horny.

'You look happy, Miss,' Lee said when she walked into the room. Perhaps strutting just a little. Her mother hadn't scared off the man who might be having a baby with her, there was reason to hope.

'Yes, I had a nice time on the weekend. Did you have a nice time?'

'Mum and I made chocolate cake. Then we ate it. I was supposed to do icing but it all came out wrong, so we didn't bother about that.'

'Even chocolate cake without icing is pretty delicious. Was it a special occasion?'

'I don't think so. It was Mum's idea.' Lee looked off into middle distance, apparently more perplexed by the question than Chloe had anticipated. Sometimes she would ask him a question she thought was innocuous and it had a profound effect on him. Once they were talking about penguins and he'd gone into a sort of quiet trance, a good half hour later he'd asked whether two boy penguins could have a baby, he'd seen something about a bonded pair in Edinburgh and seemed to have been thinking about it ever since.

Chloe liked kids, she spent plenty of time with them in her job and she had infinite patience for their outbursts and frustrations. Would she be as tolerant for a child of her own? A child she couldn't get away from. Some of the parents of her special needs kids were harried and frazzled all the time, others seemed to glide serenely through any kind of setback or difficulty. Janine had been a battler, any small setback would send her into fits of despair. Chloe had often wondered if her mother was being histrionic on purpose or if her sense of self really was so unstable.

Her mother's boyfriends were never much use, at least she'd never married any of them. One of them asked her when Chloe was fourteen; a few days before they'd had an enormous fight, the man had punched Janine fairly in the stomach and stormed out while she was doubled over. Chloe had been sure that would be the last time she'd see him but he was back two days later. He proposed marriage, got down on one knee and everything on the front step.

Janine had spent the two days crying in her bedroom, she hadn't come out for anything except to use the bathroom. Chloe had made herself food and gotten to school on the tram without disturbing her mother's misery.

After two days of pills and wine, Janine was so blurry around the edges it was a surprise she could stand up, but she said no.

'I can't marry you, but I can forgive you.' She took his hand and pulled him up to kiss him. They'd gone straight to the bedroom where Chloe could hear them making up to each other; she went for a walk for an hour and thankfully the noises had stopped by the time she got home.

*   *   *

Chloe arrived home to find her apartment empty. She hadn't asked Eddie to stay, nor had she expected him to; surely he would be out trying to get a more permanent job now he wanted to keep the baby, but she was still sad to find herself alone.

Damned hormones, she thought.

How was your day?

She sent a text to Eddie while she started on dinner. She needed to use up some of the vegetables in her fridge before they started growing fur and she had to throw them out. Growing up there were periods when she and her mother had hardly enough money to eat and now she was living on her own she had sometimes had to live off rice and soy sauce for a couple of days until her pay came through just to afford the rent on her own apartment. Chloe hated waste.

The Mother's Fault

*I had a good day. I thought about you a
lot. And the baby. I don't want you to feel
like I'm smothering you, but we could
drive up to see my parents this weekend. I
bet you wouldn't feel like such a weirdo if
you met my mad relatives.*

The words shimmered and Chloe realised her eyes
were filled with tears. She was never this emotional
usually unless it was the few days before she started her
period. It would be nice to meet his parents, and brother
and sister, and their kids. As the only child of an only
child, she had grown up without relatives except the
boyfriends, and she was never sure how long they would
stick around. Most often it was a relief when they left,
but there had been a couple of good ones Chloe had
considered calling Dad.

*I don't have any specific plans. I'd love to
meet your family.*

Her pasta started to boil over on the stovetop and she
was forced out of her reverie.

Chapter 11

Eddie didn't have a car, so they had to drive up to see his parents in her car. They shared the driving; two and a half hours or so to get to Shepparton where they a lived.

'Mum and Dad still live in the same house they bought when I was a kid. My brother, Mark, he's the mechanic, has one kid with his girlfriend, Meg. Mum and Dad want them to get married but he seems to be resisting that, God knows why. And my baby sister, Charlotte, she's a stay-at-home mum. Married to Petey, the boy who got her knocked up in year twelve. They had another couple of kids one after the other.'

'Sounds like it will be a big gathering.'

'Don't be stressed babe, they'll love you.' He put his hand on her knee without looking away from the road.

'I know it's silly to worry, but I've never really wanted something to work out as badly as this. Not since I left home and started working.' Her bottom lip trembled and she scolded herself for getting emotional again. She needed to keep it together.

They drove a while longer before coming up to a green metal sign with white text pointing to Shepparton.

'Not far now. We're on the other side of town. If you want to stop for a constitutional, get some Dutch courage—although you're not supposed to be having that, maybe a hot choccie to steel your resolve, now's the time to speak up. Mum talks a mile a minute and if she ever slows down Dad will take over.'

The Mother's Fault

She smiled. 'I think I'll be alright. I'd rather get it over with.'

Eddie nodded and they drove on in silence for a while. She fiddled with the car stereo, there were a couple of CDs in the glovebox, she pulled one out and swapped it for the radio. It was her first car to be new enough to have a CD player, a luxury for her. Maybe an audiobook would have been a good idea for the road trip, although she and Eddie never had any trouble keeping a conversation going. He must take after his mother, there was barely a moment when he didn't talk unless he was playing video games.

After another ten minutes or so, Eddie swung the car onto a wide concrete driveway in front of a wide, low, weatherboard house. It had been white once, although orange dirt came up the boards to about waist height and the upper boards were dusty and cobwebby. A veranda ran along the front, two tropical-looking cane chairs, with faded floral cushion covers, and a glass topped cane table between them sat to the left of the front door.

Chloe took a slow steady breath in and put her hand on the door handle.

'You'll be fine.'

'Okay. Let's not say anything about the baby yet, okay? I don't want the first memory they have of me is that I'm up the duff.'

He laughed, a soft guffaw. 'Alright, but they'll find out eventually.'

She clenched her jaw and pulled open the car door. Eddie slid out of the driver's seat and strode towards the door without a glance in her direction.

The pale green front door opened as they approached and a plump older woman stepped out to greet them.

'Nice to see you,' she said, wrapping her arms around her son. She wore a floral print dress with buttons down the front that looked like it had survived in her wardrobe since it was in fashion in the eighties. Her hair was cut in a bob just below her ears and was a highly unnatural shade of deep auburn, and her eyes were a dull sort of brown.

'I'm Virginia, Eddie's mother. It's nice to meet you.' She held out her hand to Chloe to shake. It seemed awkwardly formal after the greeting her son got, but then again, she was a stranger.

'It's lovely to meet you too. I'm Chloe, although you probably figured that out.'

Virginia smiled and nodded. 'Come in, I've put the kettle on for a cuppa and I've made a fresh banana bread for us to have with it. I'm sure Eddie isn't feeding you right, he was never much of an eater that one.'

'Mum…' Eddie's voice hovered somewhere between whining and teasing.

'I'm sure he doesn't bother cooking for you either, we love him dearly but he never stayed still long enough to learn more than the basics.'

Eddie sighed.

'You know I'm just teasing you, darling,' his mother said.

'I can cook steak. Dad taught me that.'

'You see how he doesn't listen to a word I say? Will you have a cup of tea, Chloe? Or coffee?'

'I'd love a coffee,' Chloe replied.

'Don't bother, Mum only keeps instant. Her tea isn't bad, if you like that sort of thing.'

The dynamic between mother and son put Chloe on edge, she found herself hovering on her tiptoes as though she might need to run at any moment, and her breathing shallow. They were family and it wasn't her place to dictate how they should be with each other, but she wasn't sure how she would come out of the weekend if they were at each other's throats like this the whole time.

'Tea then, if that's okay, Mrs Travers.'

'Virginia, please. I know how you city people are about fancy coffee, but up here we don't bother with that sort of thing. We go out for a cuppa plenty, to meet with friends or catch up on the latest around town, but I'm sure the cafés would have nothing on the Melbourne stuff you're used to.'

'Maybe we'll try somewhere on our way out. I'm sure they make a lovely coffee.' Chloe wished it wasn't so obvious she was from the city, it felt as though Eddie's mother was judging her. It was stressful enough knowing she was pregnant and unmarried, no doubt a big no-no in Virginia's eyes given her insistence his brother marry. Though Chloe wasn't sure she wanted to keep the baby yet, so perhaps Virginia need never know.

Eddie rolled his eyes theatrically. 'You like that one on High Street, don't you, Mum?'

'Yes, that one's not bad. Although it changed hands recently, and I don't think it's quite the same…' Virginia went into a long description of the new owners and the small changes she'd seen in the café. As she was talking, she took the steaming kettle and poured hot water over four teabags which she'd put into a cream and blue floral-patterned teapot. Chloe thought it was quaint and somewhat redundant to put teabags into a pot, but it was a sweet thought. The teapot looked old, perhaps mid-eighties in vintage. It would have suited her own mother's house and décor, although Janine would never have dreamed of serving tea in a pot.

Tuning her attention back to the conversation, Eddie's mother seemed to be reminiscing about his old school friends, although the scowl on Eddie's face suggested perhaps they weren't his friends after all.

'Anyway, he moved back from Albury in December. There was a job up there in a car dealership, but my friend Paula said he couldn't make the sales targets and they had to let him go. It was a shame too; he'd knocked up Paula's niece and was going to make good for the little family to move to Albury with him. They've split now, of course, and the girl has two other kids from different fathers so he's probably better off without her. He'll have to pay child support though.'

It was mind-boggling the speed with which Virginia doled out stories, and judgement, about people from around the town in hearing of a stranger. Perhaps she had better be careful exactly what details she let slip to

Eddie's family lest she be the star of the next round of gossip at the café down on High Street.

Eddie turned to her and raised an eyebrow, she frowned and shook her head. They had discussed telling his parents about her pregnancy, but it was too soon. Even if she decided to keep it, it wasn't usually done to tell people before the twelve-week mark for fear of miscarriage.

Sitting in his parent's kitchen with its kitschy cabinets, all varnished pine, and the orange laminate benches, she couldn't see herself as a mother. She wasn't ready. As much as she wanted to believe Eddie would come through with a stable job and reliable income, she would have liked to see him prove that he could before getting pregnant. Sometimes she worried about Eddie, he seemed to have trouble settling down and if she was being honest with herself, she didn't want a boyfriend who was flaky—enough of her mother's boyfriends had been like that.

'Chloe? Hello?' Eddie waved his hand in front of her face.

'Sorry, what?'

'Mum's asking you what you do for work.'

'Sorry,' she said again, 'away with the fairies. I work in a primary school with children who need extra help.'

'Are you a teacher?' Virginia asked.

'No, she helps the retards,' Eddie said.

'I told you we don't use that word.' Chloe cringed. 'I work with kids who have learning difficulties, dyslexia,

ADHD, that sort of thing. Sometimes they have behavioural issues as well, but I've found once they have the help they need, they settle down really well.'

'Except when they have a meltdown for no reason.'

Chloe stared at Eddie. 'Some students are more prone to frustration and outbursts than others. I have two kids I work with pretty intensively at the moment. You must be thinking about the time Lee was upset because his parents were fighting. It can be very challenging to work with children who have a low frustration tolerance.'

Virginia made a strangled coughing noise. 'A lot of children need to learn how to manage their frustrations.'

The kitchen fell into a tense silence, Eddie had folded his arms and was leaning way back on his chair, Virginia stirred a teaspoon of sugar into her mug, the clanging of the spoon against the ceramic sides echoed in the silence.

'Dad here?' Eddie's tone was sullen.

'He's out the back, he'll come in when he's finished pottering on whatever it is he's working on at the moment.'

'Come out and meet Dad,' Eddie said to Chloe. 'Bring your cuppa.'

'Should we take your Dad a drink?' Chloe asked.

'Nah. He'll be onto the beer, there's a fridge out there.'

Remaining in her seat, Eddie's mother pursed her lips in disapproval but said nothing. Chloe had thought her house was tense growing up, but at least their arguments had been out loud. This unspoken antagonism was disconcerting.

The kitchen was at the back of the house, out the back door, three steps to the back yard, a beautiful, well-tended cottage style garden, and a few metres from the house along the right-hand side of the property was an enormous, corrugated steel shed. Sounds of metal striking metal came from inside.

Eddie pulled a heavy sliding door to the side to reveal a glorified garage; tools lined the back wall, each with outlines drawn on the Masonite pegboard backing. The rest of the shed was uninsulated and would have been subject to any extreme weather conditions, it smelled vaguely of grass, petrol and sweat. A man in his mid-sixties was leaning under the bonnet of an emerald green Holden Torana.

'Dad,' Eddie said. The man didn't raise his head.

'Son.'

'I've brought Chloe out to meet you. Chloe, this is Dad.'

'It's lovely to meet you, Mister Travers.' Chloe went to hold out her hand to shake his but the older man still hadn't turned to them. It seemed rude to continue what he was doing when he had a guest, but perhaps Eddie's father was not keen on visitors.

'Call me Steve,' he said, looking up. His eyes were sparkling and playful and like Eddie's. Chloe stood frozen for a moment, lost in the intense gaze, uncomfortable but strangely drawn in as Steve's eyes ran her over, assessing her. 'You've done well,' he said to Eddie.

'Be nice.' Eddie stood up a little taller, whether he was proud or defensive Chloe couldn't be sure. 'This is Dad's pride and joy. I wouldn't be surprised if he saved this before any of his kids in a fire.'

'You're not wrong.' Steve smiled and his eyes were alight with mischief. 'So, you've been deigned worthy of coming up to the country to meet the parents have you? Makes you pretty special, I haven't met one of Eddie's girls since—how long would it be Eddie? Since you moved out probably.'

'Sounds right.'

'And you've had enough of your mother already, have you?' Steve raised an eyebrow.

'You know what she's like.'

'I have a big shed for a reason.'

Chloe couldn't tell if he was joking, her ability to read Eddie's father was completely thrown, something like an older, more confident and understated version of Eddie. He would have been a magnet for ladies in his youth.

'Don't mind us, Chloe. His mother likes to tease him and he's never been able to stand it. The curse of being the firstborn maybe.'

Chloe opened her mouth to say something but everything she could think of sounded inadequate or rude, so she closed her mouth again. Janine had never been much good at friendly teasing, banter some people called it, and her boyfriends had always been mean-spirited in their teasing. It did not seem a good way to demonstrate love but she had to admit the Travers family seemed more functional than hers, maybe she should reserve judgement.

While she had been standing there internally debating the Travers family dynamic, the two men had started a reasonably heated conversation about football. With only a minor interest in the sport, Chloe was happy to listen rather than try to contribute. Of course, she had a team, what Melbournian didn't, but she couldn't have recited more than two of the players' names or where the team was placed on the ladder.

The sound of conversation washed over her, more like water than words, as Chloe looked around the shed. Larger than the average garage, the shed was at least four metres wide and long enough to fit the car inside it twice over. Besides the gleaning vehicle, several workbenches were covered in the guts of various unidentifiable mechanical objects. Neat, but not fastidiously so, the floor showed signs of oil stains and a coating of black dust suggesting it wasn't cleaned often but kept tidy.

Steve and Eddie's heads were now both hovering inside the bonnet of the car, apparently having returned to the task of fixing whatever was in need of repair. Chloe wasn't sure if she was supposed to show interest, but stood and sipped her tea, waiting for them to remember she was there.

'You still here, babe?' Eddie turned away from the car to retrieve his mug.

'Yeah.'

'You don't have to hang around here like a blueberry, go sit inside with Mum, or I'm sure she won't mind if you read or something. I can't imagine watching me work on an engine is particularly entertaining.'

'Not especially, I'll see what's happening inside.' She slipped back out of the shed, up the couple of steps and into the kitchen. It wasn't how she'd expected the reception to go—in her mind the family all sat around the dining table, or perhaps in the lounge, with cups of tea, and biscuits, getting to know one another. Not that she'd ever met a partner's parents before, but that's what happened in films. She shook her head at her own naïveté.

'They working on the car, love?' Virginia said as she entered.

Chloe nodded.

'They'll be out there until dinnertime. I sometimes wonder what keeps them interested but there you go. I suppose the old rust bucket has enough going wrong with it they'll forever be fixing it.'

'Does it run?'

'Yes, Steve drives it most of the time. Ridiculous attention-seeking thing if you ask me, but of course he never does, so I put up with it. Every couple of months I wonder what would happen if I really put my foot down about the car; probably end up divorced.' She chuckled to herself and idly ran a cloth over the bench top.

The silence stretched out; Chloe wasn't sure what had happened to the talkative woman from half an hour ago. She seemed deflated, and the sparkle had gone out of her eyes.

'Can I do anything to help with dinner?' Chloe asked. It was only four o'clock but if she had a job it might alleviate some of her anxiety.

'No, that's alright. I've got it all sorted, just needs to be heated up.'

Eddie had not commented on his mother's ability to cook but his efforts were abysmal unless it was steak, salad and chips. Chloe pulled out her phone and started scrolling through Facebook. If she'd known it would be so quiet, she would have brought a book or something from work to keep her occupied. After the long drive it was a struggle to sit quietly and do nothing.

'Do you think the boys would miss me if I went for a walk?' Chloe asked.

'What, dear?' Virginia looked as though she had been startled from a daze. 'I think that would be fine. Dinner will be around six, so be sure to be back before then. There are a few nice streets around this area if you just want a stroll. The shops will all have closed by now.'

Of course, Saturday in a country town everything will have closed up early.

'Unless you want to go the pub, but I wouldn't recommend it on your own. The boys can be a bit rough and ready if you're not used to them.'

Chloe nodded. 'Thanks. I'll be back in time for dinner.' She picked up her shoulder bag and wandered out the front door. Pulling it closed behind her she had an overwhelming vision of the pub scenes in the old

Australian thriller *Wake in Fright;* men in blue workers' shorts and sweat-stained white singlets sitting at dusty bars drinking warm beers. Out the back an illegal gambling den, where gap-toothed ruffians played two-up for all the main characters wages.

A shiver ran down Chloe's back at the thought of how the men in that pub would have leered at her. She'd never understood the film but it had certainly stayed with her.

The streets around the Travers' house were not so different from suburbs in Melbourne, perhaps bigger blocks. The architecture was a bit more eclectic; fifties orange brick veneer next to turn of the century weatherboard. The gardens were similarly varied, one front yard was almost entirely concreted with a depressed, sunburnt square patch of lawn, the next overflowing with flowering trees and a jungle-like profusion of foliage.

Since she wasn't in any hurry, Chloe strolled down the streets without much thought to where she was headed. After twenty minutes or so she looked up and realised she hadn't been paying attention to the surrounds and wouldn't be able to get back to the house. She checked her phone's map app and was relieved to see she had enough reception to find her way back when the time came.

Without warning she felt a tide of nausea rise up from her belly and she had to bend over leaning her palms on her thighs to catch her breath.

'You alright, love?' a man's voice asked. She looked up at the speaker; squat and muscular, a tradesman maybe, his face crinkled with concern.

'Yes, I felt a bit sick for a second. I'll be fine.' It was probably the pregnancy, she thought.

His lips pressed together in a thin line of concern. 'You wanna have a sit down? Need me to get you a glass of water or something? I just live around the corner.'

Chloe took a slow, steady breath before answering. 'No, I'm fine, really.'

'Righto.' The man bobbed his head and waddled away, his rubber thongs rhythmically slapping the soles of his feet as he went. Chloe rested on the top of a low brick fence for a at least five minutes before the nausea faded enough and she thought she could walk without vomiting. According to her phone, she was ten minutes away from Eddie's parent's place if she went directly back. She resolved to walk slowly and to take a rest if her belly started to complain again. If the pregnancy was going to be like this the whole way through it was certainly a strong argument to terminate.

* * *

When Chloe arrived back at the Travers' house Eddie was waiting on the front veranda.

'Where did you go?' he asked, frowning.

'I wanted a walk. You all seemed busy.'

'I was worried about you.'

She put her hand on his upper arm. 'Why? I'm fine, see?'

'I couldn't find you. I thought you'd left me.'

'Didn't your mum tell you I'd gone for a walk?'

Eddie moved away from her touch. 'The way she said it sounded like a lie.'

Chloe made a noise of acknowledgement, unsure what to say. She put her hand out to touch him again and he turned away, pacing down the veranda towards the agapanthus bushes.

'I didn't leave you. I'm sorry you were worried.' She paused. 'Your family seems nice.'

Eddie harrumphed, leaning on the balustrade. She walked over to him and put her hand on his back. He didn't flinch away this time, a good sign.

'I don't have much of a gauge of what a good family is like. I'm sure yours have their issues but they seem to care about you. I am not going to change how I feel about you based on anything that happens this weekend. I promise.'

He sighed.

'If it gets really unpleasant for either one of us, maybe we should have a code word? Something that means we need to change the topic or get out of here.'

'Like what?'

'I don't know. Anything. Red alert or my hovercraft is full of eels?'

He chuckled quietly. 'That's not exactly subtle.'

'Alright then, you come up with a code phrase, smarty pants.' She smiled broadly, glad he seemed to have forgiven her for the imagined abandonment.

'Maybe say something like, 'I just remembered I have to give someone from work a call'. That gives you a reason to leave the room, and if it's really bad you can make up something where we have to go home.'

'Sounds good. What about for you?'

Eddie turned to look at her, his eyes sharp. 'What do you mean?'

'I...' she hesitated. It was a sore point for Eddie that he couldn't find ongoing work he was happy with. 'I don't know what you told your parents you do.'

'I didn't want them asking me about what I was doing for a crust constantly, so I told 'em I work for Johnno permanently.'

'That's good. I'm sure they're pleased you have a steady job.'

Eddie scoffed. 'Yeah, right. I'm a labourer, sometimes gardener. It's hardly rocket science.'

Despite his earlier laughter his mood remained dark. There would be no bringing him out of it, Chloe thought, perhaps being back at home had put him in a funk he couldn't shake. She rubbed her hand over his upper back, trailing circles over the fabric of his T-shirt. After a while he sighed again.

'Better get back inside. Dinner's nearly ready.'

*   *   *

The meal was as awkward as the rest of the day had been. Eddie's mood vacillated between civil, and barely contained rage. Chloe helped Virginia with the washing up, Eddie and his dad had gone back out to the garage after dessert.

'Are you alright dear? You've gone all flushed.' Virginia had paused her wiping of the dining table to stare at her.

'It's been a long day. I always find big car trips taxing. I'm fine.' As she said it, she didn't feel particularly fine. Her cheeks and forehead felt hot, and she was suddenly very thirsty. 'I might just have a sit down.'

'If I didn't know any better, I might put your coming up to meet us and the fact you seem pale or flushed in waves together and suggest you were about to make an announcement.' Eddie's mother looked pointedly at her abdomen.

Chloe gaped her mouth open, struggling to find the words. 'We aren't telling people yet. In case...' She hoped it sounded as though she was worried she might miscarry.

'Of course. I'll keep it under my hat.'

Instead of feeling closer to Virginia, Chloe felt a shift in the room. As a woman who thrived on gossip, having a secret like this would be currency, yet how could she have denied it? Chloe was good at a few things but lying wasn't one of them. No doubt Steve and the rest of the family would all know by the time they all sat down to lunch the next day.

'Where will we be staying?' she asked, realising for the first time their accommodations for the next couple of nights hadn't been discussed.

'Eddie's old room is set up as my sewing and crafting room, but the grandchildren often stay in the third bedroom. It's bunkbeds but I'm sure you'll be okay for a couple of nights.' She paused, a faded floral tea towel dangling from her hands. 'Tell Eddie you'll have the bottom bunk.'

The men stayed out in the shed for a long time, and Chloe decided to head to bed early. The driving, the walk, and the tension on the house all drained her energy. Not to mention she didn't want to hang out with Virginia, who was watching some terrible reality show about C-list celebrities out in a jungle somewhere while commentating on their various strengths or controversies. Her knowledge of the stars careers was truly encyclopaedic.

The bedroom room she was to sleep in was clearly made up for children; walls painted an alarming shade of mint-green, toys overflowing from the chest in the corner, and the rug on the floor had a map design that could be used for toy cars or trains.

Chloe lay down on the bottom bunk, her mouth filled with the tangy cleanness of toothpaste, and stared at the slats of the bed above her, despite having turned off all the lights she could make out quite a lot of detail from the light coming under the door. She was sure she would fall asleep immediately but her mind was churning with thoughts. About her mother, the baby inside her, about what it would mean for her lifestyle, the changes she would need to make, that Eddie would need to make if they were to have the child.

Virginia and Steve, despite whatever failings they might have had as parents were clearly committed to being good grandparents, having decked out the room so thoroughly. But they lived so far away. Janine would be unreliable as a babysitter, on good days Chloe might consider leaving the baby with her, but her good days were few and far between, so best not to count on her. Her mother had only had a few months with Chloe as a baby before the authorities took her to live with her great-grandparents. By the time she went back to Janine she was ready to start school.

Sometimes Chloe wondered how Janine managed to avoid losing her again, but perhaps Child Protection were less thorough when there weren't other relatives clamouring to take the child. She had been lonely growing up, it wasn't until late primary school that she realised how large some of the other kids' families were; aunts and uncles and so many cousins she couldn't keep track of them, while she was an only child, with no father, no grandparents, no aunts or uncles or cousins. Just her and her mother. And her mother's boyfriends.

The door opened with a creak and light spilled around the edges into the dark room. She twisted her head to see Eddie creep in.

'Hi babe.'

'You awake?' he asked.

'Yeah.'

He made his way over to the bunk and knelt down. She could smell the beer coming off him in wafts.

'Thanks for coming up.'

'That's okay. I haven't met anyone's parents before, it's all a bit overwhelming.'

'I know.'

'What were you doing with your dad? Did you talk?'

'No, Dad's not much of a talker. We just fiddled with the car, drank a few beers. He's become a real lightweight, nurses his beer for ages.'

Chloe clamped her mouth shut to stop from saying he clearly hadn't nursed his. She hoped he wouldn't try to get in with her, before realising he might be too drunk to get into the top bunk.

He leaned in and tried to kiss her, his mouth wet and searching.

'Babe,' she said, her tone admonishing.

'C'mon, it's just a kiss.'

'I know, but we're in your parent's house, in a child's bed. We'd better not.'

'I'll be quiet, I promise.' He'd found her face with his hand and trailed it down her neck towards her chest and breasts. 'Just a quickie.'

She sighed. It didn't seem worth the effort to convince him it was a bad idea.

Eddie was sloppy in his lovemaking, but was true to his word, his grunts were very soft and it was over in a few minutes. He rolled off her and almost immediately was snoring loudly and taking up most of the room in the bed. Despite being exhausted after the drive and the day with his parents, she couldn't sleep. Eddie's skin was too hot on her, and his lawnmower-like breathing right in her ear.

I could climb into the top bunk; he was unlikely to wake up. But it may not make any difference to her ability to sleep. Eddie would probably be offended to wake and find her in the other bed, and given how sensitive he was being back with his family, Chloe decided to endure the uncomfortable sleeping arrangement rather than deal with sulking all day tomorrow.

Chapter 12

Sunday morning and Eddie's brother, Mark, sister, Charlotte, their respective partners and children were all coming around later on for a family barbeque. Chloe had to be back in Melbourne that evening, as she had school on Monday morning, but Eddie had no work lined up and would probably be drinking beers with his family. She was not looking forward to driving all the way back to Melbourne after a bad night's sleep with a drunken passenger.

Mark was everything she expected a country mechanic to be; bearded, tall and broad-shouldered, he was a little chunky, but strong and fit, though they all had the same dark hair and aquiline nose. His body type was much more like their father than Eddie's, whose body was long and wiry. His partner Meg was fleshy and a few inches shorter than Mark. Her clothing appeared to be active-wear, her legs snugly wrapped in teal and orange three-quarter length leggings and her top a floaty singlet affair with more straps than could possibly be necessary. Both of them looked like they would snap Chloe in half if she stepped out of line, although as soon as she was introduced as Eddie's girlfriend, both Mark and Meg grinned lifting some of the heaviness in Chloe's chest.

'So, we finally meet you. We've heard nothing about you, Eddie doesn't tell anyone anything,' Mark said, pulling Chloe into a bear hug.

'Not that we'd given up hope of Eddie ever settling down, but it has been a long time since we got to meet anyone,' Meg said.

Given the stories about last time, I can't blame him. 'I guess he's just being careful he has the right woman,' Chloe said.

Charlotte arrived a few minutes later, her family spilling out of a minivan after her. Pete seemed pleasant, if a little scattered, trying to keep an eye on their four kids. Average height, blond, and a little thick around the middle, Pete wore jeans and a button-up checked shirt which was too small. Charlotte was in a cotton wrap dress which did very little to flatter her figure; she looked like Eddie in build; long, wiry, very little in the way of curves, and their father's nose on her looked severe rather than handsome.

The children took after Pete, blond and heavyset, and dashed around the front yard chasing each other in a squealing game for which Chloe didn't understand the rules. Indeed, watching them play, perhaps there were no rules.

Steve was on barbeque duty, a huge contraption pulled from the back of the shed, past the car, which had been covered for the day, and into the back yard. There were T-bone steaks, sausages of various sizes and consistencies, vegetable skewers and a couple of cobs of corn way up the back of the griddle. The smell wafting over on the smoke was pungent with rosemary and garlic. Chloe started salivating at the smell, the awkward family dynamics were not enough to dampen her appetite.

Charlotte and Mark stood with their mother, chatting about local dramas from what Chloe overheard, while she and Eddie were caught in a sort of no man's land between the kitchen and the barbie; they were not participating in the conversation near the kitchen and Steve wasn't a talker at the best of times.

'Now, Chloe. He must be serious about you if you're coming up here to meet us all. It's been years since Eddie's deigned to make the trip back,' Charlotte said. Her voice was warm and friendly but the deep furrow between her brows suggested she didn't feel friendly.

'You're not up the duff, are ya?' Mark asked. Chloe was sure the colour drained from her face despite her determination not to show a reaction, beside her Eddie coughed as a sip from his beer tried to go down the wrong pipe.

'Good one,' Eddie managed to say around the spluttering. Chloe was far from convinced the comment had been unnoticed. Another reason to get a termination as soon as they were back in Melbourne; lest she be known in the family as the one who tied Eddie down by getting pregnant.

In the car on the drive up, Eddie had given her the rundown on the siblings' history, Charlotte was the first to have kids, and she and Pete were pregnant before she even finished high school. It would hardly be fair for a teen-parent to judge her for an unplanned child, but

Chloe didn't want to give them anything to criticise her over.

She was doing better than any of the Travers children—with her TAFE qualification and a good, professional job, but no doubt the tradies, Mark and Pete, were earning more than she was, and that wasn't considering the shemozzle of Eddie's finances.

*   *   *

Just before four o'clock Chloe put her mouth close to Eddie's ear and whispered, 'we should think about heading home, I have work in the morning.' She'd eaten as much as she could manage, and had picked and grazed in the couple of hours since. One thing she could say about the Travers family was they knew how to cater.

'Relax, babe, it's only a couple of hours drive,' he replied, finishing the can in his hand. It was his fifth and he wouldn't be in a fit state to drive home any time soon.

'I know it's only a couple of hours, but I don't want to drive in the dark.'

'You don't have to drive all the way babe, I'll do some.' Eddied cracked open a new beer.

'After six beers? I'm glad to have met your family, and now we need to go.'

'I just opened this. Wait till I've finished and we've said our goodbyes then we can go.'

I'm leaving by five, she thought to herself, and if he doesn't want to come he can get the train back.

She sipped her tea; it was tepid and bitter. Watching the way they spoke to each other Chloe didn't understand why Eddie would want to hang around with them anyway, at least with her mother and whatever boyfriend she happened to be seeing at the time, their gatherings were quickly taken over by the television, sports usually, but occasionally Janine would have her pick, usually a trashy reality show. There was no chance of that here, the kids had commandeered the lounge room and television to play some video game they were shouting at intermittently.

'You done any work on the car lately, Dad?' Mark asked.

'Yeah, Eddie helped me on it last night,' Steve replied.

'I'm surprised you got your hands dirty, mate,' Mark said to his brother. 'I hope you were supervising his work,' he added, turning to his father.

'I know my way around an engine,' Eddie said.

'Like fuck you do,' Mark muttered.

'What did you say?' Eddie's can dimpled as he gripped it a little too tightly.

'Nothing.'

A tense silence filled the air between them. Chloe drained the last of her disappointing tea and looked around.

'I'm afraid we'll have to start making tracks,' she said, standing.

'So early?' Virginia's voice was tight with alarm. 'Are you feeling alright?'

'I'm fine, but I don't like driving in the dark. Silly I know, but this one had a few more than is wise for driving so we're on my schedule now I'm afraid.' She hoped giving him the excuse of blaming her would allow Eddie to excuse himself without losing face.

'Never stopped him before,' Mark said quietly.

'Well,' Virginia said, scrunching up her nose as though Chloe had developed a foul odour, 'it was lovely to meet, and to see our firstborn. God knows he doesn't get up here much. Must be that fancy job he keeps telling us about keeping him working at all hours.'

Chloe put her hand on Eddie's forearm, hoping to remind him they were leaving and stop him getting into an argument.

'We often get last minute jobs and I need to be around. See you soon, Mum.' Eddie stood to give his mother a peck on the cheek, Chloe did the same. They said their goodbyes, the men shook hands, grasping each other in a hostile way, and Chloe wasn't able to relax until they had pulled out of the house and were around the corner.

'Thank fuck that's over,' Eddie said. She didn't know what to say, it had been tense but nothing really terrible had happened.

'It could have been worse.'

'Everyone was on their best behaviour.'

Chloe kept her eyes on the road and waited for him to say more but he didn't elaborate. If that was their best behaviour, she wondered what they were like normally; Steve seemed the type to bottle everything up, perhaps never showing any kind of affection for the kids, while Virginia seemed likely to criticise, whether openly or subtly. It must have been tough growing up in that house, especially as the oldest. Eddie didn't finish school which was no doubt a serious disappointment for both his parents. The two younger siblings were more normal, and therefore unlikely to attract negative attention from either parent. Chloe suspected with Eddie as the scapegoat the other two got away with more. Having grown up an only child, she had longed for a sister or brother to spend time with, someone who knew what was going on at home, to be on her side, possibly to protect her from her mother's shitty boyfriends, but perhaps miraculously, Janine was only ever pregnant once.

She snuck a look at Eddie, sitting next to her in the passenger seat. He had tipped his chair back and had his eyes closed—she would have to keep herself entertained on the ride home then.

*   *   *

Eddie stayed at Chloe's place that night, he had slept most of the way in the car, and when he wasn't sleeping, he was playing on his phone. When they got home, he went straight to bed. Chloe did her nightly routine and climbed into bed next to him. His breathing was steady, but she didn't think he was asleep. He didn't try to get physical with her, and despite her reluctance the night before she felt rejected. Why he would want to in a bunkbed in his parent's house but not in her own made no sense to her.

At school her mind went over and over the weekend, trying to find the moment when Eddie had slid into his funk.

'Miss?' Lee asked.

She shook herself and turned to him. 'Sorry, what was your question?'

'I asked if you were okay, and you didn't say anything.'

'Thank you, Lee, I was just thinking about my weekend. It was a bit confusing.'

'What do you mean, Miss?'

'I met my friend's mum and dad and brother and sister. They were all nice to me, but I feel a bit funny about it. Do you ever have that?'

'Feeling funny around people?' He hitched one side of his mouth up in a sad smile. 'I get confused around people all the time. I thought it was just me, because I'm different to other kids.'

She put her hand on his shoulder. 'It's not just you. Everyone feels that way sometimes, especially when we don't know someone very well. You might have it a bit more often than other people, but you're not the only one.'

'Okay.' Lee turned back to his drawing, apparently content with this answer. She'd been surprised several times by the apparent insight her student showed, only to be reminded moments later that he was naïve to so many other things. If only she had someone to sit and explain the world to her.

At lunchtime, Chloe checked her phone. Nothing from Eddie, either he was still in a sulk or possibly still snoozing in her bed. She'd never been one to stay in bed during the day, as a kid it was much safer to be in the lounge or kitchen. On the rare occasions her mother and whoever was the current boyfriend were up before her, it was always a sign of laziness to have a sleep in. Not that Janine ever did anything with her time, apparently watching a lot of TV was less lazy than staying in bed.

Mel had texted her to say hi. She hadn't told anyone about the pregnancy but maybe her friend would be able to offer her reassurance. There was no way a baby now was a good idea. She texted Mel:

> *Hey gorgeous. Feels like I haven't seen you in ages. I need to do something but I'm avoiding it. Wanna have dinner tonight?*

The bell went to return to class, and Chloe put her phone back in her bag. If Eddie was going to be in a mood, she could take herself out with a friend and let him stew on his own for a while. Hopefully he wouldn't still be hanging at her apartment when she got home.

*　　*　　*

Chloe pushed open the door as though she expected to set off an explosion. It looked like her apartment, one bedroom, her slightly beaten-up couch, the grey kitchenette beyond.

'I'm home,' she said aloud, holding her breath for a reply. When none came sigh escaped in a whoosh of air, he wasn't there. She loved him, but given how his mood had deteriorated over the weekend she was glad to have a place to unwind in peace.

Mel had agreed to meet her in Victoria Street in an hour for cheap and cheerful Vietnamese food and they could gossip about things other than the Travers family. Chloe dropped her bag next to the couch and flopped down on it. She scrolled through Facebook for a moment, but when she looked up it was time to go. Time always seemed to disappear on social media.

The street bustled with the evening crowd despite Mondays being quieter than other nights. Her favourite place was open every day, thankfully. Mel was already standing outside waiting as she approached.

'Gorgeous girl. What a fantastic idea to have dinner, I haven't seen you in an age.' Mel threw her arms out wide and pulled her into a hug. Chloe returned it a little awkwardly, having convinced herself Mel was upset after being sidelined in favour of Eddie for so many months. 'Let me look at you; you look different. Haircut?'

Her cheeks heated. 'No, I didn't even wash it.'

'Perhaps it's love curves.' Mel pinched her cheek, it hurt.

'Maybe.' She took a half step back. 'Let's eat, I'm starving.'

All the tables except one were packed with diners, the air carried the solid buzzing of their conversations and smelled of Vietnamese mint and frying. A small, slim waitress with long, straight black hair showed them to two seats sharing a table with another duo. It wasn't the sort of place you went for personal space.

Mel leaned forward over the table to speak, her voice raised over the hubbub of chatter. 'I know what I want; pork and prawn spring rolls and *pho*. You know what you want?'

'I'll have the same.'

'Good.' Mel folded the menu and tucked it under her elbows on the tabletop. 'You won't believe what Robbo and the band got up to the other night after a show...'

Chloe sat back and allowed Mel's voice to wash over her, the details of a night of debauchery unfolding morsel by morsel. If nothing else, Mel was a fantastic storyteller, always drip feeding the juicy bits so you were hooked from the start.

'I mean they wouldn't ever admit they were into partner swapping, but that's what I call it. They're all perverts.' She laughed, tossing her head back in triumph.

'You mean you're sleeping with the other guys in the band?' Chloe frowned, sure she had misunderstood.

'Only at parties. It's not cheating, coz Robbo is there too.'

'Oh.'

The waitress with the long ponytail came to take their orders, while Mel rattled on for both of them.

'And I'll have a three-colour drink,' Chloe added just as the waitress was about to turn away.

'You love those,' Mel said.

'It's traditional, I can't eat anywhere down here without one.'

'Anyway, back to the story, I would never tell any of them, but Robbo is much better than all of his bandmates, I really only do it to be a good sport.'

Chloe frowned and opened her mouth to say something.

'Not that I'm being coerced or anything, I mean, it's all a bit of fun, but I could take it or leave it, y'know?'

Chloe closed her mouth again as her friend listed an array of people and positions she'd engaged in. It wasn't that she was a prude, but Chloe had never understood her friend's level of comfort with sex.

The story morphed into other adventures Mel had had since they last caught up, a ball of guilt started to form in Chloe's stomach as she listened to how much had happened. Their food arrived all at once, as it always did.

Mel picked up a spring roll with some mint and wrapped it in a lettuce leaf before dipping it in sauce and taking a huge bite.

'I met Eddie's parents,' Chloe said into the silence as Mel chewed. Her jaw slowed as her friend registered her words.

'That escalated quickly.'

'After I told him about the baby, I took him to meet my mum, which was surprisingly fine, and I met his family yesterday.'

'Did you tell them about the baby?'

'His mum guessed.'

'Ah, and told them all?'

'I assume so.' Chloe took a sip of her drink, thick with *agar agar*, red beans and coconut milk.

'What are his family like?' Mel said after a lengthy pause.

'I thought my family was fucked up, but they have made passing judgment a competition sport. I've never seen Ed so shaken as when he was there with his brother and sister and their kids.'

'Do you want to keep the baby?'

'I—' Chloe hesitated. 'I thought I would, but I feel nauseous half the time.'

'Does he want the kid?'

'He said he does. Reckons he's gonna turn his life around and everything.'

Mel made a humming noise, her eyes on her food.

'If you have something to say…' Chloe said.

'You might be wondering, will I have the chance again? But remember you're not even thirty yet, there will be plenty of time to have kids if that's what you want down the track. Even with Eddie, when he has his life together.'

'I feel like I'm trying to convince myself to keep it. I've never really thought through actually having a termination.' Chloe prodded a noodle in her soup. 'It's a woman's right to choose and it's not a human being for a while yet but looking down the barrel, if you'll pardon the expression, I feel… I don't want to.'

'Having the right to do something has never made that thing easy. Or pleasant.'

They were silent for a moment, Chloe's belly was suddenly very full and she pushed away her food. 'Have you ever had one?'

Mel pinched her mouth in and inhaled slowly. 'I've had two.'

'What? You never said. How long have I known you and you never told me?'

'They were both before we met. One in high school and one in first year TAFE.' She looked at the table-top and her shoulders crumpled forward.

'What happened?'

'I was a dumb teenager is what happened. My high school boyfriend refused to wear condoms, my mum wouldn't let me go on the pill and sometimes he didn't pull out. It was a disaster waiting to happen.'

'And you stayed with him after the first pregnancy?'

'No way. I had to tell my parents, they had to sign the consent forms and stuff cos I wasn't sixteen yet.'

'Oh.' Chloe didn't want to say anything, Mel seemed on the verge of tears and she wondered if there were more to the story than she was letting on.

'The second time I was on the pill but still got pregnant, I didn't really see any long-term potential, and I never even told the father. I just had the procedure and didn't see him after that.'

It took all of her concentration for Chloe to keep her mouth closed, she wanted to gape in horror at her friend. Her best friend, whom she had thought she knew everything about, seemed like a completely different person. 'Did it hurt?'

'A bit, they put me out both times and then I woke up and I was sore for a while, there was some bleeding. But if you get onto it early, you can probably just have the tablet—I forget what it's called. In the first eight weeks or so you don't need the surgery these days.'

Mel seemed to know a lot about terminations, but after her confession Chloe doubted there would be anymore secret pregnancies her friend hadn't told her about.

'Are you okay, hun?' Chloe reached across the table and put her hand on Mel's.

'Yep,' she said, inhaling loudly and plastering a smile on her face. It wasn't the time to ask her any more about it.

After they'd eaten and Chloe was lying in her bed alone, she thought about what Mel had said. In all of her thinking over and over, she hadn't come up with any good answers as to why she should keep it, except for fear of missing out. Her job was good but she didn't earn enough to have a baby alone, Eddie was a fantastic boyfriend but he lived from one pay to the next and wouldn't be any good at supporting their family. Maybe in six months, or a year, things would be different, they could try again. If Eddie managed to keep a job, or if they'd been together longer, then she wouldn't have these reservations. And with his family in Shep and her mother completely unsuitable to babysit, they would struggle to get the help they needed.

As she drifted off to sleep, it occurred to Chloe she hadn't heard from Eddie since she left that morning. She wondered what he'd done that day, whether he was alright. He was so quiet and reserved on the drive home, it wasn't like him, and he'd been asleep when she left that morning.

I'll check in on him in the morning, she thought, and rolled over.

Fleur Blüm

Chapter 13

Sleep didn't come easily, despite being exhausted Chloe's brain churned over and over the decision she had to make and how Eddie would respond. He had said it was her decision but would he be hurt or angry? Could she risk telling him before the termination, in case he tried to convince her to keep it or should she do it and tell him later?

In the morning, she hadn't heard from Eddie, she picked up her phone to send him a good morning message. Chloe stared at the screen for a long time before putting it down without sending anything. If he wanted to contact her, he knew where she was. Perhaps he was angry with her for some reason. Best to give him a little space, she thought.

The day at work was average, Lee was behaving well for once and things were ticking along smoothly.

In the staff room at lunchtime, she checked her phone; her mother had called four times.

'Are you alright Mum?' Chloe said as soon as her mother answered the call.

'You need to come over right now,' Janine said, her voice breathy as though she had been running.

'What do you mean? Why?'

'It's hard to explain.'

'Try?' Chloe pinched the bridge of her nose.

'There's blood on the driveway and I need you to come clean it off before Gary gets home.'

Chloe took a moment to process what her mother had said. 'Why is there blood on the driveway?'

'I'll explain when you get here, just come now—please?'

'I can't just leave work, especially if you aren't honest with me.'

Janine sighed loudly down the phone. 'You know Terry? The roof plumber? I had him and his apprentice around to fix the gutters, they're almost completely rotten and Gary said we needed to do something about it before it got too cold and wet. Anyway, Terry climbs down to get something from the ute and his apprentice manages to fall off the ladder and land headfirst on the concrete of the driveway.'

'Jesus,' Chloe said. 'Did you call an ambulance?'

'Yes, Terry took care of all that. The ambos came and took the boy away and then Terry left to follow them to hospital, but my gutters are still not fixed and there's a huge stain—I can't bear to look at it, you know what I'm like with blood, and I need it gone before Gary gets home or else he'll be angry.'

'Why would he be angry?'

Janine made a tsking sound. 'Please. You never help me when I need you.'

Chloe's hand tightened around the phone where she held it to her ear. 'I'm happy to help you, but I'm at work. I finish at three and I'll come after that, okay?' It didn't matter that she'd been living out of home for eight years, her mother still knew exactly how to press her buttons. Her cheeks felt flushed.

'I suppose so. If Gary gets home and sees what a mess I've made of getting the gutters fixed I'll never hear the end of it.'

All of Janine's partners and boyfriends had vicious streaks and Gary was no different. Usually he was calm and pleasant, especially in company, but Chloe had seen how he changed when things went sideways.

At Christmas last year she had reached for the gravy jug at the same time as he had and, in the confusion, the jug had slipped off the table onto the floor and smashed, spraying hot, greasy gravy all over the carpet and up both Gary and Chloe's legs.

'Sorry, Gary,' Chloe had said automatically, even though it was as much his fault as hers.

'What are you gaping at? Fucking clean this shit up.' Gary's voice was quiet and threatening. Chloe had grabbed some paper serviettes from the table and tried to scoop the gravy into the remnants of the jug before carrying it to the kitchen. He seemed jolly enough, but when he followed her away from the dining table that day, Chloe had felt small and powerless. All the times through her childhood when a man had loomed over her in that kitchen started flashing before her eyes.

'Filthy fucking pig, look at my pants. Not to mention ruining the meal.' Gary's massive frame blocked most of the arched doorway into the kitchen. Chloe stood with her hands poised over the sink, frozen. 'Just gonna stand there are you? He started to unbuckle his belt and a fresh wave of terror have thumped her in the stomach; she couldn't inhale, couldn't move, and could only wait for the blow to fall. But it didn't come, he turned and stalked down the corridor to change.

By the time he came back to the table Chloe had cleaned up most of the spilled gravy and made more from the can of powder. Gary forced himself to smile and get through the meal, but since that day she had known the veneer of pleasantness could so easily slip.

'Before I get there, give the driveway a hose. It probably won't get it all off, but the longer it stays on the surface the harder it will be to shift.'

'Alright, but hurry over after work.' Janine hung up the phone before she could say anything else. There was no way her mother would do anything to that stain before Chloe arrived. Who played the parent and who played the child in their relationship was never entirely clear, Janine almost always abdicated her responsibility to someone else. Another reason Chloe had wanted to leave her mother's house had been to put some distance between them and break out of the co-dependent dynamic.

*   *   *

The hours after lunch dragged by and Chloe found herself becoming more and more agitated for the final bell to go. As she was collecting her bags from the staff room one of the senior teachers stopped her to have a chat. She felt herself bouncing on her toes, anxious to get away.

'Sorry, am I keeping you?' the teacher asked.

'I've got to help Mum with a bit of a... domestic emergency, but I'll see you tomorrow.' Chloe bustled out the door to her car as though wearing blinkers. It wouldn't do her nerves any good to get stuck in another pleasant, but undirected chat.

As soon as Chloe parked in front of her mother's house, she saw the damage to the guttering; a long section was bent and dangling from the eaves next to the driveway. Perhaps the apprentice had grabbed the gutter to try to stop himself falling and torn it down, she thought.

The concreted patch was the size of one car, Janine hadn't been much of a driver, and usually couldn't afford to keep a car, so her boyfriends over the years had laid claim to the space. Gary's shiny grey ute was not in the space, at least she didn't have to deal with him just yet.

'There you are,' Janine said, her voice fluttery and breathless.

'I told you I'd come straight from work.'

She harrumphed.

'Did you have a go at hosing it away before I got here?' Chloe asked, despite the dark red of the stain and the bone-dry concrete around it giving her the answer.

'No, I couldn't look at it.' She turned her head away to emphasise her disgust.

'Okay, I'm here now, so you don't need to worry anymore. I'll come in and get some cleaning stuff and you can relax.' Given how highly strung her mother usually was, Chloe was surprised she hadn't taken a Valium and passed out by this time. Perhaps she didn't have any left. Janine fled back into the house without another word.

'When does Gary get home?' Chloe asked, following her mother inside.

'Usually four-thirty or five.'

She had about fifteen minutes. Janine went straight to the couch and took up her usual spot on the decrepit brown velvet couch in front of the television. Chloe put down her bag and went to the laundry cupboard, filled the bucket with warm water and floor cleaner and took the hard bristled scrubbing brush her mother had for the bathroom out to the driveway.

First she hosed down the stain hoping to move as much as she could before getting too close to a stranger's blood. The hose had no nozzle, the garden was never a priority for Gary or Janine, so she put her thumb over the end in an attempt to get a hard spray.

Other than wetting down the stain, the hose did very little, so Chloe knelt on the concrete with the bucket and scrubbed at it. After five minutes she was hot and sweaty, and the knees of her trousers were soaked through. Good thing the pants were black, and not her best; she should have used a piece of cardboard or a cushion in a plastic shopping bag to kneel on to keep the cleaning products and bodily fluids away from her. *Too late now.*

Subsequent squirts with the hose showed she was making some progress but the stain it was still clearly visible. She sat back on her heels and took a breath just as the big silver ute pulled into the drive.

Time seemed to slow down and for an agonisingly long moment she thought Gary wasn't going to stop in time. In the end he pulled up short before sticking his head out the window to yell at her.

'What the fuck are you doing there? I could have killed you.'

'Mum needed me to clean up a stain.'

'Stain?'

'Yes.' She refused to provide more information to Gary than he strictly asked for. It had never done her any good to be overly friendly to her mother's boyfriends.

'Janine,' Gary bellowed, climbing out of the cabin of his ute. The front door of the house opened and her mother stood there, swaying a little. She must have taken a tablet once Chloe arrived.

'You're home.' Janine pasted a smile on her lips.

'What have you been doing? You useless hag, can't do anything right.'

'Come inside, the neighbours don't need to hear all that.'

Gary stormed past her into the house, Janine turned to her daughter with a pleading look in her eyes. Chloe's skin crawled, she wanted nothing more than to leave right then but it wouldn't do her mother any good to be alone with Gary, especially half-baked on tablets.

She poured the contents of the bucket over the concrete, watching the rusty brown water run into the grass. *Floor cleaner won't do that any favours,* it would probably die.

In spite of Gary's angry words outside the house was eerily quiet. Janine was back on the couch and she heard Gary stomping around in the bedroom and bathroom.

The empty bucket and scrubber went back into the laundry and Chloe took a seat on one of the dining chairs. It was a quarter to five, her mother would want her to stay for dinner, which meant she had to cook it.

The fridge was mostly bare, except for a half-empty milk bottle, margarine and a crust of tasty cheese that had started to dry and crack. The freezer held a packet of thin sausages from Coles and some frozen peas and corn, and some bacon. She found instant mashed potatoes in the cupboard and had to supress a shudder thinking of all the times she'd eaten it growing up.

After moving out, Chloe had made a deal with herself to always use real food in her cooking, none of the highly processed instant stuff her mother relied on, but when she came to visit and saw the state her mother was in, her ability to cook had never been strong anyway, she lamented how Janine had ended up without an appreciation for good food. Perhaps after all the cigarettes and booze and tablets her tastebuds were no good.

Janine remained on the couch, Gary eventually emerged from the back of the house, neither of them spoke as Chloe prepared the meal.

'Tea's ready,' she said, as she laid the plates on the dining table. Gary had the seat at the head, Chloe and her mother faced each other on either side. From his place the television was still clearly visible and Gary increased the volume. Eddie Maguire's voice drifted over the room, asking questions of contestants who seemed to know less and less as the program went on.

'Thanks for cookin',' Gary said, pushing his plate away. He'd had a larger serving but still got through it faster than either of the women. He moved back to the armchair, the same fabric and style as the couch, newer, although it probably smelled just as bad.

'I'm glad you came round.' Janine put a small forkful of mashed potato and peas into her mouth.

'That's okay. The stain needs a bit more elbow grease, I had to stop when Gary got home.'

Janine mumbled something inaudible. Probably bemoaning the work she would have to do in the next few days. It seemed unlikely Gary would let a stain like that hang around, but she doubted he would do anything about it himself.

Chloe and her mother cleared the table when they had finished, Gary continued to watch his program, occasionally shouting answers at the screen. In the kitchen, Chloe filled the sink to do the dishes, knowing her mother would want to leave them for later, a habit Chloe found particularly frustrating.

'Gary didn't want to pay for the gutters to be fixed, he said I don't have the money, but I stood up for myself, it's my house and if we don't fix the gutters the walls will start to rot with the overflowing water and what not.'

'Good for you, Mum.' Chloe was surprised her mother had showed so much spine, perhaps after all the men she'd had pushing her around she'd finally learned to push back when it was important. It was a shame it was after so many years of being subservient and abused.

'Janine, bring me a beer,' Gary bellowed from the chair in the next room. Despite her newfound confidence, her mother jumped to fulfil the request.

'Are you alright, hunny?' her mother said quietly, returning from the lounge.

'Yeah, why?'

'You were frowning. And you look, I don't know, pale?'

Chloe sighed. 'I'm okay.'

'Are you right to finish that off? Gary likes me to watch his programs with him.'

'Sure, Mum.' I can't see how being there on the couch in silence makes any difference to him, she thought, but wouldn't dare say it aloud. Despite disapproving of most of her mother's romantic relationships, Chloe no longer made any comments. She tried at fifteen, when her mother's boyfriend was particularly cruel and pervy. Janine had been devastated.

'You need a father figure,' she'd said. 'Not to mention we would really struggle without Kev's contributions. I'm surprised you're so ungrateful, I thought I'd raised you better than that.'

'I don't think it's ungrateful to expect not to be abused in my own home.'

'Don't be ridiculous. It's not abuse, if you did as you were told he wouldn't have to punish you.'

Chloe was so angry she couldn't speak. She considered running away, not for the first time, but she knew her mother had left home at sixteen and how that had worked out. So she bit back her words and stayed out of Kev's way. As soon as Chloe had finished high school she was out of the house straight into scummy share houses and low paying hospitality jobs to pay her way through TAFE.

'What happened to that boy you were seeing?' Janine asked when Chloe came back to the lounge.

'Eddie? I'm still seeing him.' *I think.*

'You bring him to see us one time and then nothing. If I didn't know any better, I'd think you were ashamed of me.'

'It was only the other week, Mum. I'm not ashamed—I don't know how serious we are yet, and I don't want to crowd you and Gary.'

Janine nodded, the ad break was over and silence was needed. She seemed to have accepted the reasoning, although Chloe certainly didn't want to expose Eddie to her dysfunctional mother and her awful boyfriend more than absolutely necessary.

Once the dishes were all done and drying in the rack, she collected her bag and headed out.

'Bye Mum, Gary.' She tiptoed to the front door and let herself out quietly. In the car, she checked her phone, still nothing from Eddie. Whatever had happened, whatever she'd done, it seemed she was getting the silent treatment.

Spent the evening with mum, what fun.
Had to come clean her driveway. Long
story, I'll tell you when I see you. X

The offer of a tantalising story, especially one in which Eddie could position himself as being superior, should be enough to break a silence. She hoped he would reply as she drove home and she could write it off as a peculiarity of boys not needing to be in contact as much. Her belly folded over itself in a ripple of nausea.

I have to do something about that too, she thought. It wasn't the right time, Eddie would make a good dad in a couple of years, maybe once they were married and had a chance to plan for a baby. As she drove home in the dull grey black night rain started to fall; sudden heavy droplets like in the tropics. She slowed and put the wipers on the highest speed. Ten minutes' later the rain had stopped but Chloe didn't feel any clearer about the pickle she'd found herself in.

Chapter 14

Every day for the rest of the week Chloe sent Eddie a good morning text and another to say goodnight. He never replied.

One day they were meeting his parents, taking things to the next level, and she had considered having a child with him. Now he wouldn't return her texts and hadn't spoken to her in almost a week. Her time was running out to have the medical abortion and on Friday evening after work she made an appointment with her GP for the next morning.

Over the week Chloe had spent a time researching ways to terminate a pregnancy and had decided to go for the combination of pills, rather than any surgery. The pill was less invasive but needed to be administered within the first eight weeks. If she was going to use it, she would need to do so in the next few days.

Chloe's usual doctor was in Richmond, not far from her apartment. Growing up she had seen the same doctor as her mother in Brunswick but a couple of things Chloe had told the doctor got back to Janine and she didn't trust them. When she moved out, she found a new clinic. Surely it was against the medical code of ethics to tell her mother things about her appointments without permission, even if she had been under age for some of them, but the doctor had been an older man, whose round cheeks were always red and whose shirts seemed to strain a little more at the buttons each time she saw him.

At the new clinic she was always seen by young, attractive doctors. The reception staff and nurses were all slim and stylish. Chloe didn't believe they had hired attractive people on purpose, but the fact still made it a little more awkward, sitting on the hard, dark grey, plastic bucket chair, joined to a row of similar chairs as you might see in an airport.

'Chloe Barrett?' a tall, brown-haired young man called out.

'Yes,' she replied as she stood and followed him down the corridor. He was thin, and from the back reminded her a little of Eddie. Her breath caught in her throat and she covered it with a little cough.

'I'm Patrick. I don't think I've seen you in here before. Have you got a lurgy?' he said, indicating she take a seat in the bright, clean office down the hall from the waiting area. He closed the door before she replied.

'No, that was just a little tickle.' Chloe looked at her clasped hands.

'What can we do for you today then?'

She looked up and was surprised again how handsome the doctor was; swarthy skin that was smooth and glowing, an artistic amount of stubble, expensive-looking shirt, one button undone, and pale grey trousers.

'I need a uh...'

He leaned forward, as though waiting eagerly to hear her reason for being there.

'I need a termination. I had hoped to get the tablet.'

'I see.' The doctor leaned back. 'You're sure you're pregnant?'

'Yes, I did several home tests, all positive. And my period is three weeks late.'

'You'd say you're about seven weeks along then?'

'Yes, though I can't be entirely sure.'

'I see.' He looked over her records on the computer screen.

'I'm on birth control, I mean, I was. I stopped taking them when I found out I was pregnant, just in case.'

'They're never one hundred percent effective and probably wouldn't have done the embryo any harm had you continued, although as you no doubt suspected, it would be rather pointless.' He typed in a few things without looking at her.

'I need to make sure you're definitely pregnant so we will have to have an ultrasound and some blood work done. Once that's all done, you will be given two tablets; one to take at the clinic and one later at home.'

He described what the process would feel like. 'The medication is designed to induce a miscarriage which can be quite painful and distressing. Most people I've known who have used this method describe it as moderately worse than a very heavy period.'

Chloe's mouth was dry, and she found herself swallowing compulsively.

'You'll probably feel unwell for a day or two. Some people take a couple of days off work, but each person is different.' He smiled, but it didn't reassure her.

'Thank you.'

She walked out to the reception area to pay with the referral for an ultrasound at the hospital in the city in her handbag. It felt clandestine, a shameful secret she wouldn't want anyone to know about. As much as she believed it shouldn't be a big deal for a woman to make the choice about her own body, a voice in her head told her she should have been more careful. It sounded like her great-grandmother's voice; a nasty vindictive woman who always made it sound like she was doing the best thing for you.

Once she was back at home, it was nearly dinnertime. Chloe checked her phone just in case Eddie had decided to respond to her but the screen was tauntingly blank. Her ultrasound was scheduled for after school on Monday. Though the doctor had suggested she take a couple of days off work, Chloe didn't have many sick days and Lee would be distressed if she had more than a day off work. If it all went to plan she'd take Tuesday as a sick day and go back to school on Wednesday.

Her hands were sweaty and the left-over lasagne she'd eaten sat in her belly like a lump. She lay on the couch feeling sad but no tears would come. She watched TV all evening without taking much in, none of her usual tasks seemed important. It had been a while since she'd felt so low, but there was no other decision she could make, without the baby's father she had no hope of giving the child a better life than she'd had. A promise she'd made to herself as soon as she was old enough to think about kids was to be a better mother than Janine.

*   *   *

Chloe hated hospitals, the smell made her skin crawl and the all the shiny white surfaces made it feel like everything was too bright, too loud. A nurse strode past quickly, his shoes squeaking a little on the linoleum floor; the sound was like nails on a blackboard.

She had walked up to the desk, a young woman sat behind it, her fingernails long and vividly orange. Chloe couldn't imagine the nails were particularly practical for a person whose job involved a lot of typing.

'I'm here for an ultrasound,' she had said, her voice swallowed up by her nervousness.

'Sorry?' the receptionist asked.

Chloe cleared her throat and tried again. 'I'm here for an ultrasound.'

'Name and date of birth?' she said, Chloe gave them. 'You can take a seat over there. Someone will be with you shortly.'

The receptionist was not interested in anything else. Chloe sighed out a breath in relief; one more person who didn't need to know what she was there for. Working in the medical profession the receptionist had probably seen all sorts and nothing surprised her. The waiting area had banks of chairs stuck together, the grey buckets like the doctors' surgery, and a big TV on one wall. The sound was turned right down but the closed captions were turned on. She sat facing the TV and watched the mind-numbing afternoon game show hosts as she tried not to think about the small spark of life inside her that would soon be gone. Her phone was in her hand, she flipped it

over and over nervously for about ten minutes before
tapping in the code to open it.

> *Hey, I haven't heard from you for a while.
> I'm not sure what's going on. I hope you're
> going okay.*

She didn't expect Eddie to reply, but it seemed like
the right thing to do, reaching out one last time in case he
hadn't completely written her off. Part of her didn't want
a reply, if someone was so unreliable they would
disappear for a week at a time without a word she didn't
want them in her life but everything reminded her of
him.

Yesterday, she'd done a load of washing and the
towel he'd last used smell like him. If she saw a tall, thin
man from behind she would think of him. Each room in
her tiny apartment was full of memories they had created
together. Some of them were sad, like the time she'd
washed dishes after they'd had an argument, but most of
them were happy, hours spent cuddling on the couch, and
of course every time she caught his scent on the sheets,
she became aroused, so she changed them too.

'Chloe Barrett?' A tall, plump, blonde woman in
green scrubs called her name.

'That's me,' she said standing.

'Come this way.' The woman turned and started
walking away down the white corridor without looking
to see whether Chloe was following.

After several turns around corners to corridors that
all looked the same, the woman turned into a

consultation room. It was small, but it only had to fit the two of them.

'I'm Jane, I'll be your ultrasound technician today. Hop up on the bed there,' she didn't wait for Chloe to comply, but kept talking. 'I see here we're doing check for pregnancy and that you're after a medical termination once we've confirmed your condition. Is that right?'

'Yes.'

'Good. Lie back, that's right. I'll need to get you to pull up your top, and open your trousers so I can reach your tummy. I'll be using a gel to help make sure the picture is good quality, it will be cold, sorry about that.' The technician continued to chatter away, describing what she was doing as she set everything up and started to push the ultrasound wand across Chloe's lower abdomen.

The gel was cold, and slimy. The smell reminded her of lubricant she had occasionally used and she had a momentary, inappropriate twinge between her legs. The technician pressed the ultrasound wand firmly across her skin, making Chloe feel a bit sick, although she seemed to feel a bit sick a lot of the time these days.

'Here we are. I've found the embryo.' She pointed to the screen, and then pressed a couple of buttons on the machine. 'They're only very small at this stage, but you can sort of see a head and some little stumpy limbs. You're definitely pregnant.'

Though she had known for a while she was pregnant, seeing the tiny bean inside her made it much more real than it had been five minutes ago. And now

she was going to get rid of it. She swallowed, the
decision was made, it couldn't be any other way,
especially with Eddie being out of touch completely.

'We're all done. I've taken a still image for the file.
You can use one of these tissues to clean up your tummy,
and redress, and I'll go get one of the doctors to sign off
and come back with your two tablets. Did the GP go over
when to have them?'

Chloe nodded and started trying to mop up the stick
gel with the tissues. The technician walked out of the
room and closed the door behind her. In the cold empty
room, Chloe felt the urge to cry rising in her throat—
tight and hot, prickling upwards from her collarbone to
the back of her mouth.

The tissues made almost no difference to the mess
on her skin, and in the end Chloe just fastened her jeans
over the gloop, telling herself she only had to get home
from the hospital and then could take a bath and change
her outfit.

'Here we go. Have this one now.' The blonde
woman came bustling back through the door, breaking
Chloe's self-pitying reverie. 'The other one is for
tomorrow. I've also brought you some pamphlets, make
sure you have a read of them. The process can be quite
messy and tiring, so if you can take tomorrow and maybe
the next day off work. If you need someone to talk to,
there is a number on the back of this one you can call for
referral to a psychologist or whatever.'

'Thanks,' Chloe said, taking the tablet and a sip of
water from the cup Jane offered her.

'Have you got any questions?'

'How long does it take to, you know, work?'

'Depends, it usually isn't until after you have the second pill at home tomorrow but it might start today. It's all in the pamphlets.'

'Right.' Chloe felt the technician was trying to move her on and she didn't want to be a burden. 'Thank you for your time.'

'No worries, have a good day.'

Chloe collected her handbag and wandered back out through the waiting area to her car. She didn't feel entirely right but couldn't decide if that was a result of the tablet or psychosomatic.

*   *   *

The rest of the late afternoon and evening slid away in a blur of television and couch time. She had wanted to soak in a hot bath for an hour or so but the pamphlets from the hospital said she couldn't until the bleeding had stopped. She felt queasy, hungry and tired.

In the morning she woke up to strong abdominal cramps and found her bleeding had started. She swallowed the second tablet with the water beside her bed, along with a couple of paracetamols, before cocooning herself in the blankets again.

A cool hand worked its way around her waist, she hadn't realised she had fallen asleep but it was nice to wake up to being spooned. She pulled Eddie's hand around her and snuggled back into him. Then she realised how long it had been, she hadn't heard from him and hadn't let him in, immediately her back stiffened.

'You're awake finally,' he said, his words hot with breath across her ear.

'Yes,' she managed to say. Trying to swallow, her mouth had become a parched landscape, she pieced together what had happened. He didn't give back my key, she thought.

'I missed you, baby.'

'What are you doing here, Eddie?' she asked, keeping her voice soft despite the adrenaline rushing through her veins. She tried to breathe normally waiting what seemed like an eternity for him to reply.

'I'm sorry I didn't let you know I was coming over. I've been doing a lot of thinking and trying to get myself sorted out. Johnno offered me full-time work with him when we were on the way back from Mum and Dad's and I was wrecked at the end of the day and couldn't come to visit you while I got used to that.'

'That's great news about the job.' Chloe moved away from him, sliding across the bed to turn to look at Eddie. His face was pink with fading sunburn, no doubt from being out in the sun a little too much, but his eyes had a wild, darting quality to them.

'I'm ready to be a dad now. I've worked it all out.'

Chloe opened her mouth to say something but Eddie cut her off.

'Don't say anything, babe, I know I shouldn't have disappeared after we went to see Mum and Dad,' he was talking fast, almost panting, 'but seeing my little bro and sister with their perfect little families kind of sent me into a bit of a spiral so I texted Johnno from the car to ask if he'd take me on full-time. He always said if I wanted it, he'd give me a go at being regular with him.'

'Babe—'

'I scrounged a bit of extra speed from Max's workmate at the bar to make sure I got up on time in the mornings. Johnno was a little sceptical I could hack it but I busted my butt to prove to him I was genuine. He was so surprised when I told him you were pregnant, but I think it made sense to him that I wanted to be a responsible dad.'

As he drew breath a sharp pain rippled through Chloe's lower belly, she winced and blew her breathe out through clenched teeth.

'You okay, babe?' Eddie frowned.

'I'm alright.'

'And the baby? There's not something wrong with it is there?'

'Eddie, don't get upset.'

'What would I get upset about? The mother of my kid is in some sort of pain, of course I'm upset.'

Chloe tried to push him away from her, to pull herself out of bed so they could talk properly, but she was exhausted and the cramps were worsening by the minute. Her legs were tangled in the bedding and she ended up falling over the edge onto her bottom. Eddie had got up and walked around to where she was.

'Chloe.' His voice was cold, and his eyes were dancing with erratic anger.

'What did you think was going to happen? I don't hear from you for a week and I'm supposed to know by magic that you're off setting up your life for this baby? For all I know you're dead in a ditch, or sleeping with every woman who'll have you.' She started to cry, hot, thick tears ran down her face, making the image of him dance in front of her eyes.

'What the fuck did you do?'

'I had a termination. I told you I wasn't sure I wanted to keep it, and then you disappeared. I did what I had to do.'

'You killed my baby.'

'Your baby? What role, exactly, were you playing in its life? Drug-addled garden labourer for the moment until you crash out and can't wake up for two days and Johnno fires you? Or maybe you get so baked you lose your mind? That seems like a completely responsible thing to do as a first-time father.'

Eddie's fists were clenched by his side, and he was standing over her, his breath ragged, jaw rippling as he ground his teeth together.

'You had no right.' The words were so soft she wasn't sure he had said them. She stayed perfectly still, worried any move she made would set him off, she hardly breathed. They hung like that for a long moment before Eddie reached his arm out, like a snake, and grabbed her hair. He pulled her up, holding her face close to his.

'You had no fucking right,' he said again, before he brought the fist of his other hand up to smash across her cheek. The blow rattled her jaw and brain, like all the wires in her mind were suddenly jumbled and she couldn't understand what was happening. The ground leapt up to meet her, her elbow and hip slamming into the carpeted floor of her bedroom.

For a while all she could comprehend was pain and noise. He was shouting, screaming at her, but she couldn't make out the words. She curled into a ball to try to protect herself from the kicks and punches he was laying on her, a frenzy of pain, then something wet fell onto her face and a short time later silence.

Chloe stayed in the ball for a long time, her body screamed with discomfort at being scrunched as she was, but if she uncurled parts of her body Eddie had punished would twinge and shoot through her with agony.

In the end cold made her unfurl herself. She blinked open her eyes, which were swollen and blurry from her tears and Eddie's blows. Her cheek was slimy where he'd spat on her as he left, her lip was split and bleeding, but her other injuries didn't seem too bad yet. Chloe crawled into a seated position on the floor trying to work out what had happened.

Through the doorway she could just see the front door of her apartment was swung open into the living room. *Bastard hadn't even closed it after he left.* It needed to be closed, but the distance from her bedroom to the door seemed more difficult than running a marathon. She leaned forward onto her hands and knees and crawled to the door, halfway across the living room she stopped to retch a few times but thankfully nothing came up. When the door was closed, she took a moment to lean against it to get her breath back. Breathing hurt, moving hurt, and her groin felt wet and cold, she'd probably bled through the pad she was wearing.

*   *   *

Pain in her abdomen woke her in dark, sharp, shooting pain when she inhaled deeply.

That's not from the termination, she thought. Lying in the bed trying to ignore the sensations in her ribcage didn't work at all, she lay flat on her back, taking shallow gasps as she avoided deep breaths.

She must have fallen asleep as she was woken again by light coming through the curtains and a particularly stabby pain in her left side. The dull ache in her lower belly was still there, but it paled in comparison. Chloe ran her right hand over her left side, it was tender over the spot that hurt when she breathed.

Gingerly pushing herself into a sitting position, she swung her legs over the edge of the bed before shuffling to the bathroom. What she thought was sleepiness blurring her vision turned out to be significant swelling around her eyes. The upper and lower lid of her left eye was purple and puffy, the other eye seemed a little swollen and only a little pink. She didn't remember how many times Eddie had hit her, nor exactly where he'd made contact, only snatches of pain and confusion.

Her breath hitched again and she pulled up her shirt to look at her ribs. The same purpley-red as her eye spread in a lumpy circle across her side. The imprint of the fabric of her shirt was visible in the middle forming a rough line; a vague memory of Eddie kicking her as she cowered on the floor floated into her mind.

There was no way she could go into work looking like that and given how much it hurt to inhale she would have to go to the doctor. No doubt they would have questions and might get the police involved. Her throat tightened as she pushed down the urge to cry, it wasn't supposed to be this hard.

She shuffled back to the bedroom, swallowed two paracetamol and lay back. It was almost nine in the morning, so she called her doctor. Their first appointment available was at one o'clock, she took another couple of sips of water and tried to rest.

*   *   *

Getting down the stairs, into the car and to the doctor's office had taken her almost half an hour. She was in too much pain to want to eat anything but her stomach growled a little as she waited in doctors' surgery. It was the second time she'd been there in under a week, something that had never happened in her whole twenty-five years of life. The receptionist had eyed her bruises but didn't comment, perhaps they were trained to be un-obtrusive.

Patrick, the GP who had seen her last time, called her name and she looked up to see his bright, handsome smile slip a little as he caught sight of her.

'What's happened?' he asked, waiting until they were both in the consulting suite and the door was closed.

Chloe inhaled and winced in pain. 'Hmnn. Sorry.' She took another breath, smaller this time. 'My ex. He uh… well. I hadn't told him about the abortion.'

'He hit you?'

She nodded.

'Jesus. I probably shouldn't say that. Is that why you came in today? To look at the bruises?'

'This happened yesterday. I didn't think it was too bad but I think there's something wrong with my ribs. To be honest, I don't feel so crash hot. I don't want to get him in trouble or anything but I'll need a medical certificate for work.'

'You should go to hospital, have an X-ray if you're having pain when you breathe. If the ribs are bruised or cracked there isn't a lot that we can do, but if there is a full break we might need to make sure you aren't at risk of further complications.' He sighed. 'I can't report this to police on your behalf, you're over eighteen, but I would strongly recommend you make a report. This sort of behaviour is almost never the end of it. But let's have a look at those ribs, and the rest of you probably while we're at it. I don't want to miss anything, especially if you are going to ignore my advice to go to a hospital.'

Chloe was stood slowly, her limbs felt as though they were made from lead and wouldn't respond to her instructions. Patrick drew the curtain around the little examination table so she could undress, but as she tried to pull her T-shirt over her head she cried out in pain.

'I might need a hand, sorry,' she said.

Patrick pulled back the curtain, his face taut with worry, but thankfully he said nothing more. Once undressed to her knickers, she hadn't bothered to put on a bra, Patrick gently palpated her skin, narrating softly what he was doing to ensure she understood.

'It seems the ribs and the eye are the main injuries, although you have a few bruises forming on the upper arms… did he grab you?'

'Probably. It's a bit of a blur.'

'And you got the termination?' Patrick helped her put her shirt and pants back on before moving back to the chairs.

'I hadn't heard from him. I had assumed he was out of the picture and I didn't want to have the baby alone, but he let himself into the apartment yesterday, he still had a key, and wasn't pleased when he found out.'

He nodded, pausing to think through his next statement. 'It might not be my place to tell you what to do in this situation, but I think it's clear he is not taking your health or safety into consideration. If I were you, I would have the locks changed and speak to the police as soon as possible.'

'Thank you for the concern, but I was really here to make sure I'm not bleeding internally and get a certificate for the rest of the week.'

'As far as my examination goes, and I stress that an X-ray would be the best way to know for sure, it doesn't appear you've broken any ribs. They may be bruised or cracked. You can take Ibuprofen and paracetamol as needed, apply ice, and rest. Otherwise, take at least ten deep breaths each hour, I know it hurts, but you risk all sorts of complications if you don't. It should be healed in three to six weeks.'

Chloe blinked slowly, it hadn't occurred to her it would take so long to recover. 'And the bruising?'

'That might take up to two weeks to fully clear.'

'I can't take that long off work. I'll have to tell them something.'

'They can't legally ask you why you're taking sick leave,' Patrick said, 'however, if you say nothing, people are likely to make up their own reasons why you have bruises, so it might be better to say something.'

Chloe chewed her bottom lip. She'd never had to deal with this before. Eddie had been sulky, even angry sometimes but he'd never hit her before. There were a few slammed doors after she had tried to put her foot down about a couple of things. Maybe she should have seen the red flags sooner, surely people didn't just become violent like that out of the blue. The doctor cleared his throat and she was reminded that she had glazed over and hadn't said anything for a while.

'Sorry. I'll have to think about it.'

'Come back if anything else happens, or your symptoms get worse. I'm also just going to grab a few pamphlets for you.' He sighed before standing to leave his office.

Chloe had known it would be coming. He had a duty of care and it certainly seemed she had found herself in an abusive relationship. The only thing that worried her now was whether Eddie had gotten the anger out of his system and would fade into the shadows, never to bother her again, or if this was somehow the beginning of a different, horrible phase of her life. He'd done some work on himself, perhaps pushed himself harder than he ever had, conformed to the societal norms against his nature, to prove to her he was a good father, and she had killed his baby.

Of course he'd gone about it completely the wrong way, but when had Eddie ever been one to think conventionally? She shook her head and was rewarded with a dull throbbing pain. Changing the locks was the first step. If there were any further incidents, then she would go to the police.

Having made her decision Chloe felt flat, as though something inside her was resigned to the idea Eddie was bad news. A man she still loved, a man she'd considered having a child with, who now had to be considered dangerous. Growing up with her mother's terrible choices in men, Chloe had believed she knew better. Thought she would be able to see the warning signs, but she was just like Janine; blinded by love, or lust, or poor judgement.

Patrick walked back in and swung the door closed with a soft swish against the dull grey-blue carpet. 'Have a read of these. There are services available to help people in your … situation.'

'My situation.' She laughed, a hollow, bitter sound. 'Thank you for your help.'

Patrick handed her the medical certificate and a slip of paper to take to reception before she walked slowly back to the front of the clinic. She cringed internally to see the sadness in his eyes, that puppy-dog expression of pity she had hoped never to see again after she left her mother's house.

The certificate gave her the rest of the week off work, the way she felt after driving home and dragging herself up the three flights of stairs to her apartment she was tempted to take it all. Lee would have to cope without her, it was difficult for him but he wouldn't always be able to avoid frustrations and disappointments. Hopefully she could make it a teachable moment, though she hated the phrase. She had called in sick that morning and she called again from the couch to take the next two days off work. If she felt better, she would go in on Friday, but if not, or if the bruising and swelling were too obvious, she would have to stay home.

*　　　*　　　*

Chloe wasn't sure how time slipped by but soon it was dark and she was cold and hungry on the couch. She had used up all her extra energy to get to the GP for her certificate, and had to choose between ordering delivery from a local place or having instant noodles or porridge for dinner. After the crappy week she'd had she felt she deserved a treat and ordered her favourite foods from the Thai restaurant on Bridge Road. She ordered *pad thai,* a green curry, rice, spring rolls and *roti*. She wouldn't eat much today but it would save having to make decisions for the next few meals.

Pulling her doona off the bed, she curled into a ball on the couch, no matter what position she was in, she couldn't get comfortable, everything hurt. Despite that fact she'd dozed off and was woken by a loud knocking.

The Mother's Fault

'Hello?' A muffled voice came through the door. It must be her food.

'I'm coming.' Unwrapping herself from the cocoon on the couch and making her way the four or five steps to the front door involved a number of muttered swear words. She paused to take a breath and put a smile on her face before swinging it open.

Standing in front of her was a shaggy blond-headed man, skinny and pale. 'Max?' she said. He didn't look himself, hunched over and somehow shrunken. Her hand tightened on the doorknob.

'You look terrible,' he said.

'So do you. Do you, uh, want to come in?' Chloe couldn't help briefly looking over his shoulder for Eddie.

'I came on my own.'

'Right.' She shivered in the cool wind blowing in through the open front door. 'Come in.' Normally she would have reached out, taken Max's hand and dragged him inside. He seemed to have lost all of his spark and sometimes he needed firm instructions but her arm wouldn't obey, it just dangled beside her, useless.

Max's eyes flickered up from where he was staring at the carpet and he shuffled forward.

'Sit.' She waved at the kitchen chairs; the couch was covered in her blanket cocoon and despite it being rude not to offer her guest the comfortable spot to sit, she couldn't handle the hard planes of the wooden chairs. Max probably wouldn't notice anyway, he seemed to be entirely caught up in whatever was going on in his brain. Chloe rewrapped herself in the doona and waited for

Max to be ready to say what he had come to say. Sometimes at school she had to wait quite a long time for Lee, or her other students, to be ready to tell her something. He had clearly come with a specific purpose in mind, his hands were sitting in his lap fidgeting over each other in anxiety, maybe just as a habit he'd developed to cope with overwhelming emotions. A lot of neurodiverse people, and children in particular, used such repetitive behaviours to cope.

After a while of sitting without input from her, Max cleared his throat. She re-opened her eyes and looked at him.

'I have to tell you something,' he said.

'Okay.'

'Eddie told me what—had happened between you.' His eyes darted to the door, then the floor, before coming back to her face. 'Told me he'd done that.'

'What did you do when he said that?'

'I was really angry; I couldn't believe he would hit you. He's hit me a couple of times, but usually only when he gets a bit drunk, or high, or thinks we're playing. I've never known him to hit a woman in anger.'

Interesting he didn't say hit anyone in anger, she thought, nodding to encourage Max to continue.

'I didn't say anything. He said something like "I can't believe you're taking her side, fuck this," and stormed out of the house.'

'Right.' If Eddie had gone straight from her place back home, this had all happened over a day ago. 'Then what happened?'

'I went to work; I was nearly late because I was so upset. I tried not to think about how drunk he was.'

'When was this?'

'Tuesday.' His fingers danced over each other as he tried to formulate the next phrase. 'I got home later, like, two in the morning, no sign of Eddie. I got woken up this morning by coppers.'

'What?' Chloe said, blurting the word out before she could calm herself enough not to startle poor Max. He flinched back in the chair, his eyes squeezing shut briefly and his fingernails digging deeply into the palms of his hands. 'I'm sorry, I wasn't expecting police.'

'I wasn't either.' His mouth pulled up on one side, as though he was trying to bring some levity. 'They found Eddie.'

'What do you mean they found him?'

'His body.'

The silence stretched out between them, Chloe's mouth worked up and down, but she couldn't make any sound come out. No wonder Max looked like he did.

'What do you mean?' She needed him to say the words aloud.

'The coppers came to the house; told me he'd died. They found his address on his license but no next of kin. They said they'll tell the family but I'll have to speak to them about his, you know, stuff. I can't do it … Can you?'

'Me? No, I don't think that's right.' She sighed, her ribs twinged as she took a deep inhale and she was reminded of the blows, the last interaction she'd had with

Eddie. 'I only met his family one time. And then Eddie didn't speak to me until this, and now... how did he die?'

'Jumped in front of a train.'

'Fuck.' Her head was spinning and the image of Eddie's thin, lanky body walking out in front of the train and the sickening splat and crunch of metal hitting flesh. 'Poor Eddie. Poor driver.'

'I would never put someone through that to kill myself. Selfish.'

They sat in silence, Chloe's mind clouded with a swirling, confusing mist of emotions. On one hand, relieved she wouldn't wake up to find him in her bed, or waiting at the bottom of her stairs, but on the other hand, it was over. Really over. She loved Eddie, had thought they would have a happily ever after, with kids and a white picket fence, even if the first pregnancy was too soon. She'd always had faith that with the right love and guidance he would be able to get himself together and make a life, a real, decent, multifaceted life his parents could be proud of. Not that they would be, given their condescension the weekend she was up there. No wonder Eddie had problems with authority.

'He never said anything to you?' she asked.

Max looked up, as though coming back to the room from a sort of trance. 'I ... didn't think he was serious. He'd said a bunch of times if things didn't work out, he'd top himself, but I always thought he was being dramatic, you know how much he likes to talk shit.'

Chloe nodded. Eddie had never said anything like that in her presence. 'If what things didn't work out?'

281

'Lots of things, anything really. We've been friends for years, for a while when he didn't have money for rent, he'd say he may as well die. Of course I paid for him those times. Lately it was mainly when he was worried about you, he really wanted to have a life with you, it's why he introduced you to his family even though he said he felt sick how nervous it made him.'

'Why was he nervous?'

'You saw what they're like. Nothing is ever good enough, not to mention he's supersensitive. Was supersensitive.' Max's eyes glazed over and he was silent again.

'His parents don't know?' she asked.

'The cops said they'd send someone.'

She didn't want to talk to them; she was his ex-girlfriend, the woman who had killed his baby, according to him. Probably the thing that pushed him over the edge. She didn't want to organise his funeral and would have to turn up there with the remnants of the black eye and bruised ribs that he'd given her. It would have to be her to make the call; Max was retreating back into himself as she watched.

'I don't have their number.'

He pulled out his phone and scrolled trough for a few minutes. Handing her the phone, silently, she wasn't sure if she was supposed to use it to call or copy the number into her own phone. Part of her wanted to make sure Virginia couldn't get in touch with her, but it would mean leaving Max to field her calls and despite her resentment at being dumped with the notification, she couldn't set him up like that.

She dialled the number on her handset before handing Max's phone back. It rang and rang in her ear and she was certain it would go to voicemail.

'Hello?' a breathless voice said down the line.

'Mrs Travers?'

'Yes, of course, who is this?'

'It's Chloe Barrett. I came up to see you with your son, Eddie.' Her voice wobbled a little as she said his name.

A pause of a few moments hung between them. 'What do you want? I'm in the middle of something.'

'I'm calling about Eddie's things.'

'What things? What are you talking about?'

'Have the police been to see you yet?'

There was a strangled sound down the line. 'Yes.'

'Max asked me to contact you about his belongings, rent, his body.'

'I can't deal with all of that; I'm needed up here, I can't come down to Melbourne on a whim.'

Rage started to bubble in her belly.

'A whim? Your eldest child has died and you won't even come down to sort out his things?'

'What could he possibly have that's of any value?'

'A funeral needs to be arranged. His body is—' She looked desperately to Max for more information, she should have had this when she called, no doubt the police had his body.

'With the coroner,' Max said.

'With the coroner,' she repeated into the phone.

'The coroner? Can't they deal with it? I don't want the stain of suicide on me.' Virginia's voice was rising in pitch as the call went on.

'My God, is that your first thought? Nothing about how my firstborn child was in so much pain he had to end it all, straight to how will this make me look? You're a monster. He was never good enough for you and now even in death you're criticising.' Chloe didn't want to hear anymore and hung up without saying goodbye. If Virginia called back, she would have a long think about whether to answer. She stared at the phone; her fingers wrapped around it so hard the tips were white. Carefully she put it back on the coffee table and forced herself to take a deep breath, wincing in pain as her ribs protested.

'I'm not sure that helped anything.' Chloe said after a long pause.

'Thanks anyway. Maybe she'll come around.' Max's voice was so quiet, a whisper in the silence pressing on her in the apartment. Chloe was exhausted. So many things had happened in the last couple of days even without the difficulties her body had been through. Max seemed to have retreated into himself, she had no idea how long he might sit there, a melancholy, faraway look on his face, but she settled herself down on the couch, adjusting her cocoon and closed her eyes. There weren't many people she would sleep in front of but Max wouldn't hurt her, especially not in his current state.

*   *   *

She woke a little while later to answer the door to the delivery driver. Her body was stiff from the curled-up position she'd fallen asleep in and despite the delicious smell she couldn't eat. Max was still sitting on the chair by the table, apparently, he hadn't moved even when there was a knock at the door.

'You okay?' she asked, reseating herself, trying not to wince in pain with each movement.

'I … think so.'

'Do you have work today?'

'Shit.' Max's eyes widened slightly.

'You're not in any fit state to go in. You need me to call them for you?'

'No—actually, would you mind? I'm not really coping with things.'

She nodded, he found the number and handed her the phone. 'What's the manager's name?'

'Pippa.'

'Max, tell me you're on the way in.' The young woman's voice sounded breathless and hurried down the phone.

'Um, my name is Chloe, I'm calling on behalf of Max.'

'What? Why?'

'I'm afraid we've had some very bad news today, and he's not well enough to come into work.'

'Fuck, I don't need this today. What kind of bad news could possibly put him off work? He loves work.'

'His housemate was found dead this morning.'

Pippa made a choking sound, then gave a short laugh. 'Good one, I was worried for a second there.'

'I'm not joking. I don't know how long Max might need off but perhaps you'd better find someone else for a couple of days. There are … arrangements that will need to be made.'

'Shit, you're serious. Okay.' Pippa mumbled something to herself. 'Thanks for letting me know. Send him my condolences and we hope to see him in a few days.'

Chloe handed the phone back. 'She thought it was a joke. Some prank though.'

Max nodded and put the mobile into his pocket mechanically.

'You're going to stay here for a bit, I have this Thai food but I'm not sure I can eat it?'

'I'm not hungry.'

'Have you eaten today?' she asked.

'No.'

'Right, well, you need to eat, even if you're not hungry. I probably should too.'

Chloe put the TV on and they ate in silence. Max seemed to chew his meal mechanically, barely paying attention to anything outside his mind, while she forced herself to eat something. At least once she started it was tasty.

As she put the remains of the meal in the fridge, she realised she felt surprisingly normal. Her body hurt, she felt anxious and exhausted but it didn't seem to be any more so than before she heard Eddie was dead. Perhaps she was too numb to feel anymore, perhaps she'd hit rock bottom, or it would hit her later. On the other hand it could be that she'd mourned Eddie's loss in the time he hadn't spoken to her, having been worried he'd meet a terrible end, having it confirmed was oddly calming.

'I'm going to bed. I'll get you some blankets and a pillow, you can sleep on the couch if you don't want to go back to your place.'

'Thank you. I don't think I want to be there on my own right now.'

She nodded, found the spare bedding and retreated into her room. Usually, she would sleep with the bedroom door open, but tonight she closed it. The bathroom was only accessible through her bedroom, but she didn't want to think about that. Things would be better in the morning, that's what she had always told herself, and it was a rare occasion when it wasn't true.

*   *   *

When she woke the next day, she could hear Max's gentle snoring in the next room. At least he was still there and had managed to get some sleep. She'd fallen into a dreamless exhausted sleep almost the moment she pulled the covers up but had been woken in the early hours of the morning by pain in her side.

What would need to be done to deal with Eddie's death, she wondered to herself. Virginia hadn't shown much interest in the practicalities, though Chloe probably shouldn't blame her, losing her eldest child like that wasn't conducive to rational decision making. She used the bathroom, pleasantly surprised that her body didn't scream in protest as it had the day before. Though it was probably because the painkillers she'd had were still working it was a welcome relief.

The lounge was dimly lit, Max's breathing remained steady as she tiptoed through to the kitchen. It would be impossible not to wake him in the small space but she would try.

Kettle on for coffee, bread in the toaster. The lino was cold against her bare feet as she stood with her hands folded into her armholes of her dressing gown. The kettle became noisier and noisier as it neared boiling and she heard Max take a sharp breath before mumbling something.

'I didn't mean to wake you,' she said. 'I'm about to put coffee on if you want one.'

'Yes please.' Max sat up, his naked chest revealed as the blanket slipped down. Bare legs stuck out the bottom as he put his feet on the ground. He was more muscular than she had expected; thin, but solid, like a gymnast. Chloe had never known him to exercise but perhaps it was just something they'd never talked about. Turning away to make coffee she tried to push the image of his torso from her mind, but she found her mind drifting back to it. Knowing it was there just behind her. It shouldn't have been tempting, she'd never found Max attractive, or unattractive, before, he was just there. The coffee plunger was ready to push down and when she turned back to the lounge Max had put his T-shirt and pants back on, though it did little to stop her imagination now she'd seen his skin.

She stared at the bathroom mirror; her face was very swollen and purple with some of the bruises fading to brown and yellow. Good thing she'd called in sick until next Monday. Sounds of Max washing out his cup in the kitchen sink drew her back from her reverie.

'Do you need help to sort out, y'know, Eddie's stuff?' she asked walking back into the lounge area. He didn't have that much stuff, and what he did have was barely fit for giving to a charity shop, but it was all Max had left of the best friend he'd had since school. In their own way they had tried to look out for each other, Max kept Eddie grounded, paying his bills when things went sideways, and Eddie helped Max move in the world giving him confidence and a social circle. At work he seemed to have a groove, a routine and role he would slip into, perhaps since he was getting paid he was able to put more energy into appearing normal, masking his natural feelings and tendencies, but in other situations, at home when it had just been the three of them, Max had slipped back into being his real self, quiet and painfully shy.

'I hadn't thought of that,' he said, not looking up.

'It can be overwhelming dealing with an unexpected death. I haven't had much experience with it myself, only the time my great-grandparents passed when I was a little kid. I can imagine there will be more stuff to do than you first think, especially if Virginia and Steve won't step up to help.' She paused, leaving a space for Max to say something. 'How long has he paid rent till? Will you need to find a new housemate?'

Max's eyes widened and he looked up at her. 'I've never lived with anyone else. I don't know how I would cope.'

She put her hand on his shoulder and he didn't flinch away, he wasn't usually into physical touch but today he seemed to need it.

'He's paid till the seventeenth; about three weeks,' he said.

Chloe made a sound of agreement. She hadn't thought of how hard it might be for Max to find someone to live with. He was such a sweet man, Eddie had teased him and been strangely jealous of her spending any time with him, so she felt as though she barely knew him. After a good breakfast and with her coffee starting to kick in, she felt almost well enough to start on Eddie's stuff, though a couple of painkillers would be welcome.

'Shall I come home with you now and get started? Do you have work tonight?'

He nodded.

'Let me shower and dress and we'll get stuff sorted.' She lifted her hand from his shoulder, he slumped a little as though her presence had been keeping him upright.

Chapter 15

The inside of Eddie's house looked much the same as it always did but the smell hit her as soon as she followed Max over the threshold; like sweat but also like a cat had peed somewhere.

'Oof,' she said.

'Sorry. I can't figure out where the smell is coming from.'

She opened Eddie's bedroom door and the smell was worse inside. 'I think I know.'

Max turned and came back towards the bedroom. 'What is that?'

'He said he'd taken some speed to get through the days at work. It smells like meth.' She hoped he didn't ask how she knew what it smelled like. 'I'm surprised Johnno let him on site if he was off his tree.'

'I didn't know he was using anything—then again I barely saw him recently, he was out of the house before I got up and I had to leave for work before he was home. I can't believe I missed that.'

'It happened so quickly, and for him to be—' her breath caught in her throat, she swallowed and went on. 'Dead. I don't think any of us thought this is what it would lead to.'

Chloe went to the window and opened it to clear some of the stale air. On the floor were clothes in various states of cleanliness, some covered in dirt and grass, others looked clean enough except for the odour. She collected the laundry basket from the other end of the house and put all the most soiled garments into a hot wash. Even if it was all going to charity, she couldn't send it dirty. There were enough clothes scattered around the floor for a second load, which she left in a pile in front of the machine. *Perhaps I'll take them to the laundromat and use the dryer*, she thought.

'Other than the bedroom stuff, is anything else Eddie's?' she asked Max, who had settled on the couch and looked ready to doze off. *He must have had a rough night.*

'Not really, I bought all the furniture. The Xbox is Eddie's, as are most of the games, the TV is mine. Do you think his family will want any of these?'

'I doubt it.' She would have to contact Virginia again and ask what she wanted done with all the stuff. It seemed a forlorn hope to think Eddie would have a will of any kind, all his possessions would revert back to his parents unless anyone challenged it. She had no intention of doing so, the thought of keeping anything of his seemed repellent after what had happened; she didn't need anything to remind her of their time together.

Chloe stripped the bed; the doona was a dirty beige colour and there was a yellowish stain on the top of the mattress no doubt caused by an accumulation of sweat. It was possibly not even Eddie's stain, he was likely to have picked the thing up from the side of the road. No charity would want that, she thought, it would have to go out in the hard rubbish. There were enough people in the area as desperate as Eddie had been so it probably would be picked up without her having to call the council disposal service.

Aside from clothes, Eddie had a few novels, assorted beaten up tools in a tattered black canvas bag, and an acoustic guitar with no strings. Hidden inside the sound hole, taped below the pick guard, was his stash of drugs; tiny white crystals, they looked a little like rock salt except for the very subtle blue-grey tinge. The bag was small, only a few centimetres on the long edge, and about a third full.

Chloe shook her head. He must have been in a really bad way the Eddie she knew would never had ended his life with that much still in his house. Then again the only thing keeping him going was to get money together to help raise his child, a child she had terminated. Her mouth was dry, breathing was hard, and she found herself wishing she felt something other than relief. Relief and shame.

It would never have worked, he would have exhausted himself, become dependent on the drugs, or both, and then where would she and the baby be? Of all the terrible men her mother had brought into the house as she was growing up, none of them used meth. A few dabbled in pot and most had an unhealthy relationship with alcohol but nothing harder. Perhaps it was a sign of the times but Chloe wondered if she had managed to choose a man who was worse than all of her mother's. She shuddered. Fighting the urge to smash the guitar, she dumped it on the bed and went to the toilet to flush away the drugs.

'Where do you think he got it?' Max asked as she returned to through the lounge.

'Sorry?' she said.

'The drugs. He had a contact for weed, everyone has a contact for weed, but I wouldn't know where to get harder stuff.'

Chloe shrugged. 'I don't know. There's a lot about Eddie I didn't know.'

'I thought I knew him. We've been friends long enough I thought I knew how far he'd go. Just goes to show how unobservant I am.'

'Don't be so hard on yourself.' She took half a step forward, hovering, unsure whether to sit down or not. 'You couldn't have done anything. I think he—' she stopped herself. 'There was nothing anyone could have done if he'd decided to end it. Blaming yourself for what he did isn't going to help. He's dead, feeling bad about yourself won't help Eddie and it will make you miserable—   more miserable than you are now.'

Max said nothing, the Xbox controller hung in his hands as though forgotten.

'You've lost a good friend. It's normal to feel sad. And the way he did it doesn't help. Don't blame yourself, is all I'm trying to say.'

'You too.'

'Hmm?'

'It's not your fault either,' he said, raising his eyes to hers. 'I know you think you pushed him over the edge with the... abortion.'

How could he have known? Had Eddie told him? 'I thought you didn't see him much lately?'

'He left a voicemail. The night he died. I was at work.'

Part of her wanted to hear it, to ask for more details, but another part of her knew it would only lead to more self-hatred.

'It was long and rambling. He wasn't making much sense,' Max went on. 'I've listened to it a lot since the police were here.'

'Maybe you shouldn't listen to it anymore.'

'You're probably right. But it's the last thing he ever said to me.'

'Even so.' She knew how cruel Eddie could be when he was on a roll, Max would be using the message as self-flagellation. She perched on the arm of one of the couches, the energy she'd found earlier had left her and she felt as though her limbs were filled with mud.

The room swam before her eyes as though she couldn't focus on what was in front of her. Hot wetness trickled down her face and she realised she had started to cry. Everything seemed to be happening all at once but at the same time not happening at all. She felt so many emotions she could barely identify them, she could barely breathe, but the urge to howl in pain became so strong she had to clamp her mouth shut to stop it.

How had things gone so wrong so quickly? One minute she was considering having a baby with Eddie, the next minute he wouldn't take her calls, or return her texts. She had to terminate a baby she had always longed for because she couldn't raise it on her own, only to find out Eddie wanted to keep it. And now he was dead. She sobbed loudly.

Max made a strange squawking sound and she wiped her eyes to look at him. 'Are you alright?' he asked.

'I don't think so.'

The silence felt like another person in the room, she knew she should fill it, reassure him, but she couldn't.

'Should I, umm, make you a cup of tea or something?' he asked eventually, his face was white, he looked at her intensely as though trying to figure out what he needed to do.

'That would be lovely... it's just hit me. Eddie's gone.'

He exhaled. 'Yeah, sometimes I think he's going to come in or something and then I remember he's never coming back. And then I feel bad about forgetting he's dead.'

Chloe had no energy to say anything comforting back, she merely nodded, hoping it would be enough to convey her thanks and empathy. Max stood slowly, as though each movement was deliberate and careful, perhaps trying not to startle her, and walked into the kitchen. She listened absentmindedly as he switched on the kettle, opened and closed cupboards, clanked the teaspoon against a cup.

He returned to the lounge with two cups, placing them on the coffee table which looked sticky and desperately needed a wipe down. When Chloe took her first sip, she nearly choked he'd put so much sugar into it. 'Thank you,' she said.

'I couldn't remember how you have it, so I made it the same as mine. Sorry.'

'It's fine.' She slid down to sit on the couch properly, both hands wrapped around the cup. Feeling as though she was being swallowed was strangely comforting and familiar. The sweet tea was soothing, as was the warmth in her hands, it was calming to focus on the feeling in her fingers, the taste on her tongue. Perhaps things weren't as bad as she thought they were only minutes ago.

*   *   *

The afternoon passed and neither Chloe nor Max moved much from the couch. Her desire to get things sorted only extended to getting up each time the washing machine beeped to indicate it was done. In the end she had an enormous pile of clean, wet fabric that she couldn't bear to hang on the line or take to the laundromat.

'Do you have work?' she asked. Her throat was a little scratchy after having sat silent, weeping on and off, for several hours.

'No. I took a few days off.'

She nodded. 'I'm supposed to be back on Monday but I don't know if I can face it. They'll probably think I'm making it up but I don't think they'll have heard my ex-boyfriend just killed himself too often.' Chloe intended the comment to lighten the mood but the heaviness lingered. Her belly growled.

'I'll order pizza,' Max said.

'You don't have to do that.'

'I know. It's all I'm capable of doing at the moment. And staring at the TV.' He'd switched off his game hours ago and changed it to one of the commercial channels; a fishing show and some news were all Chloe could remember, not that she'd been watching, though the voices of the hosts made it feel less empty.

'Do you mind if I sit on the couch with you?' Her neck was stiff from turning, she stood and moved to the couch facing the TV without waiting for Max to respond. She resisted the urge to rest her head on his lap but appreciated the warmth and proximity of being near another human.

Max ordered two pizzas, one plain cheese and Napoli sauce and the other a *marinara*, with bits of seafood. The smell was enough to remind her body that she had barely eaten all day. After she'd gorged herself on about six slices, she felt sleepy and lethargic. It would be hard to go back to her apartment, the emptiness of it made her shoulders bunch together in worry. She sighed heavily and her ribs twinged, reminding her to have some more Panadol.

Maybe Max wouldn't mind if she just stayed on the couch until the morning; being alone in the dark wasn't something she could handle today. Tomorrow would be better.

At some point she must have fallen asleep, she woke to find the TV still on, her tongue dry and teeth furry with plaque. Max was still next to her, his head laid back at an awkward angle, his breath gently rattling his soft palette. It had never occurred to her before but he was quite attractive in an awkward way, she wanted to protect him and his quiet comfort today had been just what she needed. No doubt he needed the company as badly as she did. This time she gave in to the desire for human contact and laid her head on Max's lap, closing her eyes again.

Epilogue

Six months later

It took a long time for Eddie's death to really sink in, but Chloe found herself less and less affected by it every day. Max proved to be a staunch friend and, as they spent more time in each other's company, their connection deepened.

Chloe was surprised the first time she found herself kissing him. He didn't make her tummy flutter or her knees weak, he didn't make her blood thrill with every touch, but he was always there. Always safe. No matter what she did, he was there. Sometimes he didn't know what to do when she cried or yelled, either at him or at the universe, but once it became clear he wouldn't run away or turn nasty she stopped yelling.

Theirs wasn't a stormy or passionate romance but a steady friendship which blossomed into a surprisingly satisfying physical relationship. He cared whether she was satisfied, and despite not having had a steady girlfriend before her, Max knew how to find her pleasure buttons and remembered them for next time.

'Do you want to meet my mother?' she asked one night as they sat in her apartment. It was a balmy evening in December. 'Mum said you could come to Christmas if you wanted.'

'Oh.' He became still the way he always did when something unexpected happened. Chloe had learned if given a few minutes to work things through in his mind, he would come back to the conversation.

'I know you worry about your mother and about how people might change their opinion of you if they meet her,' he said eventually. She didn't reply, but was surprised, she hadn't thought he'd been listening when she talked about her mum.

'I would like to meet her. It seems like the sociable thing to do. I want you to know I won't judge you because of her. I know you're different, your kindness and empathy and some of your less functional behaviours stem from growing up with Janine, but all in all I think you turned out okay, so she can't be too bad.'

'I'm glad you have so much faith in me,' she managed to say. She was always astounded by the amount of thought went on, silently, inside Max's brain. It was a bad habit to think just because someone was quiet meant they were dumb and even in six months she hadn't managed to recalibrate her ideas. She squeezed his hand where it was lying on top of her thigh. The little bubble of love in her chest swelled every time he said something gentle. 'I'm glad you love me.'

'I always loved you.'

She turned to him; he had said he loved her before but this was new.

'Even when you were with Eddie. I thought you could never love me back, so I put the feeling away in a box inside, but when you were there after he died, I started to wonder if I was wrong.'

'I never knew. It must have been awful to see me with Eddie.'

'I didn't mind. You seemed happy, and that was enough for me.'

She made a murmuring sound of agreement. If only she'd known then what real happiness felt like, not the excitement or drama she felt with Eddie but the quiet, safe contentment she felt now. Her upbringing had affected her more than she liked to admit.

If she found herself pregnant now, there would be no second thoughts. Max would be a great dad, and they would make a home, a family together, but she wasn't in any rush. She kissed his cheek, smiling, and they went back to watching a cooking competition in silence.

Keep reading for a sneak peak of:

Sins of the Father

By Fleur Blüm

Out now

1. Goodbye Daddy

Janine Barrett was too hot in her black dress. Her mother, Vicky, had made her wear stockings even though it was the middle of February, the hottest month of the year.

'I won't have you looking like a tramp at your own father's funeral,' she'd said.

Janine had crossed her arms and put on her best pouty face, but in the end, she'd given up. Mum had bought her the new dress for the occasion. Shiny black polyester, off the shoulder with a big bow across the boobs rustled as she walked. She was surprised her mother had allowed it, the dress was tight-fitting and only came to mid-thigh.

They hadn't had much time to get things ready; Vicky was in full crisis mode and didn't care much what Janine was doing. Unless it included 'slutting around'.

As if she was innocent at my age, Janine thought as she sat in the hot chapel beside her mother. She wasn't listening to the droning voice of the minister. He must have been even hotter than her in all that getup.

Her father's coffin was closed. One side of the chapel was filled with men in uniform. If they hadn't all been Dad's pals she might have found them attractive. Janine loved uniforms. But on closer inspection they were all salt and pepper haired with bulging bellies.

The booklet in her hand had a photo of her father, taken when he'd been promoted to sergeant. Even on the other side of forty, still handsome, with broad shoulders she'd always loved riding as a child. When he was home that was.

The job in the army meant he was away from the family for most of the year. He'd be placed on some project or other around Australia, sometimes in the Pacific. 'Godforsaken deserts and bug-infested jungles' he'd called them.

Her mother never allowed them to visit him. She didn't care for any of it. Janine wasn't really sure why they had married at all sometimes. She'd always wanted to see what her dad did to experience the challenges and meet the natives he always spoke about. *No chance of that now.*

Janine was surprised she didn't feel particularly sad. She'd cried a little when her mother had broken the news, but mostly she felt numb. Maybe it would have sunk in better if she'd been allowed to look in the coffin, but the army guys said she'd better not see it. Something about bloating and discolouration.

It was patronising—just because she was a girl. She wasn't a child anymore and he didn't get shot or anything. Her mother didn't want to see him.

Her dad, big strong man that he was, had died of pneumonia. In the desert, somewhere out the back of nowhere in the Northern Territory doing secret army stuff, and he'd stood on a rusty nail. His tetanus shots weren't up to date, and the army doctor had run out. While they'd trying to treat him, he developed pneumonia and drowned in his own fluids.

Her mother snuffled into a hanky. She hadn't stopped crying in the three days since they'd found out. It had to be for show; her parents were hardly close.

Bill, her dad, had only been home one month out of every six, sometimes all at once, sometimes only a week before he was sent off somewhere else. He always brought Janine a present.

'You're my special girl,' he'd say, and kiss her.

At the front of the chapel, the minister clutched the pulpit. He swayed slightly, Janine narrowed her eyes.

I bet he's drunk. Her mother would often have several glasses of wine with dinner, before dinner, and after.

'Bill would have been proud to see his daughter growing into a woman. I'm sure he will be watching over her as she develops. I'll call on her now to read from Corinthians.'

Janine stood, the back of her legs damp with sweat as she walked the short distance to the pulpit. She'd practised the passage repeating it over and over to herself to make her father proud.

They weren't a religious family, her father had believed in God, they went to church at Christmas, Easter and for special occasions. This was the first time Janine had spoken to a congregation.

She cleared her throat. '*I declare to you, brothers and sisters, that flesh and blood cannot inherit the kingdom of God, nor does the perishable inherit the imperishable,*' she said.

The celebrant nudged her and pointed up. She swallowed and tried again, louder this time.

'*Listen, I tell you a mystery: We will not all sleep, but we will all be changed— in a flash, in the twinkling of an eye, at the last trumpet. For the trumpet will sound, the dead will be raised imperishable, and we will be changed. For the perishable must clothe itself with the imperishable, and the mortal with immortality. When the perishable has been clothed with the imperishable, and the mortal with immortality.*'

Janine's hands were trembling as she read. She grabbed the sides of the pulpit, just as the minister had, and swayed a little.

'You're doing fine,' he whispered.

'*Then the saying that is written will come true: Death has been swallowed up in victory. Where, O death, is your victory? Where, O death, is your sting? The sting of death is sin, and the power of sin is the law. But thanks be to God! He gives us the victory through our Lord Jesus Christ.*'

She staggered back to her seat on legs made from jelly. She'd done a good job, heads in the crowd nodded, and she felt a silly urge to grin. She pushed it down and set her mouth in a stony line.

Grownups don't grin at funerals. Her father would have understood she was pleased and relieved, and her mother would use it later.

As she sat down, her mother dabbed her eyes with a sodden handkerchief and replaced her hands in her lap.

Several of the men in uniform on the other side of the chapel spoke. Her father's superior spoke of how he was a credit to the army, how he had been a committed soldier for twenty-five years and that he would be sorely missed. *I bet he says that every time someone dies.*

A man, about the same age, and whose face was weathered and sunken from long working in the sun, stood at the front and told stories of how he and Bill had played pranks on the new recruits, created rapport with the locals, and always left their mark on the people they had helped.

Janine was both fascinated and bored hearing about her father's life. Still, the sadness didn't come.

Finally, it was her mother's turn. Janine had offered to help her mother write the eulogy but had been told to keep her fat nose out of it.

'I met Bill through my brother; they were both in the cadets and he thought we'd get on. He was right, of course, we got on like a house on fire. I had hoped—' she broke off to blow her nose with a honk.

'I had hoped that we would grow old together. That when he finally finished gallivanting around saving the world, we would find a little cottage and keep bees.'

Janine stifled a snigger. Her mother in a cottage with bees? She was a rigidly reputable woman with champagne taste. She liked nice things and used them to feel superior to others. Retirement spending every day with Bill? She was clearly delusional. Whenever he was home for a month straight, they were bickering and hounding each other within a fortnight. Her mother nagged incessantly; she'd had no idea how to give Dad what he needed.

'Bill was a good man, a good provider, and when he was with us on leave, a great help around the house.

'Now all we have of him are memories. Our daughter will always be a reminder of the man I've now lost. Along with all the half-finished projects in the shed!' There was a smattering of laughter, and the men in uniform nodded.

The service ended with a hymn. Some rubbish the minister had chosen. Her mother didn't sing, she said it was undignified. The sweltering chapel filled with the droning of fifty men who would rather do anything else.

Outside was much cooler, a late afternoon breeze swept past Janine. The sweat collected inside her dress had soaked through her knickers and strapless bra was chilly against her skin. She followed her mother back to the car.

'How did I do, Mum?' she asked.

'What?'

Janine jogged a few steps in her teetering black stilettos to catch up. 'The reading, how did I do?'

'You weren't a complete embarrassment. Stiff as a board and barely audible, but we can't do much about it now.'

Janine's smile faded. She should have known better than to expect praise from her mother, but maybe this day, of all days might have been the exception.

*   *   *

The wake was held at their family home in Camberwell, a large, single-storey, cream, weatherboard Edwardian house. Her father's parents lived in a similar house around the corner and it had been his idea to buy there. Her mother constantly complained about the snobs in the area.

Her grandparents had insisted on having the wake catered, and the black-clad staff were waiting outside the house when they arrived.

'You're here. I thought someone would have let you in already. Keep the canapés coming and stay out of my way,' Vicky barked at the closest.

The woman, in her forties, dark hair pulled back in a severe bun, held a clipboard and looked to be in charge. She widened her eyes slightly, then nodded and started giving instructions to the staff.

Her mother poured herself a glass of red wine as soon as she walked in the door.

'Do I have to be at this party?' Janine asked. She was tired and watching the coffin be lowered into the ground had released some of the sadness she'd pushed down.

'Yes. You will not humiliate me,' Vicky stared out the kitchen window. 'Go put on some perfume or something, you smell like a pig.'

'Can I have some wine?'

'No. You're fifteen.'

'You never let me do anything,' Janine whined. 'It's Dad's bloody wake. Can't I just have one glass?'

'Let her have one, Vicky, it can't do any harm.' Her father's mother, Claire, had let herself in behind them.

'Fine. It's on you if she does anything stupid,' Vicky said. She refilled her glass and stalked off toward her bedroom.

'Don't mind her, she's had a hard day too.' Her paternal grandmother was Janine's favourite. The one who spoiled her, she barely saw her mother's parents.

'She's so mean.'

'I know, sweetheart. Don't let it get to you, eh?' Claire put her plump hand on her shoulder. 'Have some of this.'

She poured out a glass of red wine and held it out to Janine. 'Sip it dear, like a lady. Make it last.'

Her grandmother wore thick glasses, her grey hair was cut short against her head, and she was almost as round as she was tall. It was grandma who brought chicken soup when they were sick, and gave Janine secret chocolate. Her mother wouldn't keep any kind of junk food in the house.

It wasn't Janine's first taste of wine, but it was her first whole glass. She used to steal a little when her mother was nodding off on the couch and drink it furtively in the kitchen. She'd never had enough to get drunk, and wondered what it would feel like to have to hold onto something to stand upright.

Guests started arriving in dribs and drabs. Everyone who had been in the chapel, and at the cemetery, of course, as well as a number of her mother's friends who had had to be left off the guest list to fit all her father's army buddies.

Only once the wine was being sent around with the wait staff, and the smell of the hot nibbles wafted through the house, did her mother made her appearance. She'd redone her makeup and changed into a floor length gown of deep navy shot through with flecks of silver. Janine thought it looked like she'd tried to wear the night sky, although looking glamorous at your husband's funeral was tacky.

*   *   *

Janine nursed her glass of wine; her grandmother had topped the glass up a couple of times. 'It's still only one glass if you top up before you finish,' she said.

Janine's cheeks were flushed, the tight dress and thick black stockings felt suffocating. It was nearly midnight when she stood up and moved quietly towards her bedroom.

'Where do you think you're going, you little slut?' her mother whispered at her elbow, appearing out of nowhere. She was quite drunk now; her teeth and lips had turned purple from the wine and rage burned in her eyes.

'I'm going to bed, Mum, it's late and no one is talking to me.'

'More important to be entertained constantly than to show any kind of respect?' Vicky's words were blurred at the edges.

'No. I'm just—it's boring and I'm tired.'

'You think you're tired? Twenty-seven years with your father and now I have to make conversation with the men who made him the way he was, you think you're tired?'

'I'm sorry.'

'You will be sorry. What do you think they'd do if I told them what you get up to, eh?' Vicky had hold of her elbow, her fingers digging in and tingles ran down her forearm.

'I'm sorry.' Janine looked down at the floor. She'd never seen her mother this bad before. She had no idea what she was supposed to say.

'I know you about you and your father. Don't think I didn't see how you looked at him.'

Janine looked at her mother's face. 'You knew?'

'Of course, I knew. I knew every hole your father ever poked and he wasn't picky.' Her breath stank of sour wine. 'A word in the ear of the right people and no boy will ever come near you.'

'He told me I was his special girl.' Janine's eyes stung with tears.

'You weren't special. Get out of my sight.'

She released Janine's arm and walked away. She barely swayed if you didn't look too closely.

Janine ran to her room, slammed the door and lay face down on her bed. He'd said what they did was special, it was pure. All those nights he'd come into her bedroom, the camping trips.

Her mother had known. She'd known it was wrong and had never done anything about it. She thought Janine had seduced him. Everything he'd said was a lie. Everything her mother had done was out of spite and jealousy.

Janine's hands trembled with rage. If it was so bad, telling anyone would make them hate her, why had her mother let it go on? She didn't know anything about keeping a man happy and now he was gone she deserved to be left alone with her wine and diets.

Janine decided it was time to leave home, there was nothing tying her there now. She got up, stripped off her dress, sticky from a long sweaty day, and peeled off her tights.

She slipped on her thin cotton nightie and lay on top of the bed. It was too hot to have even a sheet over her. In the dark, she planned her escape. She couldn't stay with her grandparents; as liberal as her grandma might seem she wouldn't abide having her stay. She didn't have a job and couldn't leave school until she was sixteen. Maybe Gerry, who hated being called Geraldine and was Janine's best friend, would let her stay for a while. A few of the other girls at school might let her stay over. Maybe she could set up a sort of roster. She could tell each of the parents that her mother had to go away for work, now that her father was dead. Janine guessed she might be able to get away with a week at a time.

She would leave all her school things in her locker, then she'd only need to carry some clothes and a couple school uniforms. She drifted off to sleep going over everything she might need to take with her.

Sins of the Father

www.ingramcontent.com/pod-product-compliance
Lightning Source LLC
Chambersburg PA
CBHW030529120726
47904CB00005B/1688